A DANCE AT ALMACK'S

"Miss Stone, how can I possibly predict what the Fates have in store for me?"

"How indeed?" replied Pamela, laughingly. "Don't you dislike being weighed and inventoried in the Marriage Mart? I do dislike it, terribly—I think everyone must have already been told just exactly how old I am, how tall I am (though in my case, how tall I am not), and what was my birth, and exactly how large is my portion."

The Honorable John Whyte laughed in recognition of his own position as prey for predatory mothers, and then his laughter transformed into a quite dazzling smile.

In a lowered voice meant for the two of them alone, Mr. Whyte added, "One might just as well admit that the entirety of our London society revolves around the ancient traditions of seeking and finding mates. Save for that, what would be the reason of gathering so many people in such a comparatively crowded space at such great expense, and serving such insipid beverages? It would all fall apart in a moment!"

"A brutal assessment, but true, I fear," she replied, smiling. As she did so, John Whyte found himself suddenly entranced by the shine in her sea-green eyes, a vision that left him momentarily speechless.

Miss Pamela Stone, on her part, was finding herself powerfully magnetized by the Hon. John Whyte.

Mr. Whyte and Miss Stone finished the set with a distinct desire to encounter one another again at the earliest opportunity.

ZEBRA'S REGENCY ROMANCES
DAZZLE AND DELIGHT

A BEGUILING INTRIGUE (4441, $3.99)
by Olivia Sumner
Pretty as a picture Justine Riggs cared nothing for propriety. She dressed as a boy, sat on her horse like a jockey, and pondered the stars like a scientist. But when she tried to best the handsome Quenton Fletcher, Marquess of Devon, by proving that she was the better equestrian, he would try to prove Justine's antics were pure folly. The game he had in mind was seduction — never imagining that he might lose his heart in the process!

AN INCONVENIENT ENGAGEMENT (4442, $3.99)
by Joy Reed
Rebecca Wentworth was furious when she saw her betrothed waltzing with another. So she decides to make him jealous by flirting with the handsomest man at the ball, John Collinwood, Earl of Stanford. The "wicked" nobleman knew exactly what the enticing miss was up to — and he was only too happy to play along. But as Rebecca gazed into his magnificent eyes, her errant fiancé was soon utterly forgotten!

SCANDAL'S LADY (4472, $3.99)
by Mary Kingsley
Cassandra was shocked to learn that the new Earl of Lynton was her childhood friend, Nicholas St. John. After years at sea and mixed feelings Nicholas had come home to take the family title. And although Cassandra knew her place as a governess, she could not help the thrill that went through her each time he was near. Nicholas was pleased to find that his old friend Cassandra was his new next door neighbor, but after being near her, he wondered if mere friendship would be enough . . .

HIS LORDSHIP'S REWARD (4473, $3.99)
by Carola Dunn
As the daughter of a seasoned soldier, Fanny Ingram was accustomed to the vagaries of military life and cared not a whit about matters of rank and social standing. So she certainly never foresaw her *tendre* for handsome Viscount Roworth of Kent with whom she was forced to share lodgings, while he carried out his clandestine activities on behalf of the British Army. And though good sense told Roworth to keep his distance, he couldn't stop from taking Fanny in his arms for a kiss that made all hearts equal!

Available wherever paperbacks are sold, or order direct from the Publisher. Send cover price plus 50¢ per copy for mailing and handling to Penguin USA, P.O. Box 999, c/o Dept. 17109, Bergenfield, NJ 07621. Residents of New York and Tennessee must include sales tax. DO NOT SEND CASH.

A Gentleman's Daughter

Isobel Linton

ZEBRA BOOKS
KENSINGTON PUBLISHING CORP.

ZEBRA BOOKS are published by

Kensington Publishing Corp.
850 Third Avenue
New York, NY 10022

First Printing: May, 1995

Printed in the United States of America

One

In a corner of Almack's, a vision of unsullied innocence: in high-waisted gowns of palest pastel and whitest muslin, young girls of quality waited patiently—or impatiently—for desirable partners to be presented to them. Adjusting a sash here, pulling up a long white glove there, or nervously fingering an heirloom necklet of matched pearls, these well-bred young women had come to Society's inner sanctum to toss their hats into the ring at the Marriage Mart. In short, they were come to find themselves husbands.

Among these hopefuls were two attractive young cousins, one full of good sense, and one largely free of it. The latter was truly a diamond of the first water, who, as our story unfolds, was unaccountably absorbed in fiddling and fussing with the set of blue silk ribands that adorned her elegant Vergere gown.

"Lie *down!*" cried she, apparently addressing her ornaments directly. "How provoking! These odious bows simply will not lie as they ought!"

Standing patiently next to the preoccupied speaker was Miss Pamela Stone of Easton, a brunette whose glossy curls had been dressed so charmingly as to frame her thoughtful oval face. She was a young lady graced with an air of natural kindness which seemed to shine forth from her teal-green eyes. Miss Stone, listening to her cousin, allowed a sigh to escape her lips. She whispered, in reply to her distressed relation, "Victorine, cut line! Pray do not fall into distempered freaks, here at Almack's, of all places! Try for a little conduct, won't you? Your behavior is most unbecoming."

"To the contrary, my dear cousin, it is these bows that are unbecoming, I tell you!" replied the petite blonde, her brow continuing to darken. Miss Wells was an inexperienced, overindulged only child easily overset by the tiniest deviation of reality from the ideal. "I cannot think *how* I allowed myself to be talked into purchasing such a dowdy style by that odious, money-grubbing Madame Vergere. She claimed these bows are in the very first style of elegance, but of course, they're not so, not at all! And, as if deliberately to add insult to this injury, they've each one of them been sewn on crooked! My whole evening is ruined! I swear I shan't dance tonight! I shan't!"

There was a flutter as Victorine's fan was pumped back and forth, in an apparent brave attempt to hold back an oncoming flood of tears. This attempt to attract solicitous attention proving unsuccessful, she was forced to resort to speech.

"Mama? Did you hear what I said?" she asked in the high, nasal tone of the perpetually oppressed.

Victorine's mother, Lady Charlton, raised an eyebrow, then sighed and quickly murmured some requisite words of sympathy in order to achieve a decorous silence. An attractive, silver-blonde woman of forty years who had been standing back in the second row talking with the other chaperones, she was only too well-used to Victorine's tantrums and related eccentricities.

Lady Charlton had moved quickly to conceal Victorine's lack of proper comportment; it was, of course, essential that her daughter be beyond a breath of criticism and gossip. If not, how would it be possible for Almack's to function as it must to achieve her aims? Here was concluded the most serious possible business for females—it was here above all that, in indubitably good society, a young lady of quality might meet as many eligible men as possible, dance with them, make herself agreeable to them, and induce them to offer for her hand.

Without knowing why she could not rid herself of such a fearful intuition, Lady Charlton could not help feeling that in the search to find a husband for her twitter-headed daughter, and despite Victorine's beauty and considerable fortune, there was not a moment to lose. Thus Lady Charlton was glad to have her level-headed niece Pamela present to assist her in this onerous and exacting task.

The presence of Miss Pamela Stone in their party in London had occurred rather as an afterthought, as a kindness to Lady Charlton's beloved brother, Thomas Stone, a widower. Mr. Stone was unable to see to Pamela's coming-out himself, so Lady Charlton had undertaken to launch Pamela into society. Her ladyship was carrying out her promise most admirably, though there was really little to be done for Pamela beyond serving as her chaperone. Pamela's manners were exquisite, her comportment always upstanding; she was neither shy nor coming. Her taste in gowns was excellent; it was, in many ways, the easiest thing in the world to present her to polite society.

A lucky thing this was, however, since her own daughter was such a handful. Lady Charlton's very understandably preeminent concern was trying to hold Victorine in line just long enough for her to make a real conquest, and secure the grand match her mother very much desired.

Miss Stone, on her part, was not really come to London

on the lookout for a husband, but rather to begin to brush with more sophisticated persons, in accordance with her father's wishes, and acquire the feminine equivalent of town-bronze.

Pamela, dressed in a simple, but well-cut gown of white muslin, her late mother's favorite golden cross around her neck, was content to look with real pleasure at the glitter and whirl of the ballroom. She felt perfectly satisfied merely to be present among the well-turned-out couples who defined the London Season, ornamenting the dance floor with their intricate silks and smiles.

When she turned her attention toward her cousin, Miss Stone could not help but stare in mixed amusement and dismay. Her cousin Victorine's eyes had actually begun to fill with tears at what Pamela could hardly consider a deep disappointment. The silly child could not seem to cease fussing about her dress.

Pamela noticed a group of impeccably-dressed gentlemen approaching them. As they made their way toward the ladies across the highly polished floor, she whispered to her cousin, "Compose yourself, Victorine! Lord Balmore is coming, and bringing with him several gentlemen! It will not do anything for your marital prospects to be discovered in deep misery over a set of crooked ribands!"

Victorine flashed Pamela a look of mild surprise and hurt. Pamela thrust the sword home by adding, "Besides, Victorine, if those tears turn to sniffles, your eyes will get puffy, your nose will go red, and you'll look just like the curate's daughter come down with hay fever."

Horrified at this possibility, Victorine instantly stifled her tantrum and blinked back her tears. In fact, the poor child barely had any time at all to concoct a fetching smile to greet the newcomers.

A debutante of several weeks' standing, Miss Wells had had quite sufficient time to master the most essential social graces—such as cultivating the stunning smile that appears suddenly, out of thin air.

Victorine Wells was a doll of a girl with cornflower-blue eyes and golden hair arranged in a shower of curls at each side of her head, who, when not pouting or sulking, was considered one of the great new beauties of the year. It was an unsurprising event for gentlemen to go out of their way to seek an introduction to such a divinity. The surprise to all, and no less to that young lady herself, was that no one of consequence had offered for her as yet. In fact, no one had made any offer at all.

Lord Balmore, who was leading the approaching party of gentlemen, was a tall and stately man of sixty, with a kind smile and excellent address. He was accompanied by three younger gentlemen   one raven-haired and blue-eyed, dressed in the pink of fashion; another brown-haired and green-eyed, very tall, with a kind face, a man dressed well and without ostentation; the third man young and sweet-faced, but portly and beginning to bald.

Lord Baltimore bowed as he said, "How do you do, Miss Wells? Where is your delightful mother?"

Victorine looked around her, surprised, and then shrugged, shaking her bouncy curls.

"How do you do, Lord Balmore? Mother was just here an instant ago; she must have wandered off. Pray wait a moment; she'll return directly."

"Certainly, child. I could hardly come to Almack's and miss the opportunity of dancing with her."

"Present me to the child now, would you, Balmore?" said the raven-haired man.

"She just said her mother will return anon."

"There's no need to be so stuffy about it, Balmore. Pray, go ahead and have it done with, won't you? One does not have all day."

"Miss Wells, allow me to present to you Lord St. Clare."

The dark-haired gentleman bowed slightly at this, and with his slightly hooded eyes looked as ravenously at Victorine as might a cat when regarding a young and delectable sparrow; his eyes did not meet hers, as Victorine's had been demurely cast down toward the ground. The Viscount, however, by no means lessened his intensive inspection of the charms of the golden-haired miss.

"Miss Wells, allow me to present to you his lordship's younger brother, Mr. John Whyte."

The man with the gentle green eyes made his bow. Pamela noted that the cut of his clothes was perhaps not of the very first stare, but the man's figure was impressive in itself: a broad, deep chest, a high, thoughtful brow, well-muscled legs, powerful shoulders that naturally filled out a tight-cut coat. His hair was brushed in the fashionable Brutus style; his white tie had been expertly wound around in a classical fashion she did not recognize, which was, perhaps, his own invention.

"And my own nephew, Mr. Charles Bellfort," continued Lord Balmore, introducing the balding young man who sported an engaging smile, as he swept an elegant bow to Miss Wells.

"How do you do," said Victorine, prettily dropping a curtsey, so that all her golden curls bobbed prettily along. There were polite smiles all around, followed by a slight, awkward pause.

"Miss Wells," said Lord Balmore, "I believe we have not yet had the pleasure of making the acquaintance of the young lady who accompanies you?"

"Oh! Oh! Of course! How stupid of me!" said Victorine. "I thought Mama would do so! Now, what has become of my mama? It is generally she who would introduce my cousin, but she seems to have become otherwise occupied. It cannot signify, I'll do it myself . . ."

Just as Victorine was about to continue, her eyes encountered those of the Viscount St. Clare, and she ceased speaking, leaving her pretty mouth wide open for several seconds. Victorine found herself momentarily stunned by the dark-blue depths of the Viscount's eyes, which were boring into hers most directly.

Victorine then started, and shook her head, as if shaking off a slight trance, saying finally, "Forgive me. How very rude of me. I was about to say that I—I should like to make known to you all my dear cousin, Miss Pamela Stone."

The gentlemen bowed again, and seemed for a moment to be perplexed, since there were four of them, and only two ladies. Mr. Bellfort was suddenly hailed from across the hall by his own mother; after having asked both young ladies to honor him with a dance later in the evening, he excused himself and disappeared.

Lady Charlton reappeared out of nowhere in a flutter of feathers and silk, and Lord Balmore applied successfully for her hand for the next dance. Viscount St. Clare was then able to lead away to the dance floor a still-entranced Victorine.

His younger brother John was left with Pamela and graciously begged to be allowed the honor of dancing with her. Pamela smiled her assent, but without any great expectations, since she, really quite lovely herself, but by no means in a class with her cousin, had grown inured to serving as the second-choice dance partner for the excess of Victorine's suitors.

Although she was only seventeen, she had always been characterized by her family for possessing as much good sense as her cousin was renowned for lacking any sense at all. Pamela's father was a renowned gentleman-scholar of medieval literature; since his wife's death and a disabling hunting accident, he had for some years been confined to his home where Pamela, his only child, looked after him. Mr. Stone had very much desired that his beloved Pamela have a proper come-out in town, and asked this favor of his favorite sister, Lady Charlton. In this way, Pamela accompanied her cousin to London.

The Hon. John Whyte was a tall man, of grave but pleasant mien. He danced well, although perhaps without great liveliness, and had a direct, engaging manner. He began to converse with Pamela just at the proper juncture of their dance.

"You will be remain in London for some time, one supposes, Miss Stone?"

"That is my aunt's intention, Mr. Whyte."

"And your own?"

"To see more of London, and enjoy even more of its delights—I hope to go to see the Exhibition at the Royal Academy."

"I have seen it. I find Turner's work, in particular, exhilarating."

"I look forward to seeing it."

Pamela found that Mr. Whyte was an accomplished partner, one who moved with a grace that was a pleasure to complement. Mr. Whyte's manners were so gentle and assured that talking to him seemed the most natural thing in the world, and she was forced to let her natural shyness slip away into ease.

"Your family is from Lincolnshire, I collect."

"Yes. I live with my father, whose health no longer permits him to spend much time in company. His nature is retiring, and is much involved in scholarly pursuits. I enjoy literature myself very much—which is Father's field, but I cannot pretend to be anywhere near so accomplished as is he. He is a most learned man, and I, his only child, keep house for him, my mother having died long ago. And you?"

"There is just Miles—my brother St. Clare—and myself, and my father, Lord Cleremont of Haverford. My father, not unlike your own, is used to living rather a secluded life, these many years since my own mother's death—and that of his previous wife, my brother Miles's mother. Father rarely ventures into society anymore.

"However, Father believes that St. Clare and I should do so, so here I find myself. Lady St. Clare, my sister-in-law, whom you have yet to meet, is French; she takes an excessive amount of pleasure in balls and the premier gatherings of society."

"I don't believe I've seen your sister-in-law in town."

"It would hake been unlikely that you would. St. Clare and his wife have only relatively recently returned to England. They met and married on the continent, and stayed in Brussels till a few months after Waterloo. Since the time they set foot on English soil, they have been socializing with a vengeance I find almost frightening."

"Do you indeed?"

Mr. Whyte inclined his head slightly, and Pamela, for some reason unclear to herself, blushed. She soon rallied, and readied herself to continue the conversation.

"I collect then, sir, that I may see here before me a man shocking enough to come to London during the Season lacking any serious social intentions. Further, do I intuit that you are come here to dance at Almack's quite against your better judgment? Can it be that you, unlike so many fine gentlemen present, are not at present looking to get—how is it said?—'leg-shackled'?" said Pamela with an audacious gleam in her green eyes.

"Miss Stone, how can I possibly predict what the Fates may have in store for me?"

"How indeed?" replied Pamela, laughingly. "I certainly harbor no such wishes, this being only my very first season. However, my Aunt Charlton wants very much to see her daughter wed just as soon as may be, and the intensity of her search for a suitable *parti* sometimes quite overwhelms me. I think that is the case with many in this company—they are fascinated by their all-consuming search for a suitable spouse."

"Very much so."

"Don't you dislike being weighed and inventoried in the Marriage Mart? I do dislike it, terribly—I think everyone must have already been told just exactly how old I am, how tall I am (though in my case, how tall I am not), and, what was my birth, and exactly how large is my portion. Do you not find it as intrusive and exasperating?"

The Honorable John Whyte laughed in recognition of his own position as potential prey for predatory mothers, and then his laughter transformed into a quite dazzling smile.

In a lowered voice meant for the two of them alone, the Mr. Whyte added, "One might just as well admit that the entirety of our London society, its whole *raison d'etre,* revolves around the ancient traditions of seeking and finding mates—for oneself or for others. Save for that, what would be the reason of gathering so many people in such a comparatively crowded space at such great expense, and serving such insipid beverages? It would all fall apart in a moment!"

"A brutal assessment, but true, I fear," she replied, smiling. As she did so, John Whyte found himself suddenly entranced by the shine in her sea-green eyes, a vision which left him momentarily speechless.

Mr. White and Miss Stone finished the set without further discussion, but with a quiet pleasure in each other's company, and a distinct desire to encounter one another again at the earliest opportunity.

As the music ended, the dashing Viscount St. Clare was seen by all the company leading Miss Wells back to her relations, Victorine with a look of triumph and awe on her face. The two brothers bowed when they came upon each other returning the two cousins to their party, and then retired together to rejoin their own party across the ballroom.

"Oh, Pamela," said Victorine, as she watched St. Clare's gorgeously dressed figure disappear into the crowded room again, "How can I possibly express the perfection of such a man as the Viscount St. Clare. His manners! His address! His air of fashion! His coat—cut to an inch! His tie—most skillfully done! Lord St. Clare is in every way the very model of a distinguished gentleman, is he not? Pamela, you're not attending—isn't his lordship exquisite?"

"He is indeed, if you like pointy-collared dandies. And the Viscount St. Clare is not merely exquisite, Victorine, he is also married!"

"Oh, he isn't!" A look of shock and horror passed over Victorine's pretty face. "How could he be?"

"I have it on his brother's authority!"

"Oh, no! If he indeed has a wife, how *could* he contrive to flirt with me like that! My heart, I declare, my poor heart is breaking!" Tears once again began to gather up in Victorine's eyes, following a well-worn path.

"Don't take it so hard, cousin. If your mother had been present, she would have warned you. Besides, I'm sure his lordship wanted to meet you because he has someone very eligible in mind for you. These great men often serve as stalking-horses for one another."

"But I don't want another man! I was quite taken by *him!* I shall kill myself! No, I shall go into a long, languid decline, and quite waste away until St. Clare sees the wicked folly of his ways. But by then, it shall be—too late! Oh, Pamela! I'm crushed! Utterly crushed!"

"Victorine, *please*. Do lower your voice, or you will bring censure on us all," said her cousin, looking around to see if Victorine's behavior had been noticed by any of Almack's high-in-the-instep patronesses. Luckily, the closest of these great ladies to them, Sally, Lady Jersey, was deeply engrossed in conversation with the Duchess of Dorset, and had not noticed Victorine's lapse in conduct.

She whispered to Victorine, "Pray, do try harder to keep your foolishness under wraps. There are many gentlemen here whose greatest desire would be to offer for the hand of a lady as beautiful and well provided for as you are. Viscount St. Clare, however, is not one of them."

"No one has even tried to offer for me," she pouted again, having apparently, for the moment, forgotten her desire to put an end to her life, "and the season is almost over. Well, nearly over, that is. Whatever shall I do?"

"Victorine, you are beautiful, you are wealthy, you are well-born; you are young, and fresh, and mildly shatterbrained. Surely, you will find someone who loves you for what you are," said her cousin with an arch smile.

On the opposite side of the ballroom, the Viscount St. Clare tipped back his aristocratic nose and, into its delicate retrousse peak, inserted some devastatingly expensive, specially-blended snuff. He nodded knowingly to his younger brother, "That's the one, John. Have no doubts."

"Which one is *what* one?" replied the Hon. John Whyte, rather wearily.

The Viscount bristled; sudden irritation totally transformed his normally handsome, manly countenance.

"I'm talking about Miss Wells, you fool! She'll bring with her a hundred thousand in the funds at the very least! Inherited from her late bachelor uncle, George Morton, a Nabob among Nabobs! Miss Victorine Wells, in addition, is perfectly lovely, as you can quite well see for yourself."

"And, as accompaniment to her lovely looks, she has the wit of a turnip, as I can quite well tell for myself also, thank you so very much, Miles."

"John, were I in your position, I would not be so meticulous."

The Viscount looked down and became momentarily involved in tracking down and dusting off a bit of strayed snuff which had fallen onto his finely cut evening coat.

"Happily for you, you are not in my position, Miles, but are in yours," said the Hon. John Whyte, his voice rising in not-quite-imperceptible contempt.

St. Clare ignored this, and went on, with a sniff, "The younger son of an earl! You are an Hon., John, and have nothing more to hope for. I have tried and tried to make you conscious of your duty to yourself, and indeed, to

the family. With Father being the way he is—and with
me being the way I am—really, there is nothing else you
can do to better your life save for seeking out and marrying yourself off to some luscious, well-bred heiress."

"Indeed?"

The Hon. John Whyte made no more reply than this.
In order to avoid his elder brother's eyes, he swept the
dance floor with his own. He saw the Countess of Grafton
animadverting her brother's sallow-faced daughter on deportment; he perceived the Dowager Marchioness of
Plimpton casting a jaded eye over the company in general.
The once-powerful, but now debt-ridden Mr. Brummell
had appeared, along with other of the more notorious
London crowd, but the presence of these persons could
hold no possible interest for Mr. John Whyte.

His eyes were captured by the sight of the petite Miss
Stone coming down the set; he noted how becomingly
she appeared dancing with Mr. Charles Bellfort.

Mr. Whyte's attention was reclaimed by his brother's
continuing admonition.

"I don't see that you *have* any other choice, John, since
Father has refused to allow you to enter any profession. He
wouldn't allow you to purchase a commission in the army
or the navy, or to go into the diplomatic service, and he
won't allow you to take holy orders, but merely is pleased
to have you dangle at his side like the perfect country gentleman that I admit you are, running his estates." The Viscount yawned at the thought of such imprisonment.

"Someone has to take an interest in the family lands,
since you do not," replied John.

"But why should I? For my own personal estates, I
have a man of business. That's why they exist, John,
hadn't you heard? All that interests me is just how much

money I have to spend. Why should I care for Father's lands, and Father's income? What has it to do with me? Do you, John, like having succeeded to being Father's man of business? For that's precisely what you've become, since you've been permitted to become nothing else. I find it rather an embarrassment."

"He is my father. I merely acceded to his wishes. Besides, had I really wished to enter a profession, I am sure I could have come up with the funds one way or another. I simply preferred to act responsibly and honorably in terms of the interests of my family."

"Boring. Dead boring, John. Spineless, and boring. Now, were you to take matters in your own hands and marry a nice, rich, beautiful child like Miss Victorine Wells over there, it would be much more responsible in terms of acting in the interests of your family. If you would offer for her, I'm sure I could possibly be persuaded to provide you with something interesting and lucrative as a wedding gift."

"As a bribe, you mean?"

"Let us say—as an inducement."

"And why ever should you care what becomes of me, Miles? You never have before, or I should have been off fighting on the continent or leading a mission long before now."

"You can't forgive me for not having helped you years ago, can you? Your own personal fortune was to have come from your own mother; but when, so very oddly, it turned out that all her money had somehow been placed in the most excessively bad investments, I found it shocking. I don't know why I didn't lend you the funds you desired. I suppose I simply thought I should not help you to run away from your disgrace."

"It was hardly my disgrace, Miles. I was but a child

when Mother died. Who should hold me responsible for having no fortune?"

"Oh, John, in our circles, losing some money is no disgrace, but losing the whole sum of it means virtually losing one's position, one's social rank. That certainly is sufficient grounds for self-annihilation. Yes, I judged you must be depressed about your fate, and wished for death. That was the entire reason I thought you wished to enter the army, and why I chose not to help you do so. You seem to be doing a bit better for yourself these days. You could still throw your life away if you really wish to, still. However, there was and is Father to think of."

"And you're *such* an affectionate son, Miles," said the Hon. John Whyte, with unconcealed sarcasm.

"Yes, aren't I?" said the Viscount with a nasty laugh. "It is a constant surprise to me that Father should prefer me to you, but—there it is. Perhaps it's because I'm his heir. Or could it be my dazzling blue eyes? I don't know. I certainly can't see any other reason."

"Nor can I, Miles."

The brothers having said more than either one had wished, speech between them ceased entirely. Then, the Hon. John Whyte, requiring some fresh air, struck out to find more solitary circumstances.

With a heavy scent of musk and roses preceding her, the Viscountess St. Clare, the former Marguerite Perigord de la Tour, came to her husband's side, and put her small, beautifully manicured hand possessively on her husband's elbow. He had been rapt in discussion with Viscount Campden of the strengths and weaknesses of a certain team of chestnuts, but that young gentleman bowed and withdrew when he perceived that St. Clare's wife wished to engage him in private conversation.

Her ladyship's gown was a dazzling confection of thin, jonquil-colored silk cut low over her ladyship's ample bosom, with tiny puffed sleeves, and a matching gauze overskirt dampened to cling to and draw attention to her excellent figure. Her jewelry consisted of the fabulous Cleremont diamonds, a set of jewels that had been a wedding present from her fond father-in-law, the Earl of Cleremont. Her ladyship's dainty feet were shod in classical sandals—with a daring touch of polish glimmering from her nails. She was a stunning woman.

"You have been arguing with John again, Miles?" she said in her lilting, attractively accented English. "That will not do. John is so tall. Now that I have come to know him, I almost like him."

"I do not. I never have. John is a fool, and worse, a bore."

"It is of no importance. But, to argue in society with one who is so very tall and memorable and distinguished—not to say related to oneself—makes one appear—*tiens,* almost vulgar, do you not agree?"

"Doesn't matter a bit, my dear."

"I beg to disagree, dearest. This is Almack's. The British ladies are so punctilious about their manners. They are not relaxed, as we are on the continent, but always pushing and shoving and struggling to maintain their rank."

"You are quite right, my dear. I forgot myself, and will not do so again. But more to the point, love—did you like her?"

"Like whom?"

"The little girl I found. How could you not notice her—the one I was dancing with—*that* one, the blonde

with the bouncy curls. See? There by the pillar? The one
with the riband bows on her dress all askew?"

"That one? Mm, now I see. *Zut,* those bows! The poor
child should find herself a new dressmaker! But otherwise, yes, very nice. She is certainly acceptable to me.
You are telling me that you feel some sort of personal
interest in her, my love?"

"I do, my dear. That I do."

"What about the other one? The one on the other side
of the pillar? The not-as-pretty one? She seems even
younger, and thus even more to your taste."

"Miss Stone? Yes, she's certainly good-looking enough
to tempt me, but Balmore tells me that the girl has no
money, so she's useless pursuing as a wife for John—
which is, as you are well aware, the sort of thing, given
the chance, that I prefer to do with my quality discards.
It is a point of honor that my grandfather taught me—use
them, lose them, and marry them off. If she had a fortune
of her own, I would agree with you she might be prefer-
able. She would do very well indeed for a few spots of
fun, I should wager."

" 'A few spots of fun'? How intriguingly you put it,
mon cher amour. I do so love the way you perceive things.
Tiens, is it that to possess those ladies by the pillar is
your current dearest wish? My love, if you desire them,
you must have them. Not just the one, but both if you
wish it. We shall determine what is required, and they
shall be yours. I love to see you have whatever you desire,
my dear—whatever!"

She planted a kiss on her husband's cheek, whispered,
"Je t'aime toujours," and moved off to circulate again
around the ballroom.

Two

The morning sun spilled over into Pamela's bedroom while Helen Fraley was fussing with the closures on Pamela's apple-green morning dress, and scolding her young mistress along with every one of them that she fastened.

"Miss Pamela, I can't say what Lady Charlton thinks herself to be about, letting a young girl like you fritter the night away at balls, and then expecting you to rise up and take calls so early on the very morning after without taking no proper rest. You'll ruin your health, you will! And your looks! It's shameful, say I! Shameful!"

Helen bustled about the bedchamber, looking to see what else remained to complete her young lady's toilette, but her high color flaming into the very roots of her red hair was an indication that her irritation had by no means come to an end. Pamela tried to temporize, dependent as she was, on maintaining the goodwill of her faithful servant.

"I think, Helen, that Aunt Charlton merely wants to spend the remainder of the season here to best advantage. The point of going to balls and assemblies, after all, is precisely to see who becomes sufficiently interested in Victorine to wish to pay her a visit on the very next day. Therefore, Victorine and I must not lie abed, no matter how late it may be when we come home."

"Oh, Miss Pamela! That Victorine! She has her head stuffed full of novels and wads of cotton wool—*that's* why no one's offered for her!"

"Helen, you know that's not the case!"

"Hmmf!" Helen sniffed, "Well, who knows, perhaps it's not the case. Yes, you may be quite right, Miss. Your cousin Victorine's so completely cabbage-witted mayhap she can't read well enough to *have* her head stuffed full of novels!"

Pamela could not help but choke back a great laugh, shaking her head in disbelief at her maid's infectious audacity.

Helen Fraley had been Pamela Stone's companion-maid for her entire life—as Helen's mother had been to Pamela's late mother, their two daughters having been born within some months of each other, and brought up not quite as sisters, but surely just as close as those below and above stairs could ever be. Thus, there was between the two of them an intimacy that utterly transcended the boundaries of class.

Helen as well had been sent to London not merely to look after Miss Pamela, but to look out for a husband for herself. There were several sons of family friends working as grooms or footmen in distinguished households whom she, not unlike Pamela and Victorine, was expected to meet, get to know, and to choose a good mate from.

Therefore, the subjects of marriage and the proper qualities to be desired in a mate were uppermost in Helen's mind as well. It was clear that her time in the Wells household had not led her to think highly of Victorine's marriage prospects, and she was never one to conceal her disdain diplomatically.

"Helen! She's not really as foolish as all that!" said Pamela. "What a terribly unkind thing to say!"

"I've always spoke plain to you, Miss, and plain I'll speak to you always, same as me Mum and Dad. I know that Miss Victorine has pots and pots of blunt, but I'm telling you that any man of sense what marries *her* ain't got no sense to start with."

"Helen, you mustn't be so unfeeling. Victorine can be perfectly sensible when she puts her mind to it—she just doesn't bother to do so very often, so she is a bit, shall we say, out of the habit."

Helen snorted in derision as she folded some clothes and put them away.

"Besides, Helen, consider this—there are quite a few well-bred, dim-witted bachelors about London, now, aren't there?"

"You mean, like will get along with like? You see? You do recognize her for what she is just as well as I do, Miss, don't you? There are some dull fellows, bachelor gentlemen, in town like that this season, to be sure, but not so many ever so dull as your coz', Miss Victorine. What Miss Victorine needs is one of them poor old inbred dukes what can barely spell to sign his own name. That's about all as'll do for her."

"Oh, Helen. I do love you, but you're really very hard on my poor cousin."

"T'aint no more than the truth, miss. That girl will get herself and all of us in a peck of trouble with her silly foolishness, you just mark my words. She's too pretty by half, and too rich by half, and too pigeon-witted to tie up her own laces. She ain't got no pa nor brother here in London to look out for her, neither. That's a deadly combination, Miss Pamela—you just mark my words if it ain't."

* * *

Not long after the conversation in Pamela's bedchamber, the first visitors of the day at the house on Brook Street were announced. There was no small surprise in the upper floors when the callers turned out to be the Viscount and Viscountess St. Clare. Lady Charlton was very satisfied with this attention, Victorine was thrilled by it, and Pamela Stone could not account for it at all.

The Viscountess looked stunning in a morning dress of cream beige muslin, with a spencer decorated with bands of ruching caught down with narrow cords, a high-brimmed bonnet trimmed with matching beige-silk ribbons, and a fringed silk shawl. Lord St. Clare had on a teal morning coat—evidently by Weston—with biscuit inexpressibles and brilliant Hessians. One could hardly fail to feel honored to receive the visitation of two such magnificent social animals.

St. Clare made known his small, dark-haired wife to Lady Charlton, Victorine, and her cousin Pamela. Victorine was appalled to find herself in the presence of such a graceful French beauty—and one who was the *wife* of a man toward whom she had already developed a frighteningly strong attraction—an attraction which had not lessened one whit since their meeting the previous evening.

Lord St. Clare began to converse amiably with Pamela and Lady Charlton, while the Viscountess unaccountably drew Victorine aside to a chair in the corner of the salon, and proceeded to spend the visit deliberately making much of her, shamelessly inflating the poor girl's sense of self-importance.

"Such a lovely child you are, my dear Miss Wells. Thoroughly charming. So fresh; so naturally beautiful; so unaffected."

"Thank you, your ladyship."

"Oh, *do* call me Marguerite."

"Oh, but I couldn't."

"Oh, but I assure you that you can. Let me say that I am so very pleased that my dear St. Clare called my attention to you. It can be hard for an *emigrée* such as myself to meet English young women with that very special continental flair and grace. Yes, my dear, you, with your manners and grace, remind me of aristocratic days now gone forever from my native France."

"Ma'am, you surely cannot recall precisely—"

"I was an impressionable young child at the time of the Terror! As you must understand, those events scarred more than one generation. It is best, of course, not to think of it."

The Viscountess sighed, shifted her position, shifted the subject, and continued her praises.

"Yes, Victorine, meeting you is a lucky thing! I am sure that we will become the very closest of friends. We must make many plans! We shall shop, and I shall introduce to you my *modiste.* No one can design robes as we French can. The acquisition by English society of so many pairs of hands skilled at needlework is perhaps the only lucky outcome of that terrible Revolution. I believe I myself inherited from my sainted mother my own expertise with needles *in utero,* when I was barely a gleam in the eye of my dear father, the Comte de Perigord!"

The Viscountess gave a gurgle of laughter, and pressed Victorine's hands reassuringly. Victorine was torn between jealousy of the Viscountess and admiration for her vivacity and confident *bon ton* manners.

"Yes, I see that there are so many things that we can do together. And later on, perhaps you—and of course Lady Charlton and your little cousin there—might honor us with a visit to Haverford at some convenient time? In the near future, it is to be hoped? Haverford is a small place, just a country kind of house belonging to my father-in-law, Lord Cleremont, and it is so nice when we are able to receive visitors there. It is a bit out of the way for most Londoners, but perhaps you would not mind to journey a trifle far away from your family?"

"You are too kind, ma'am," replied Victorine, her initial jealousy now having vanished, completely overwhelmed by the sophistication and *élan* of the Viscountess.

Even Victorine was well aware that, though Haverford was situated deep in the countryside, it was no "small, country kind of house" but an immense estate belonging to the Earl of Cleremont, almost regal in its dimensions. The thought of spending time there under the aegis of the Viscount St. Clare, heir to the earldom, was nearly overwhelming in its condescension and attentiveness. No sane person could refuse such an invitation—much less one so utterly besotted with the dashing Viscount as Victorine.

"Always I think it is important," went on the lovely Viscountess, "to introduce new and fresh blood into one's inner circle, and such beauty and *joie de vivre* as you possess in such abundance is an occasion for celebration for all of us, do you not agree?"

Lady St. Clare was smiling so charmingly at Victorine, and holding her hand with such sympathy and understanding, that her flattering words were accepted by their recipient quite without question. Indeed, Victorine was unable to render any judgment upon them beyond their face value. Thus having been praised to the skies, she innocently—and foolishly—assumed that she was deserving of it, and that it was given without any ulterior motive.

An opportunity to spend more time in the company of Lord St. Clare was very appealing to her—even if he did, so very apparently, have a wife! The Viscountess was being so very kind to her, and was herself such a model of beauty and ideal sophistication, that it seemed only natural to try to pursue the acquaintance. To be invited to stay as a houseguest at such a grand estate! It was glorious!

Meanwhile, from a velvet-covered chair in his corner of the room, St. Clare was intently pursuing a conversation of his own, turning his regal head away from his listeners only occasionally, to check the progress of his wife with Victorine. Seeing that the two of them were getting along nicely, he turned back with a smile toward his other intended quarry.

"Miss Stone, I understand from Lady Charlton that you enjoy riding, do you not?" remarked Lord St. Clare. He was taking careful note that Miss Pamela Stone was significantly more attractive than he had at first noticed at the assembly.

"I do, your lordship," replied Pamela with careful politeness. She had to work hard to conceal her amazement that these noble people were seeking out her cousin and herself. What could possibly be the reason for it? Married couples did not generally befriend unmarried girls. It was most peculiar, she thought.

St. Clare was involved in thoughts of his own. Yes, so long as she is not standing directly next to her cousin Victorine, Miss Pamela Stone is really most delectably suitable, he realized with considerable pleasure. Miss Stone is a bit younger—always a delight—and just as untouched and innocent—a virtual necessity for the Viscount to be pleased. Miss Stone seemed to differ only in possessing a trifle less physical perfection and a trifle more intelligence, which, St. Clare assumed, would not prove much of an obstacle. It never did.

Pamela went on, "At home, at Easton, I had the opportunity to ride almost every day."

St. Clare noticed how Pamela's eyes sparkled at the mere mention of riding, and surmised that he might have found the key to the girl's consent.

"Ah, well, then, since your coming to London, you must miss the opportunity of taking up such exercise very much indeed. I hope that you and your cousin may join Lady St. Clare and myself for a ride in Hyde Park. I can provide you both with very suitable mounts. For your cousin, I have a gentle bay pony very suited to a young lady: I'd love to see her on it. For you, I think, the grey mare would prove challenging. Fifteen hands high and spirited."

"You are excessively kind, your lordship, but—"

"Perhaps we might go out together tomorrow afternoon, if that would be agreeable to you?"

"Well, although it would be excessively pleasant to ride once more—I hesitate to accept your very kind offer. I am not sure of our coming engagements," murmured Pamela, who found herself unaccountably torn. She wished to ride, but somehow she felt reluctant, even though any public connection with the Viscount and Viscountess St. Clare must result in an all-important entree into the higher reaches of the *ton*.

From the point of view of furthering her own interests, as well as Victorine's, any gestures of condescending friendship from the St. Clares ought to be immediately and gratefully accepted. Pamela was thus surprised by discovery of her own reticence.

Word about income, reputation, and expectation travelled like summer lightning through London Society. In the short time since she had made their acquaintance, she had been apprised of the fact that Lord St. Clare had more estates than seemed possible for any single peer, so many that, even if he were to remain in England year-round, it would barely be sufficient to permit short stays at all of his seats in a single year.

Lord and Lady St. Clare were an extremely fashionable, fast-moving couple who had spent much of their married life on the continent, mainly in Germany. They were childless, though they had been married for (it was said) nearly six years. The Viscount was the heir to the Cleremont earldom, of course. The couple had re-entered English society at the Duchess of Richmond's ball in Brussels, and been entirely welcomed.

While Pamela Stone was lost in these considerations, Lord St. Clare approached Lady Charlton to ask for her permission to take out the young ladies for a ride in Hyde Park; Lady Charlton, unlike her niece, was not reluctant and quickly granted permission.

"How very kind of your lordship," said Lady Charlton, as visions of her daughter's ascent up the ladder of high society spun in her head. Victorine had so many assets—beauty *and* wealth. Surely a great match could be made for her! After all, Maria and Elizabeth Gunning, with no fortune, and with only beauty to pave their way, had succeeded at snagging a Duke and an Earl, in years not so long gone by——why should not Victorine be as lucky? Merely through mentally entertaining such a divine possibility, Lady Charlton was in alt.

Pamela looked at her aunt, whom she loved, but of whose tendency toward exaggeration she was all too well aware. She realized that the St. Clares's rank and fortune was clouding her aunt's perception, and that there was nothing to be done but accede to Lord St. Clare's invitation. And besides, her own equestrienne's heart wanted nothing better than to be set free on an excellent mare after such a long time of missing that most desirable sport.

Pamela turned her attention back toward the Viscount St. Clare. She became suddenly aware that, when St. Clare had his own ice-blue eyes strongly set on hers, she found herself very much attracted to him. Perhaps, she realized with some guilt, her reticence to accept his Lordship's invitation was mere jealousy of the Viscount's obvious preference for Victorine.

Or was it something else? Lord St. Clare's manners were impeccable, his address genteel, his conversation lively and sophisticated. Yet at the same time that she felt the flattering intensity of his personal magnetism, and even enjoyed it, she was conscious of a distinct sense of unease.

Was this jealousy, indeed? Was she unwilling to watch him, like so many others, prefer her cousin to herself? Perhaps it was that the St. Clares were just too involved with fashion for her taste, or perhaps she was just being missish. Perhaps her unease reflected the fact that she was merely an unsophisticated country girl at heart.

"Oh, Aunt, do you truly think it would be the thing to go?" asked Pamela, attempting to cry off, despite her longing to sit smartly on a well-bred horse once more. "Neither Victorine nor I have ridden in quite a while. Also, knowing so few people in London, perhaps it would seem encroaching to avail ourselves so freely of his lordship's hospitality. Perhaps we would be a bit—out of our depth."

You will be out of your depth, indeed, Miss Stone, thought St. Clare. *At least, that is my fervent hope.*

But aloud he said, "My dear young woman, then you must depend upon those who understand the ways of the ton, and who can both protect you in society and lend you countenance. My wife and I would be very pleased if you would allow us to undertake this trifling, but important task. Do give us your consent."

St. Clare found young Pamela's reluctance appealing. He swiftly overrode all her objections; he was quick to remind Lady Charlton that their proposed ride in Hyde Park would be well-chaperoned by the Viscountess St. Clare, and by the St. Clares's servants. There could be no question either of impropriety or of danger. The suggestion that their acceptance of their sponsorship might appear encroaching, he dismissed out of hand.

"Oh! Pamela! Don't be such a country goose!" cried her aunt. "I am sure there can be no difficulty in the two of you riding out with Lord and Lady St. Clare tomorrow. In fact, I think it would be just the thing, particularly for Victorine, to take in a bit of fresh air for a change. She's such a delicate child, you know. So sensitive. So naturally attractive. So very refined. Of course you must accept their kind invitation."

At this point, Harkins opened the salon doors, and announced the arrival of Lord Balmore, the Hon. John Whyte, and Mr. Bellfort. The usual half-hour limit for visits having been used up, the St. Clares rose to take their leave, and gave way to their successors, who were just then being shown into the room.

As St. Clare passed his younger brother on his way out, he whispered so as to be heard only by him, "That's the ticket, John! Pursue your acquaintance with Miss

Wells, and your present and future will be assured! And in addition, you shall please me very much indeed, and please Father as well, and put yourself in a position to enjoy the fruits of our generosity."

John Whyte's face turned red and then pale with repressed rage. He made no reply to his elder brother, but merely bowed icily. Making his way to his seat, next to his friend Mr. Bellfort, he found himself barely able to contain his rage, and left it to his friend and Lord Balmore to begin the niceties.

Sitting perched on the shot-silk loveseat, he listened vaguely to the conversation Mr. Bellfort was pursuing with Miss Wells and Miss Stone. Lord Balmore was entertaining Lady Charlton. Mr. Whyte was infuriated, as he had been many times before, with his elder brother's incessant attempts to interfere in his life.

It was very much the case that John felt trapped by his birth and by his lack of fortune and by his family. Under the circumstances, however, the only course open to him was to hold his tongue and to bide his time—a course unsuited to a man of his strong character, but one that he felt to be unavoidable.

Pamela had noticed Mr. Whyte's preoccupation; she wondered why he seemed cast into a black mood by the apparently unexpected meeting with his elder brother. She kept half an eye on him throughout the pleasantries she was exchanging with Mr. Bellfort, thinking to draw him out of his dark reserve once given an opportunity to do so. She wondered what troubles Mr. Whyte might have that would lead him into such evident distraction.

Pamela noted as well the admiration Mr. Bellfort was showing toward Victorine; she formed the opinion that the poor man had fallen for her cousin head over heels.

Looking to Victorine, she could note no great partiality on her cousin's part toward her admiring interrogator, but Mr. Bellfort, pudgy as he was, could not really hope to fulfill Victorine's fantasies of romance and grandeur.

Out of sympathy for the kind Mr. Bellfort, Pamela sighed audibly, and this soft sound served to break Mr. Whyte out of his self-absorption.

"Miss Stone? Is there anything the matter?" asked John Whyte. "I must apologize for my own preoccupation. I am afraid I have not been a very amiable visitor. Do forgive me."

"You need not apologize, Mr. Whyte. I merely sighed aloud, my mind wandering. I was quite lost in my own thoughts. It is a common human failing, is it not? I refer to the habit of falling into preoccupation with oneself."

"Indeed so, ma'am. Most regrettably. I was in just such a state, only moments ago."

"Yes, you did not seem quite the thing, I noted."

"You are most perceptive, Miss Stone," said Mr. Whyte with a raise of an eyebrow. "I had not realized that we were well enough acquainted for you to read my moods so easily."

Pamela colored attractively, and went on, "In my own opinion, if we could all become somehow more absorbed in others, and less self-absorbed, it would be better for the world."

"True enough."

"In a broader sense, I think that if everyone could only put the interest of others before their own selfish interests, perhaps we would find our own happiness would naturally come to pass."

John Whyte was agreeably surprised by Miss Stone's observation, and took the opportunity of a pause in the conversation to study her countenance more closely. She seemed a person worth coming to know better, and yet she was really so very young. Just seventeen, if memory served him. How could her reflections be so cogent when her experience of the world must necessarily have been so limited?

Pamela, for her part, discovered herself once again admiring both the general attitude of Mr. Whyte and his comportment; she was no less taken by his gentle green eyes and by his pale, long-fingered hands. Although she tried to hide her growing admiration, it was a task far more difficult to carry out than she had anticipated.

Pamela found herself wishing that it was Mr. John Whyte, and not Lord St. Clare, who had asked her out to ride with him in Hyde Park. Inexperienced as she was in London society and with the male sex, she decided to test the waters just a bit.

Miss Stone ventured shyly, "Your brother, Lord St. Clare, has been kind enough to invite my cousin and myself to ride with him in the Park tomorrow afternoon."

If mention of his brother was unwelcome to him, this time he concealed his feelings masterfully, and the idea of joining his brother's party for a jaunt in the park held considerable appeal.

"Has he, indeed, Miss Stone? And do you intend to go?"

"My aunt Lady Charlton accepted his kind invitation on our behalf, yes. And I do like to ride, sir, very much indeed. It has been a sad trial to me to have had to confine my exercise while in London to window-shopping on Bond Street."

Mr. Whyte seemed amused. "Yes, I can well imagine that Bond Street lacks the thrill of the hunt."

"That's not entirely true, you know, sir," replied

Pamela, her eyes lighting up with a gleam of mischief. "Women in London, I believe, do indeed spend their time in Bond Street shops pursuing the hunt. It is merely that the town-quarry is different."

The Hon. John Whyte laughed aloud.

"I see! So—although, as I recall, you denied that you are presently husband-hunting in the style common to London town, I collect that you *do* participate in hunting the more traditional prey when in the country. You were used to do so at your home, then?"

"Yes, my father was for many years known as a great rider, and he taught me all he knew. Unfortunately, due to a hunting accident—not by any means his own fault, mind you—he became an invalid, and has been unable to hunt these many years."

"Hunting can be a very dangerous sport, I know. I enjoy it myself, but I have seen good friends of mine badly injured by trying to make for themselves a reputation of being a 'bruising rider.' "

"Victims of vanity again—yet, aren't we all?"

"You are of a contemplative temperament for a girl in her first season, Miss Stone."

Pamela let loose a trill of laughter.

"A hit! You have identified my besetting sin! Now I must hang my head in shame. It is too bad, sir—have you so little compassion? You encourage me to babble on, and now I have given you cause to think me a shocking blue-stocking! And a pious moralist as well!"

"No such thing! How could a blue-stocking and a moralist ever possess such a charming smile?"

Pamela gave him a direct, but quizzical look, and colored once more. Attractive, teasing man! Her heart gave a thrum, and she tried to still it, but it would not do. She wished very much to look at Mr. Whyte.

"Let us turn the subject, if you don't mind. Tell me, Miss Stone, is your cousin enjoying her time in London as much as you seem to be?"

Pamela released another delicious gurgle of laughter.

"Victorine? Victorine is such a droll thing; she would have a good time under any circumstances, I expect. She is quite in awe of your brother and sister-in-law, you know."

"Is she?"

"She is excited as a schoolgirl, and wants to copy all of her ladyship St. Clare's fashions."

"Now, Miss Stone, I don't mean to be presumptuous, but you are hardly out of the schoolroom yourself, if I am not in error, aren't you? How is it that, unlike your cousin, your head has not been turned by your time in London?"

"It is true that I am hardly out of the schoolroom, but I am already turned seventeen. However, my life has had in it rather more responsibility than Victorine's."

"I had forgotten. Your needing to take your mother's place at an early age would account for it, of course."

"Yes. It is so. I am thought to be rather sensible for my age."

"I see."

"I suppose that makes me rather boring."

"Not at all, Miss Stone," he replied. "Not at all. Believe me, it is refreshing to meet a girl in her very first season whose understanding has not been utterly obscured by frills, furbelows, and French fashions."

A last trill of laughter was Miss Stone's sole response, and their conversation came to a natural halt; the two of them looked at one another for just a moment.

Miss Stone smiled and Mr. Whyte smiled in return. He felt exquisitely comfortable in her presence. Being with his family, which consisted of his irritable father, his self-absorbed brother and his brother's fashion-crazed wife grated on him almost beyond endurance. Save in the company of good friends such as Charles Bellfort, John Whyte had come to regard himself as being something of a misanthrope.

But in the company of Miss Pamela Stone, it was different—not only had he no desire to escape into solitude, he wished to prolong whatever contact he had with her as long as possible. He somehow felt he had come home at last.

Miss Pamela Stone, on her part, was finding herself powerfully magnetized by the Hon. John Whyte. It being the very first time these feelings had arisen in her, she was rather unsure of what she was supposed to do, or how to conduct herself. She could only hope that Mr. Whyte was taking some pleasure in her company, and that he would seek her out in order to come to know her better.

Pamela wondered if the pleasure she felt in Mr. Whyte's company and the tug of wanting she felt in his absence might be precursors to a serious, enduring affection. She wondered whether she was too young for Mr. Whyte to consider as a suitable possibility for matrimony; whether he would want to seek her out; whether he liked her as well as she liked him. Her mind flew on in just such a fashion; indeed, she could not help herself.

Mr. Whyte surprised her reflections by speaking out suddenly, saying, "Miss Stone, I wonder if you will be attending the next Assembly at Almack's?"

"Why, yes, Mr. Whyte, I believe that is my Aunt Charlton's intention."

"Then perhaps I may see you there, and have the honor to dance the first dance with you? If it is available?"

Pamela blushed with pleasure. "Yes, of course you may. I shall be very happy."

Mr. Bellfort, inspired by example from the Hon. John Whyte, then applied for the hand of Victorine for a dance on that same evening, and was accepted. Pleased, the two men rose and took their leave.

In the carriage passing through Grosvenor Square were Mr. Bellfort and the Hon. John Whyte, each lost in a personal reverie. Mr. Bellfort was thinking only of Victorine Wells's magnificent presence, and how he could possibly contrive to have such a celestial creature turn her heart toward such a simple, dull, ugly chap as himself. It did not seem possible and his heart was sore and troubled.

Mr. Whyte was remembering Miss Pamela Stone with pleasure, but was also thinking along more practical romantic lines. To pursue an acquaintance with Miss Stone he heartily desired—but wondered whether such an acquaintance might not be unfair to her. The most that could be said for his eligibility as a suitor was that he was, technically speaking, his brother's heir, and second in line for the Earldom of Cleremont.

High-sounding expectations as they were, any such expectations were unlikely ever to come to be fulfilled. Miles, Viscount St. Clare, was in excellent health, and, sooner or later, a son was almost certain to be the product of his marriage to the Frenchwoman.

Apart from that most slim of prospects, the Hon. John

Whyte had no fortune at all. He was not in any financial position to put himself forth as a serious suitor. What ought he to do? Were he to shower his attentions on Miss Stone, as he had begun to want to do, he would be pre-occupying her attentions away from more eligible suitors, more suitable gentlemen who could provide her with the home and position young ladies of quality require.

Still, she was young yet. She had already said that she had no real intention to seek out a husband this season, and her aunt seemed to be pushing for a quick marriage for her own daughter, not for Miss Stone. It should be possible to pursue the acquaintance at least on a casual basis, for a little while, without any harm being done to the young lady.

One could not, of course, live in her pocket, or cut out other gentlemen if they should appear and court her—that would not do at all. But to initiate a warm friendship? Yes, it would be possible. And certainly, from the point of view of the Hon. John Whyte, desirable. Who knew what might, in time, occur? Perhaps his own circumstances could suddenly, magically change for the better? These things can happen, it occurred to him. Nothing is written in stone.

John Whyte then pulled his thoughts back in, away from such rhapsodizing. Things such as sudden reversals of fortune *could* happen, of course, but they did not seem to happen to men such as himself, he thought with a stab of pain.

They happened to men like Miles, he reflected, his heart's expression cloaked by a smile at once wry and bitter.

Three

It was a fine day for a promenade in the park. It was a fine day to ride. It was a fine day to drive a sleek curricle and a pair of match-bays, and that is precisely what the Viscount St. Clare did. He had sent a note along well before nuncheon, begging Miss Wells's pardon, and inquiring whether she would mind driving rather than riding on horseback, as the horse originally intended for her had, very regrettably, developed a lame forefoot overnight.

The Viscount had brought along with him—his lovely French wife, Marguerite, and the dashing continental couple was accompanied by rather an extensive retinue. To Pamela's delight, the Viscount's brother John Whyte had sent along his own note, expressing the intention of himself and Mr. Bellfort to join the company.

From an upstairs window, Pamela could see Mr. Whyte, astride a capering chestnut stallion. Apparently, he was himself a skilled horseman, for he handled the powerful beast with a hand so light as for his mastery to be invisible to the uninitiated onlooker.

Near him, was the Viscount's groom, riding a bay gelding. By a length of braided leather, he was leading the grey mare that Lord St. Clare had spoken of to her yesterday. Pamela's heart leaped at the sight of the beautiful creature.

Just following the group of riders, she saw Mr. Bellfort being driven in his brand new barouche. She'd assumed that, since the pony destined for Victorine has gone lame, the besotted Mr. Bellfort had been contacted by the Viscount, and that Bellfort was hoping to offer a seat in his carriage to Lady Charlton and her lovely daughter, Victorine Wells.

Pamela had wondered for a moment who Victorine would choose to accompany, given a choice between Lord St. Clare and Mr. Bellfort, but the outcome seemed all too certain. Poor Mr. Bellfort! It was lucky St. Clare had brought along his wife. Victorine would certainly have sought to ride with him if there had been room in his lordship's curricle.

Victorine's wishes played clearly on her lovely face. Her manners were really not under the kind of control what they ought to be, Pamela thought. But what could be done about that?

The girls let their abigails finish dressing them; Victorine raced to the front steps to meet the riding party, her cousin following decorously behind.

"Oh! Good day, Lord St. Clare!" cried Victorine. "Good afternoon, your ladyship! What a splendid pair!"

"Aren't we?" purred the Viscountess, showing her teeth. "And the match-bays as well, to be sure. But, I beg of you once more—do call me Marguerite, my child!"

Victorine blushed. Somehow she felt dreadfully inexperienced in the presence of the exquisite Lady St. Clare.

"Are you ready to enjoy this glorious morning, young ladies? Where is Lady Charlton?" inquired Lord St. Clare.

"Oh! Mother has the headache and cannot come with

us today, your lordship. There will only be myself and my cousin."

"You will not mind serving as our chaperone, will you, Lady St. Clare?" asked Pamela, not without a certain wary reserve in her voice. "Lady Charlton thought it would do, but perhaps you think it not fitting?"

"Why ever not?" inquired her ladyship, with raised brow.

"You are so young," replied Pamela, in all innocence.

"I'm not nearly as young as I seem, my dear child!" said she, laughingly. "I would be perfectly happy to chaperone you both. Indeed, it cannot be but a pleasure to me. And mind you, I shall be extremely severe, so polish your deportment and your manners!"

Everyone laughed but Mr. Whyte and Miss Stone. No one but the two of them noticed this.

Mr. Bellfort was nearly overcome by the intense felicity of being able to take Miss Wells up in his carriage. They would be almost unaccompanied—save for John Coachman. Savoring this thought, Bellfort stood in a state of extreme agitation and excitement on the sidewalk, waiting to hand his favorite in.

As he took Victorine's small hand in his, he marveled at the way her outfit became her. She had chosen to wear a spencer over a walking dress of cotton muslin that showed off the demure elegance of her figure. In her new watered silk bonnet with riband bows, and silk flowers, she looked utterly angelic; his heart was stolen by the divine Miss Wells all over again.

Mr. Whyte dismounted from his chestnut in order to throw Miss Stone into the saddle. She was wearing a flattering sea-green riding habit, a hat perched rakishly on her head, and she was looking very gay indeed as she took her seat on the mare.

"How are you this afternoon, Miss Stone?" he asked, as he helped her take her seat.

Her eyes shone. "Well, sir, thank you."

"And your cousin?"

Her lips curled up in a pretty, mischievous line. "I believe you'll find Miss Wells, as well, is well."

The corners of Mr. Whyte's mouth twitched just a little, as Miss Stone continued to speak.

"What of you, Mr. Whyte? Better than yesterday, I trust."

"Much better, thank you, my dear," he replied appreciatively. "And in your presence, even better."

He bowed briefly, and disappeared to remount the chestnut stallion.

I do believe that gentleman is flirting with me! thought Pamela, with no small pleasure, as she urged the mare into a jog-trot. *How extremely satisfactory! I wish he may do it again!*

The party then went on though the busy cobbled streets of London, the riders, though paired together, beyond speech, having to concentrate hard to keep their horses from shying at the various obstacles that thrust themselves in their way. There were hawkers, pedestrians, carts, and children running into the streets, coaches careening this way and that on the way to their intended destinations at high speed. In a way, riding the streets of London could be as difficult as riding cross-country following a pack of hounds.

Finally they all, riders and carriages as well, made their way to the comparative peace of Hyde Park. Even though it was not quite the hour of the grand strut yet, Hyde Park had become a fairly lively place, filled with the many members of the ton who had been drawn there to see one another and, of no less importance, to be seen.

A few stylish young ladies eager to win admiration promenaded arm in arm, discussing matters of great import, their abigails following respectfully behind. Young married couples strolled along the ways displaying to all in the area the distinct advantages of having made advantageous marriages.

Elderly ladies showed themselves off in carriages, criticizing the dress or deportment of the young. Gay young whips showed off their prime goers, keeping them moving at a spanking pace, hoping to win admiration of some lovely and eligible young lady.

It was, in fact, little more than an outdoor Almack's: it was the Marriage Mart once again, it was society at its most critically acute. Within the charmed circles of the ton, everything was noticed, and nothing forgiven.

The party stopped a short distance within the park at the Viscountess's behest. She had expressed to her husband a wish to stroll about and take the air a bit. The party was delighted to oblige her and they parked at a pretty knoll for some minutes.

Mr. Bellfort had the pleasure of handing Victorine down from his barouche. Her hand was soft as a dove's.

"You are looking very fine this morning, Miss Wells."

"Thank you, Mr. Bellfort."

"I had hoped to take this opportunity to ask if you would join me for a turn about the park."

"Yes, that would be most pleasant."

Mr. Bellfort's heart surged in his breast; he smiled shyly as he offered her his arm.

Miss Wells stole a glance at Mr. Bellfort just at this

time, and noted that her companion's face had changed with a kind of interesting radiance.

Short though he is, and bald though he is, there is something very warm and comfortable about this man, Victorine thought to herself with some puzzlement. *He seems so safe—and rather attractive in spite of his height and his lack of hair. And yet he's nothing like St. Clare, of course. But I do like him.*

Almost as if he could hear the way the girl's thoughts were running, Viscount St. Clare regarded the conversation between Bellfort and Victorine with a darkening brow. He exchanged a whispered word with his wife, who smiled understandingly and nodded.

Having herself just been handed from the curricle by St. Clare's diminutive tiger, the Viscountess began to sway dizzily and dangerously as she approached Mr. Bellfort's barouche.

"Oh my dears, I find I have changed my mind after all! Do not let us walk about in the park just yet! Driving in that London commotion has made me excessively giddy! So much so that although I very much wish to, I am not at all able to walk about at just this time. I should like very much to continue our drive in your barouche, Mr. Bellfort! Would that be acceptable to you? The curricle is too much for me. Too fast, you know. Too fast. I ought to have known. Silly me."

Mr. Bellfort's heart sank to a depth equal to the heights to which it had but recently risen. But there was nothing to be done. There would be no walk arm-in-arm today with Miss Victorine Wells.

He dutifully handed her ladyship up into his barouche.

The Viscountess went on, "And perhaps, dear Victorine, you would be kind enough to keep poor St. Clare company. You are not frightened of racing curricles, I collect?"

"Oh, no, your ladyship, not at all," replied Victorine, although she knew herself to be very frightened indeed. Her pleasure at having the opportunity of accompanying the divine St. Clare, however, overshadowed all else.

"You *must* call me Marguerite. I have already asked you to do so twice, I believe."

"Oh dear. I am so very sorry."

"In future, I hope you will be more amenable to my heartfelt wishes."

"Yes, of course, ma'am—Marguerite, I should say."

"Then it is all settled."

And St. Clare lifted Victorine by her waist into the curricle—light as a feather, he thought, and he jumped up beside her, brushing her skirts lightly as he did so. Victorine's pulse was racing. Their knees touched slightly, since there was not very much room, and St. Clare had angled his body to make the most of any possibility of contact.

He was close enough to Victorine to hear that her breathing had quickened. St. Clare felt desire arise within him. How he loved the thrill of the hunt! He felt that hunting was particularly amusing just at that turn-of-mind time when the fox begins to be aware of the danger that it is in. St. Clare loved every moment. Beginning, middle, and then the end-game—it was enough to set a real man's blood racing!

Pamela watched as St. Clare handled the reins, driving off. She had exchanged a wondering glance with Mr. John Whyte at the sudden turn in the seating arrangements, and then thought no more about it. They were in a large party, after all, in the middle of Hyde Park. There was no reason to suppose that anything could go amiss. They were in a public place, in company with persons of quality known to them, with a matron present as chaperone. There was no reason to assume that anything was wrong.

She turned her attention toward Mr. Whyte as they began to walk their horses together as a pair, thinking once more how attractive he was—a tall man with chestnut-colored hair on a tall, regal chestnut stallion. Very attractive, indeed. High cheekbones dominating a face filled with character, displaying a combination of gentleness, discipline, and strength.

This man, John Whyte, was clearly a cut above the rest of the young men she'd met so far in London. So many of the others were so uninspiring—over-bred fops, feeble wastrels from the gaming-hells, idiotic sports-mad Corinthians.

This man was quite another thing altogether. For one thing, she found him absolutely gorgeous. His skin was pale, but pale with refinement, not dandyish weakness. He had the most lovely long fingers she had ever seen. His eyes were grey-green, like the color of the North Sea on a stormy morning. His shoulders were broad and strong; he was tall, soft-spoken, and manly. She began to be aware of a strong instinctive stirring of her heart.

Mr. Whyte interrupted her thoughts by speaking.

"That mare St. Clare chose for you seemed spirited enough early on, but has little wind or staying power. You merit a far finer animal; I am sorry St. Clare has so badly underestimated your abilities as a rider."

"By no means."

A raising of an eyebrow told her he had not bought her polite denial. She raised her own in response.

"Are you accusing your brother of having mounted me on a slug?"

"I am."

Pamela choked back a giggle and said, "This is due only to a difference in perception. One man's 'slug' may be another man's 'well-mannered hack suitable to a lady.' In any case, this mare has lovely manners, is sweet-tempered, and will probably show much more energy once she knows she can trust my hands. I think there is a bit more to her than meets the eye. I'm sure I can get a bit more forward action out of her—she actually seems a little unbalanced, which is odd, unless Lord St. Clare normally uses her for driving. Do you know, that quiz of a brother of yours actually described her to me as spirited?"

"Miles is no great rider, though he thinks he is. He is almost always over-mounted. Lacks the knack of it, lacks the hands."

"Nor is he a good judge of horse-flesh, it seems. But it would be surely uncivil to look your brother's gift-horse in the mouth."

The Hon. John Whyte broke into laughter, adding, "I'm not so sure. Knowing Miles, I'd look if I were you."

"Indeed so? At any rate, I am truly happy merely to be able to ride again—you can have no idea how happy. It is the first time in so many weeks. Victorine doesn't care for riding above half, nor does Aunt Charlton—for them it is another one of the necessary social accomplishments, like music or needlework; consequently, I am the only one in the house who really suffers from not having horses to hand."

"We must come out together again, then."

Pamela rewarded him for this excellent suggestion with

a darling smile. He almost blushed upon its receipt, and tried to cover it by continuing to speak.

"I wonder why Miles did not bring a suitable pony along for Miss Wells. I thought he made such a point yesterday of wanting to see both of you mounted."

"He did. There was some mention of a pony having gone lame, but I thought I understood that your brother had a very large stable of horses available to him. Yesterday, he seemed to intend to provide horses for us both, but today prefers to drive Victorine."

"Perhaps he does so because he likes to show off his skills as a whip to impressionable young ladies."

Miss Stone made no reply, unable to do so without being uncivil.

"Tell me, what do you prefer to do, Miss Stone, in London?" he inquired.

She turned toward him with pleasure, slowing her mare down a bit.

"I am not much intrigued by the life of the ton, but I enjoy the cultural life in London. I like the musicales, and the opera, and the theater, and the museums. And I do enjoy dancing—that kind of frivolity is close to my heart. So if you think, as a result of our conversation, that in addition to being a boring moralizer, I am a horrid little Puritan, I must protest."

"Never would I say such a thing! May I say instead that you dance very prettily, and I recall your dancing perfectly clearly. I look forward very much to the pleasure of dancing with you again as soon as I may. *You* must recall that I have already solicited your hand for a dance at the next Assembly."

Pamela looked inquiringly at Mr. Whyte, and was pleased to find her glance met his, his dark eyes seemingly filled with admiration. Could it be so? Was she merely imagining it? The Hon. Mr. Whyte seemed deliberately to be paying her the most distinguishing attentions.

Pamela felt herself very happy as they bid their horses break into a slow, rocking, well-controlled canter. She was thrilled that she had not been so foolish and missish as to have turned down Viscount St. Clare's kind offer to ride out on horseback today. Riding in Hyde Park had its distinctive pleasures after all.

In the curricle, St. Clare was pressing his advantages to the limit. Unless one was up close, no one could see what liberties he was attempting to take with his fair passenger. His tiger was there, of course, but he was his own boy, and as such, very much used to his master's predilections.

So far in this drive, his lordship had already availed himself of the opportunity to tell Miss Wells of his admiration of her figure, and her features, and her character. To this end, his knees had been set against hers for some time now, and he had been keeping his horses going at a good, fast pace in order to keep the finer details of the picture obscure to any onlookers, and to foil any attempt of the young lady to escape from his attentions by bolting from the carriage.

But this one seemed to have no mind to do so. She seemed mesmerized by him and this pleased St. Clare no end. What a flat! It was going to be easier even than he had supposed.

He transferred the reins to one hand, and grabbed the girl's hand tightly with the other. She blushed and trembled. St. Clare's desire surged up again—he loved the sensation of a female trembling beneath him.

He turned round a bend where there were trees and bushes and no one else in sight. He took his chance, keeping his eyes on the road as his lips brushed her cheek. St. Clare whispered in her ear, "Victorine! Dear Victorine! You must, of course, forgive the shocking conduct of a man who finds himself so violently in love with you!"

"In love with me? Are you?" Victorine lifted her chin to look up at St. Clare, astonished and thrilled.

"My dear girl, how can you doubt it? I have already mentioned at length my admiration for you in every possible way!"

"Oh, my lord!"

St. Clare transferred his reins expertly and pressed a hand against Victorine's thigh till she blushed scarlet. She looked back at the tiger, but he was St. Clare's, and remained impassive, as if he had seen nothing amiss.

"Oh, do forgive me, my dear child! You must realize it is difficult to control one's passion when it is so overwhelming!"

"Oh, dear. I did not know! I dared not hope."

"My dearest Victorine. I had thought it impossible—can it be that you harbor tender feelings toward me?"

"Oh, dear. Oh, dear. I blush to admit it, your lordship, but, yes, I do! However—we must not say these things. You are a married man!"

"All the more tragic for me!"

St. Clare squeezed Victorine even more tightly, casting her a glance filled with passionate anguish.

She fairly jumped at the unaccustomed contact, then settled back as from St. Clare's mouth poured forth a torrent of romantic reassurances, soothing her fears, and heightening her sense of being loved with a passion that passed all bounds.

Again she looked behind at the tiger, who acted as if nothing was happening, which, oddly enough, gave Victorine courage. Perhaps this fondling was not unacceptable behavior in Hyde Park among the fashionable set? She had heard that many of them harbored extremely advanced ideas. Certainly Lord St. Clare was behaving in a way that seemed extremely advanced to Victorine.

"It is a terrible tragedy for us," St. Clare went on, as he made a sudden turn and drove over the turf for a few yards into a small clump of trees that would mask them completely from the view of others. His lordship had been here many times before. It was one of the few such spots in the entire park, and had taken him a long time to locate. "My dearest Victorine we are victims of a tragedy of love that must not be!"

"Oh, dear St. Clare—you are right, this is a tragedy for both of us!" said Victorine, beginning to weep with emotion.

St. Clare glanced at the girl with annoyance. He wanted to set the stage for a seduction, not to have this idiot child turning into a useless watering-pot whose tears might attract the attention of the members of the ton. There was a time and a place for everything.

"Stop crying—right now!" St. Clare hissed angrily.

Victorine was taken aback by his abrupt tone. He smiled hastily.

"We must be discreet, my dear. Any inappropriate public behavior would bring censure on both of us."

"Oh, of course, your lordship."

The Viscount smiled a tight smile of approval.

It had occurred to St. Clare that he could suggest that the chit call him Miles, but decided that, all in all, he preferred that he call her by her Christian name and that she refer to him by his title. It put power where power was due.

Once well within the grove, St. Clare pulled his horses up, and put his hands around Victorine's tiny waist. At a gesture, the tiger got off and walked away into the trees.

"Oh, but we must not, your lordship."

"I can't help myself, Victorine. Do you not understand the kind of love that is overpowering? I love you, I want you; please do not be so cruel and unfeeling as to withhold yourself from me, my dearest little love. I would die for you, a thousand times over! Favor me with but a kiss!"

The Viscount began kissing Victorine, nibbling at her neck, pressing his body close against hers. And she, poor little fool of a girl, began shyly to return his attentions with all her heart. Viscount St. Clare, as anyone can understand, was in alt.

Life, it seemed to his lordship, was sweet.

In the barouche, the Viscountess was boring Mr. Bellfort down to a grinding death. Many minutes past, he had lost sight of dear Victorine, for her ladyship kept insisting on going in another direction completely. He knew he was beginning to develop the headache, and would probably suffer from it all of the night.

How could the Frenchwoman prattle on so? How could anyone endure such nonsense? How could he stop this witless babbling of hers before he was driven quite mad?

He began looking desperately for the curricle, or for John Whyte, hoping to find a way to change the seating arrangements. It was torture for him, nothing less.

He still could not find Lord St. Clare and Miss Wells,

but he spotted John and Miss Stone far away, apparently chatting with some animation.

Mr. Bellfort greatly envied them. He wished devoutly that he were not a man of such habitually impeccable manners.

Miss Pamela Stone pulled up her grey, and suggested that they should let their horses walk and rest. Thinking to draw him into conversation, Pamela asked, "Tell me more about your family home, Mr. Whyte, if you would. My aunt tells me it is something quite out of the ordinary."

His face grew dark and cautious. Pamela was a bit taken aback, as she had thought this subject would be a fairly innocuous one.

"The family estate—one cannot call it a home, not in any sense—is called Haverford. My father has lived there alone since he became a widower for the second time, though very recently, since Miles and his wife have come back from the continent, they sometimes stay there with him as well."

"What is it like? I've never been in that part of the country."

"Haverford's great house is very grand and very drafty, and I don't care for it particularly well, or, rather, I should say that I don't like it as it is currently arranged. The drapes are too dark, the furniture far too thick, clumsy, and ornate. It reminds me somehow of the death of my mother, and so I go there as little as possible.

"I live on a small farm nearby called Melfield, which is quite pretty, with many trees and shrubs that one of my late uncles imported from the Far East. I spend the bulk of my time at the Melfield farm, pottering about and trying to improve the yield of the land. I'm most interested in crop rotation—the very pattern-card of a gentleman-farmer, I suppose. Except when I have particular business with them, I generally spend little time in the company of the rest of my family."

Miss Stone raised an eyebrow.

"Forgive me for speaking so frankly, but it is the case, and I see no reason to hide it from you or from anyone. Although I manage my father's estates, my father and I do not enjoy an easy relationship—not by any means. St. Clare, my elder brother, has been away from England for so many years that I can scarcely say I count him among my acquaintances. He is an enigma to me, in appetites and in manner; we have very dissimilar tastes in all respects.

"Now that Miles has returned from the continent, he and his wife have the use of Father's townhouse. We try to maintain a civil relationship, but even that takes effort, quite frankly. When I am in town, I generally stay with Charles Bellfort or Lord Balmore, not at the family's house."

"I see," said Pamela thoughtfully.

"But, let us speak of other things than these," said Mr. Whyte. "What do you enjoy most when you are at home at Easton, other than riding?"

"Simple, homely things. I fear I am a very simple sort of girl, sir."

The Hon. John Whyte favored Miss Stone with a faintly amused glance, saying, "Somehow I feel I should never be tempted to characterize you as 'simple,' Miss Stone."

"Why not, sir? I must protest: I cannot see myself as being intricate. If, your sister-in-law, say, is like a *fleur-de-lis,* I am a plain garden rose. If Victorine is like lace, I am like plain wool."

"Don't try to pull that 'plain wool' over *my* eyes, Miss Stone. I'm not so green."

Pamela grinned, and said, "I do protest—I am speaking naught but the plain truth, sir. I'm a simple young lady from the country, and I am fond of very ordinary occupations. I like needlework, I like tending my gardens, I like drawing and painting. I like walking in the woods, I like riding—as you perceive. I like visiting friends in the neighborhood of Easton, I like writing and receiving letters, and I am fond of reading."

And I am fond of being in your presence, Mr. John Whyte. I am fond of listening to your voice; I like being with you, Pamela was on the point of saying. Instead, she ran her hands along the smooth silky neck of her horse.

Her companion regarded her for a few moments with an appraising glance.

"You are not at all like your cousin Victorine," said Mr. Whyte. "Are you?"

Pamela blushed attractively. "No, I'm afraid not, not a bit. I am no heiress, much less a diamond of the first water."

"Miss Stone! That is not at all what I meant! It is perfectly true that your cousin is unusually beautiful, but there are other facets of character that can elicit admiration. For example, to say that Miss Wells has, for example, small interest in learning would be a vast understatement, would it not?"

Pamela gave forth a delightful trill of laughter.

"No, dear Victorine will never be regarded as a needle-witted bluestocking, I fear."

"Nor will you, Miss Stone, ever be regarded as an antidote. Please give me leave to say that you are at once a very lovely and a very intelligent young woman."

"Why, Mr. Whyte! Now I *am* shocked indeed! Are you quizzing me again?"

"By no means, Miss Stone. I am attempting, in my crude, unpracticed rural manner, to pay you a compliment."

"Then I think you must be flirting with me. But you must not! Remember, I am but a green girl in her very first season."

Mr. Whyte's eyes narrowed and an unusual gleam arose in them. His lips turned up in an appreciative smile.

"No, Miss Stone. I am no flirt and never have been."

"Indeed?"

"I merely—well, what can I say? I am no ladies' man; in fact, in my district I am known for the soberness of my character. You may ask any of my acquaintance; I am sadly lacking in romantic qualities. Miles is forever reminding me of what a dead bore I am."

"How horrid of him!"

"Be that as it may. My point, Miss Stone, however clumsily put," and here he looked genuinely embarrassed. "Keep in mind that I am only an impoverished younger son with nothing to offer any lady but my good character, I hope you will allow me the kind opportunity to come to know you better. As a friend."

Pamela smiled back at him with delight.

"I would like that very much, Mr. Whyte."

"Shall we canter on, then?" he said, very satisfied, and both took off together at a rocking canter, slow enough not to violate the sedate rules of equestrian propriety in Hyde Park, and set all the old town tabbies talking.

Viscount St. Clare helped Miss Victorine Wells, no longer quite the innocent child she had been perhaps a quarter of an hour before, but still in full possession of her virtue, to rearrange her guinea-gold hair. He signalled then for his tiger to mount up behind. He snapped the reins, bringing his horses to attention.

Miss Wells was at once flushed, elated, and confused. Gently bred as she had been, she really had no knowledge of the world or of worldly ways. She knew, in a vague way, that her behavior had gone rather far beyond the bounds of what she had previously thought proper, but she was a confirmed romantic, and was no good critic of her own behavior. She had always depended on the good advice of others to make her decisions in life and to advise her on her deportment.

At this point, such advice as she was receiving was coming from the lips of the Viscount St. Clare. He had told her that these torrid flirtations were quite the thing, perfectly acceptable, the way of the ton. He suggested that all ladies had their flirts, and that no one's reputation could be injured by acting as they had just done. It seemed reasonable enough, under the circumstances.

A doubt or two still nagged at her mind. Should she consult her sensible cousin Pamela? Pamela always seemed to know what was permissible and what was not.

Of course, what if Pamela did not approve of an innocent flirtation between herself and the Viscount St. Clare? She might not like the idea of stolen kisses. Perhaps Pamela would not approve. Pamela might be missish about the whole thing. She might scold her and that would not be pleasant at all.

It would be very bad if her mother found out, for certainly Lady Charlton would not understand about sophisticated behavior. Yes, that was a distinct danger. Perhaps the right thing would be to discontinue seeing the Viscount?

But it was impossible, Victorine immediately realized. Because she, Victorine Wells, loved St. Clare. And since her love was true, she must follow her heart. In fact, she *would* do so! Just like the heroines in her novels!

The Viscountess, silent for a moment, espied Pamela Stone and John Whyte riding together, apparently completely delighted to be in one another's company. Her lips pressed together till the blood nearly ran out of them. Her breath quickened. She found herself staring fixedly at the happy couple, and her small, perfectly formed teeth began to grind back and forth together.

A kind of strange, gnawing pain began to grow within the breast of Marguerite Perigord de la Tour.

"How odd," said the Viscountess to herself. "I am beginning to take a distinct dislike to that chit of a girl, Pamela Stone, although I know I did not dislike her last evening. Or even earlier today. But now I find I am disliking her very much indeed. I do hope Miles will ruin her."

Her lovely arched brows furrowed for a moment and then relaxed. She smiled to herself, thinking, "Even more to the point—I think I would like to have the Honorable John Whyte all to myself for some time. I find I have a liking for tall men."

The petite brunette checked the perch of her bonnet, which had cost a small fortune; she felt it made her look not a bit matronly, merely experienced. Which she, of course, was.

She smiled again. She turned her dainty face away from Mr. Bellfort, whom she had been trying unsuccessfully to put out of countenance purely for her own amusement, and stared wistfully out the window of the carriage.

"I feel sure," she went on silently to herself, "that that nice tall John Whyte would very much enjoy me. *Pour quoi pas?* What real man would not enjoy a woman who is not a child?"

Oh, oui, *Miles likes children—that is just his peculiarity. And I love Miles, dearly. But I like men. And men— like me.* She smiled again.

Mr. Bellfort began wondering what in heaven's name the Frenchwoman could find to grin about so often? He was beginning, truly, to lose his grip on civility, and that was something he prided himself on never doing. He wished to put his hand around that small white neck and throttle her.

Viscountess St. Clare turned to Mr. Bellfort, showing her pearl-like teeth in a dainty smile, saying, "Let's catch up with Mr. Whyte and Miss Stone, shall we?"

Before Mr. Bellfort had time to react, Lady St. Clare had leaned over and thus instructed the coachman, who sprang the horses forward so fast that the two within the carriage were thrown back against the seat, and against one another. Mr. Bellfort recoiled from her in an instant.

"Just one of my odd whims, Mr. Bellfort. *Zut alors!* So sorry! I own that I forgot this is your carriage and that I have behaved most improperly. Do forgive me. St. Clare indulges me so, I fear I am become quite dreadfully spoilt."

You are indeed, thought Mr. Bellfort with disapproval. *Vixen. I'm glad I don't have the charge of you.*

John Whyte and Pamela Stone, having pulled up their horses to a walk, were surprised to see Mr. Bellfort's carriage being driven up to them at breakneck speed. The two riders halted, amused at being the object of such pursuit.

The tiny lady St. Clare alit in a flash, and sidled up to them; she was followed by an incredulous Mr. Bellfort. She stood near to Pamela's grey mare and gave her brother-in-law John her most brilliant and beautiful smile.

"Oh, do come down, John—how you say *een English?*" remarked the Viscountess to Mr. Whyte. "Do come down off your high horses and keep me company for just a moment—John dear, please? I have a wish to be private with you."

Puzzled, John Whyte dismounted and approached his sister-in-law. He did not notice Lady St. Clare's eyes narrowing with a dangerous glitter of jealousy.

Pamela began to dismount as well, and lifted her leg over the upper pommel-horn of her side-saddle. She was in this precarious position, her left foot still using the left stirrup for balance, preparing to jump down to the ground when Lady St. Clare seemed to slip for a moment, her knees buckling down in a swoon.

Her ladyship's exquisite bejeweled hand, on which was a ruby ring with a short, sharp pin concealed within it, raked across the grey mare's flank deeply. To any casual observer it looked as if Lady St. Clare had merely put her hand out in an attempt to regain her footing.

A sharp cry issued from Pamela's lips, as Pamela's mare reared suddenly and bolted.

"My God—Pamela!" cried John Whyte, who immediately started to run after her. Lady St. Clare blocked his way.

"Oh, *mon dieu!*" said Lady St. Clare, letting herself fall into a deep faint into John Whyte's arms, making him stumble. "I can't see! I'm dying! *Aidez-moi!*"

Her ladyship's eyes rolled in their sockets, and she appeared to lose consciousness entirely.

Almost nauseated by the thick scent of perfume she wore, John tried to put off Lady St. Clare onto Charles Bellfort, and go to the aid of Miss Stone. He could hear the awful hoofbeats of Pamela's horse thudding off into the distance.

"Get off me, woman!" he shouted.

Pamela's horse was galloping off. Her foot had gotten caught in a stirrup, and she was being dragged behind her horse at a terrible rate over the greensward.

"Pamela!" shouted Mr. John Whyte once again, depositing his loudly objecting burden in the unwilling arms of poor Mr. Bellfort. "Madam, be still, will you?" he said curtly to her as he mounted his horse and spurred it into pursuit.

"John! How dare you! I need you! The groom can go after that creature! I want you here!" cried Lady St. Clare, but her words were lost in the dust as John settled into the saddle, shortened his reins, and sped off, calling back, "Miss Stone may be killed. I must assist her!"

"You must assist *me!*"

But her words were lost as he disappeared into the distance, riding as fast as his horse would take him.

Her ladyship was furious. *John Whyte will pay for this insult,* she thought to herself. *He shall suffer for this, and I shall see to it myself. I'll destroy his impudent strumpet, I swear it! And this man shall be made to watch and suffer as I do so!*

The Hon. John Whyte whipped his stallion after Pamela's mare, although his brave animal needed no such artificial encouragement. John saw Pamela's foot at last fall free of the stirrup; she collided heavily with the ground.

Miss Stone lay transformed into a mere crumpled heap of green velvet on the lush grass, left behind by the grey mare who, freed of its burden, galloped on.

John dismounted his horse and approached the motionless velvet heap. Knowing how falls from horses could seem terrible and turn out well, or seem terrible and prove fatal, his heart hammered in his chest. He steeled himself to see how Miss Stone fared. *I pray she not be dead,* he whispered to himself.

What he first saw—and what gave him hope—were her thick lashes, fluttering ever so slightly. Not broken her neck, thank God, and not unconscious—though very near it.

He looked over his shoulder and motioned behind him to the groom on the bay gelding, who had automatically come as well in pursuit of the runaway horse.

"Fetch a doctor—and be quick, man," John Whyte said roughly. The man wheeled his mount and was gone in an instant.

He looked at Pamela's face. It was white as fog. He brushed a strand of hair off her forehead, and her eyelids fluttered again. She moaned. He touched her hand gently, afraid that any bone he touched might be broken, afraid that he would only hurt her more than she was hurt already.

It must have been at this moment that he realized how precious Pamela Stone had become to him, and how desolate he would feel were he to be forever deprived of her company. It was an enlightening experience.

Her eyes opened. She moaned again, and reached out. He took her hand in his and chafed it.

"John. John."

"Hush, now, it's all right. It's all over."

"Took a—a bad fall."

"Very bad," he agreed.

"Wind—knocked—right out of me."

"Hush, now. The doctor's coming.

"Where does it hurt?" he asked, wanting to prolong her state of consciousness by engaging her in conversation.

"Here. My wrist. It hurts so."

"It may be broken. Don't try to move it."

"Oh, John. I'm so dizzy."

Mr. Whyte was profoundly pleased to hear her, in her delirium, address him by his Christian name. He replied with tenderness, "Lie back. Don't try to sit up. The worst will soon be over."

A small smile crept into her pale lips. "Such a calm man, John."

"Yes, Pamela."

"So very—reassuring."

She smiled sweetly again before losing consciousness. John Whyte, impatient, swore under his breath—when would the doctor arrive? When could they take Miss Stone to safety? When could he be sure she would be alright?

Pamela wakened again into consciousness of Mr. John Whyte having scooped her up in his strong arms; she clung to him like a child as he began to carry her back to the carriage.

From a distance, the Viscountess St. Clare looked on the tender scene dispassionately.

Pity the chit's not dead, Lady St. Clare thought to herself. *Perhaps next time.*

Four

Pamela's accident had a number of effects—that of putting an end to her enjoyment of the pleasures of the London season for some time, and that of bringing the party of persons who had gone to Hyde Park that day in closer contact—whether they wished that it be so, or not.

John Whyte, of course, was the most constant visitor to the house in Brook Street, keeping daily watch over Pamela's progress recovering from a concussion and a sprained wrist. He visited on the very next morning after her fall, and each day thereafter for a week. Helen Fraley noted his constant attendance with some measure of satisfaction; Lady Charlton tolerated his visits, though she did not take him seriously as a suitor for her niece.

Mr. Bellfort was also a frequent caller, though it was clear to all that, much as he wished for Pamela's swift and complete recovery, her injury had given him just the excuse he needed to call on and spend time with Victorine as well. Victorine saw him as a kind friend, but nothing more, and Lady Charlton thought him a true gentleman, wealthy and of good family, but thought her dear daughter could look far higher for a husband.

Seven days after the accident, the Hon. John Whyte called, in the morning, rather earlier than he was used to do. Pamela had stayed abed later than was her habit, and when the footman knocked to announce the visitor's arrival, Pamela's suite was set into a sudden rush of activity.

"Mr. Whyte's come, lazybones, and you're still not dressed, Miss Sleepyhead," scolded Helen Fraley. "Best get that wild hair of yours up, and I'll get you into your lace dressing-gown."

"Do you think I can receive him in bed? Ought I?"

"I'll call Lady Charlton to join you. You certainly can't go downstairs, not like that. Should I deny you to him? You've not time to dress proper. He's come so early. What could the man have been thinking of? Think he's come to make you an offer?"

"Stop it, Helen. Don't talk like that; don't send him away. Help me with the robe, will you?"

She allowed herself to be dressed in the gown that had once been her mother's. It was an exquisite confection, and Pamela loved it dearly. She felt that it still carried some of the magical aroma of her mother with it—the scent of cinnamon and jasmine.

Lady Charlton came in to her bedchamber just after Mr. John Whyte, greeted him amiably, and motioned for him to sit on a small gilt chair the housemaid had brought over to the bed. She sat nearby at the window seat, took out some embroidery, and began to work it.

John Whyte took Pamela's hand, and pressed it, briefly. "How good it is to see you this morning. Are you well? I see your wrist is still bound."

"Dr. Gordon saw her yesterday and said she is still mildly concussed," interjected Lady Charlton, "And should stay in bed for another few days. The swelling on her wrist has gone down by half."

"Is it still painful?" he asked Pamela.

"Yes, but nothing to signify."

"I am so sorry it happened, and I am glad your injuries were not worse. There is little other than flowers and sympathy that I may offer."

"It is nothing, sir. I've been tossed off horses often enough before, I can tell you."

Her visitor's brow clouded, but he said nothing more until Lady Charlton received an urgent message from Cook with regard to dinner. More than a little flustered, she excused herself, and left the two young people alone.

"Your aunt trusts me to sit alone with you now, does she?"

"Apparently. I suppose she thinks that no one would take advantage of an invalid young lady not in her best looks," said Pamela.

"Fishing for compliments? Unworthy—but I assure you that you look very lovely today, Madam Invalid."

"I protest! I was not fishing for compliments at all!"

"Methinks the lady doth protest too much."

She colored prettily, and denied his charge once again.

"Please, Mr. Whyte, you are wrong. The doctor and my aunt keep telling me how pale I look, and it frustrates me, for I am very anxious to be out and about again. I think my health suffers not so much from my injuries, but from all this vexing restriction of activity. I am used to being an active person, and being confined in this room for so long is near to driving me mad.

"I was very much disappointed that the doctor thinks I must spend even more time in this dreadful, boring bed. I'm quite recovered, and am near to being irritable about it. Everyone is being far too solicitous of me, and I wish they would stop."

"I understand your chafing at the bit, and I sympathize with you entirely."

He paused, as if unsure how to continue.

"Miss Stone, I am glad we can be private with one another today. I have something I particularly wish to say, and I have been waiting all this long week to say it to you."

Pamela raised her eyebrow in silent inquiry, and Mr. John Whyte colored faintly. He wasn't going to make her an offer, was he?

"It actually concerns that grey mare you were riding when you fell."

Miss Stone flushed suddenly with painful embarrassment. What a goose she was! How could she think that he would propose to her? How lucky she had managed to keep her countenance and held her tongue before she made a complete fool of herself in front of Mr. Whyte. She succeeded in controlling her disappointment masterfully.

"The grey mare? What about her?"

"I went over to St. Clare's stables the morning after your accident, and inspected the grey mare thoroughly. I found there was a six-inch superficial gash on her left rear haunch, and a puncture wound as well. I don't know how such wounds could have occurred. I didn't want to mention it in other company, or even to you until your health was better."

"A gash, do you say? Impossible. More like a scratch, from a branch, perhaps. A nail, a thorn. Something of that sort, to make her bolt in such a fashion. So much for that vaunted slug! I am so ashamed that I lost my seat. I should have known better than to let my boot get caught like that. It was really inexcusable. The whole thing was entirely my fault."

"I'm afraid that I do not agree with you at all." His grey-green eyes were staring at her, very grave.

"What do you mean? What are you saying, sir?"

"I'm saying, Miss Stone, that your accident was nothing of the sort. The injury your horse suffered, if one could call it a scratch, a vast underestimation in my view, was inflicted intentionally by person or persons unknown. It was an injury that must have been painful to the mare, and that accounts for her having bolted, not some fault of temperament in the horse, or any fault of expertise in yourself, the rider. I am saying, Miss Stone, that I think you should be very careful."

"What do you mean, 'careful?' How can you think that someone harmed that horse on purpose? Surely, no one could have wished that horse to bolt on me. What have I ever done to anyone that they should wish me ill?"

"I'm sure I cannot imagine. The possibility that someone does wish you ill, however, must be kept in mind."

"But who could have done such a thing? Who would do so? It cannot be, I tell you. Think back—there were very few people there at the time—the groom, your sister-in-law, Mr. Bellfort, yourself. People with whom, at that time, I was barely acquainted.

"The injury must have occurred after I fell off the horse, or after the mare bolted, not before. No, Mr. Whyte, I am terribly sorry, but such a theory defies all logic. I cannot believe that that entire incident was anything but accidental."

"Perhaps I'm wrong, then, though I believe I am correct. I am sorry that you think my theory 'defies all logic.' I simply thought that you should be apprised of all the facts of the situation."

"Why? To scare me out of my wits?" said Pamela, with some asperity. "Thank you so much!"

Mr. John Whyte, cut to the quick, stiffened with sudden anger.

"Frighten you out of your wits? By no means, ma'am. Believe me, had I known that merely to raise this possibility in discussion would cause you such immoderate distress, I would certainly have kept the information to myself," he said with chilly distance. "Having previously presented yourself as a sensible young woman, I could have had no idea that by mentioning this admittedly distasteful subject you would fall into a distempered freak."

Pamela felt this insult's sting very much, but tried to keep her temper.

"I do not believe it is at all fair to describe my reaction as a 'distempered freak.' Forgive me if I was uncivil, Mr. Whyte, but I must believe that your theory is incorrect. It is perhaps a result of an overly fanciful turn of mind."

"Fanciful, am I?" he replied even more coldly. "If so, that's the first time I've ever been characterized as such. Why then, I am so sorry to have troubled you, Miss Stone. There is nothing more to be said. It was entirely wrong of me to foist my absurd theories on you. I do apologize, ma'am, and shall remove myself from your presence directly. Good day."

Deeply offended, the Hon. John Whyte bowed and left.

Pamela spent the rest of the night alternately chiding herself for having insulted the person who had become a dear friend, and then in imagination reproving Mr. Whyte for indulging an oversensitive and irritable nature.

But neither train of thought availed her: the next morning, her previously constant caller made no appearance, and Miss Stone was cast into the megrims with full force. She tried to defend her actions, and at one moment could do so, and the next could not. Cooped up in that room, she knew that she herself had been in an irritable mood from the very beginning of the interview.

She tried to be objective: Could he have been right? Could anyone have wanted to harm her? None of those people knew her—there could be no motive at all. No, it was impossible!

He had been wrong. However, she was truly very sorry to have injured Mr. Whyte's feelings while informing him of the incontrovertible fact that he was wrong.

In another week's time, Miss Pamela Stone, Miss Victorine Wells, and Lady Charlton found themselves back at Almack's dressed to the nines, waiting for their dancing partners to appear, just as if nothing had ever happened. Victorine had finally been the recipient of two offers of marriage—both of which she had rejected.

However, Victorine was pleased at least to have finally been able to fix the interest of a few eligibles, and her mother was pleased by this as well. Lady Charlton thought that, sooner or later in this very season, a suitable husband was bound to appear, and the thought was a great comfort to her.

"For you see," she confided to Pamela, "If Victorine does not marry by the season's end, what am I to do with her? She grows ever more willful and more flighty. If my husband were still alive, she would mind him, but she simply doesn't mind a word I say. It's not that she bears me no affection, it is just a slight weakness of her character. Do you perceive what I mean?"

Miss Pamela Stone perceived precisely what her aunt meant, and, out of the love she bore her Aunt Charlton, forbore to speak of her cousin's obvious defects.

This particular evening, in fact, Miss Stone was worrying more about her own defects of character—such as a tongue that could slip into waspishness, a dislike of being commanded, and other similar weaknesses. It was these, she thought, that had so seriously undermined her relationship with the Hon. John Whyte.

In keeping with the promise he had made prior to her accident, Mr. Whyte had come over to collect a dance from Miss Stone the very next time they encountered one another at the assembly at Almack's, but this dance, a quadrille as it happened, turned out to be a very different event from the one previously anticipated by both parties.

He deliberately held himself apart from her, and made a show of putting his attention fully on the intricate dance steps. His questions and answers reflected nothing more than impersonal, superficial civility. Though she tried to turn the subjects and change his mood, he was very unresponsive, and, finally, she gave up, and merely went through the motions of the *pas de zephyr,* and the rest of them. She felt discouraged, and not a little angry at his stubbornness. Of course, being inclined towards stubbornness herself, she could understand his having withdrawn—but that understanding did not make the situation any less painful.

The worst part, of course, was when she watched him dancing with Lady St. Clare, who indulged herself by flirting with him outrageously. He had asked her for the waltz, which, in all fairness, the pair performed expertly.

His strong arms encircling the Viscountess, she whispering in his ear, her lips just an instant away from Mr. Whyte's skin, now brushing against his skin as they whirled around . . . it was unbearable for Miss Stone to witness, and yet she watched as if transfixed as they continued on. Lady St. Clare was laughing and telling jokes that drew responsive laughter from Mr. John Whyte.

Pamela felt herself reddening with humiliation as they made themselves the talk of the assembly, and finally, she withdrew and walked over to the corner where the chaperones were sitting, and tried to hide her mortification and her jealousy.

John Whyte hardly understood why he was allowing her ladyship to flirt with him so shockingly within full view of the ton. He knew he was angry with Pamela, and deeply hurt by her dismissal of his just concern for her well-being.

Serve her right, then! Calling him fanciful . . . as if he could not tell the difference between a scratch to a horse and an injury.

Yes, he knew all about injury, and he felt that he had allowed himself to be wounded. Why he had allowed a pretty face to overcome his better judgment, he did not know. He regretted having fallen victim to Pamela's charms.

He had no money. He had no prospects. There was no place for a woman in his life. No place at all. It was better, far better, to remain aloof and uninvolved.

Far better to succumb temporarily to the lures of his sister-in-law than to the wiles of some little chit who had no sense of gratitude. He required no such multiplication of his problems.

If she wouldn't allow him to express his concern for her welfare—so be it. His conscience was clear. He had tried, and been rebuffed. No more needed to be said or done.

The flirtation was over, and it never should have come to pass at all.

Her aunt found her in a sheltered corner, disconsolate, sitting on a thin, gilt chair.

"Whatever is the matter, Pamela? You are certainly acting very strangely this evening, I do not scruple to inform you."

"I am perfectly well, Aunt Charlton."

"It's my child who is thick-headed, not I, my dear. What is the matter?"

"I protest, I am perfectly well, Aunt."

"Don't take me for a ninnyhammer, for I'm not, you know. I collect that the cause of your upset must be that John Whyte, who used to visit us so often, and now visits us so rarely."

"In fact, he comes no more."

"What, have you two quarreled?"

"Yes."

"What about?"

"Nothing that signifies. We have discovered we do not suit, that's all."

"That's a whisker, if ever I heard one. You suited perfectly well for weeks, but—well, I suppose it's all for the best."

Pamela stared at her relative, uncomprehending.

"Don't look at me so, Pamela. He seems an amiable young man, but I have it on his brother's authority that he hasn't a penny, so he's useless as a candidate for marriage."

"You mustn't say that. It's unkind and mercenary."

"I am casting no aspersions on his character. Don't be ridiculous, dear—if you were an heiress like Victorine, you would be able to indulge your whims and pay no attention to money when you choose your husband. However, you've not much more than a penny yourself. Upon what did you two expect to feed your hopeful family? Suckle them on good character? Perhaps you two thought to collect a fee for your dual intelligence to pay for your sons to go to Oxford? I believed that you had more sense. No, it's a very good thing that you have quarreled."

Pamela began to realize that their mutual faults of character might have very unfortunate consequences for both herself and Mr. Whyte, and that a failure to heal this breach might end in disaster.

"I think Charles Bellfort would make a nice husband for you. Let me call him over."

"No, Aunt Charlton! Please! I am promised to him for the next dance in any case!"

"Don't be missish! Let me invite him to talk to you a bit before the dance. You mustn't behave in this heedless, care-for-nothing manner. Who knows if your father can afford another London Season for you? Remember, marriage is business."

Is it, indeed? wondered Pamela. *Men and women with fortunes can marry where they pleased; persons such as myself and Mr. Whyte must sell ourselves and our freedom or never marry at all.*

"I am not ready to marry this season, Aunt Charlton!"

"You may not be ready, but you may not be able to afford to wait. Who do you think is going to come to you, living as you do, all the way out in Lincolnshire, tucked away at Easton? Do you nurture the belief that Prince Charming makes calls at country houses?"

Aunt Charlton was right, of course. A good man is hard to find, particularly for a sensible girl such as herself, and princes do not grow on trees. She sighed with regret. Why, why had they let themselves fall into that stupid quarrel?

Just then, Mr. Charles Bellfort came to claim his dance, and Miss Pamela Stone enjoyed no further opportunities for reflection.

From the opposite side of the room, John Whyte watched as his best friend took Pamela in his arms, and waltzed her around the assembly rooms. She had long since been given permission by Almack's haughty Patronesses to do so, and she looked every inch the excellent dancer that she was.

He watched her dance with mingled pride and envy. He had eyes for no other than that green-eyed, slim creature wearing a simple white sarsenet gown, a slight trimming of lace at her bosom and sleeves, a pearl necklace ornamenting her long white neck, a few flowers ornamenting her luxuriant dark-brown hair.

Why had they quarrelled? Had it really had anything to do with that runaway horse? Upon sober reflection, John Whyte perceived that it was he who had forced the quarrel on her. In the common run of things, he was never so irritable and sensitive as to react with anger merely because his judgment had been called into question. No, there was far more to it than that.

First, he had reacted too deeply out of genuine concern for her safety. Second, his nerves had been raw because of how deeply he cared for her—and that he had qualms about fixing his interest with her, lest to pursue her might injure the person he so much cared for. That was the explanation, after all: he had been trying to detach himself from her.

The Hon. John Whyte was bitter, but reconciled to it. It was as well a quarrel had occurred. He was in no position to dangle after any woman save an heiress. Charles Bellfort was a kind-hearted man, possessed of a sizable fortune, and would make her a good husband. He wished them both happy and was glad to be out of a race he ought not run.

Five

Lord and Lady St. Clare, a few days later, invited Victorine and Pamela to ride with them once again in Hyde Park. As an experienced rider, Pamela knew that she should take advantage of this opportunity to get herself back on horseback before irretrievable damage was done to her seat, her hands, and her equestrienne's nerves. With this in mind, she accepted their offer with alacrity.

Victorine accepted because Lord St. Clare had faded into the background in the weeks after Pamela's fall. She saw little of him, and heard even less of him. Thus deprived, Victorine was very anxious to spend time in his lordship's company, even if it did mean spending some time atop some smelly beast of a pony.

Lord and Lady St. Clare arrived at Lady Charlton's house in the early afternoon, both husband and wife mounted on superb animals, Lord St. Clare experiencing some difficulty keeping his stallion under good control. Pamela winced as she watched his lordship jabbing at the beautiful creature's soft mouth, and beating its hindquarters with a tailed whip. Why, she wondered, do people who ride so badly so often buy horses they have no hope of handling?

Viscount and Viscountess St. Clare were accompanied by a groom leading two horses, both bays, one a large pony, and the other a horse, a spirited, full-size gelding. Pamela did not recognize the groom—he was not the same one who had accompanied the party on their last fateful outing.

She had hoped it might be the same man, so she might question him. Although she could not for a moment believe John Whyte's outrageous theory, she believed that it would do no harm to pursue the matter just a little bit. However, that possibility was now closed to her, at least for the time being.

As the new groom tossed her into the saddle, she asked the Viscount, with forced gaiety, "Where's my miscreant grey mare? You've not sold her for glue, have you? She was an excellent, gentle animal."

"Nonsense, Miss Stone," replied St. Clare imperturbably. "She was clearly a distempered beast, and I took good care to have her sold the very next day. I do not tolerate evil beasts in my stables, I can tell you. That nag was on the auction block within twenty-four hours of bolting on you, and is likely pulling a wagon on a country farm. Or is being mounted by a fat country squire."

"Which she so richly deserves," added the Viscountess, with a chilling smile toward Miss Stone. "Distempered country creatures have no place at all in London."

Pamela was dumbfounded at this vicious remark, obviously aimed at herself. Why would the woman say such a thing? Somehow she seemed to have offended Lady St. Clare—perhaps it had been a mare of hers, that her ladyship had been fond of? Perhaps she resented her husband for having gotten rid of the horse? That was all that Pamela could think of. Or perhaps she hadn't properly heard what her ladyship had said.

The group made their way to the Park, and, to Victorine's jealous distress, Lady St. Clare herself took charge of her, while his lordship paired himself off with Miss Pamela Stone.

St. Clare took great pains to make himself amusing to Miss Stone, until he had her coaxed into peals of gay laughter. His object was to carry out his flirtation close enough to the other ladies that Miss Wells would be aware of it, and feel the full rush of feminine envy.

St. Clare was proud of his tactics. Very good, thought he. *Let the little girl develop a hunger for me, and, in time, that hunger will be satisfied.*

The day went on without further mishap. The Viscountess's coldness toward Pamela Stone continued unabated, but no untoward incidents occurred during their ride out in the Park. Friends were met and hailed, horses and riders well-exercised.

St. Clare took the opportunity of having one private word with Victorine to the effect that, much as he regretted it, and as deeply as he cared for her, he had reconciled himself to the fact that their love was forbidden, and that they must see each other henceforth only as friends. Victorine took this opportunity to weep briefly, and tried bravely to put the dashing Viscount out of her mind.

No more was said; the young ladies were returned safely home to Brook Street, with no harm done.

That evening, the ladies were engaged to attend a particularly splendid affair at the Earl and Countess of Grafton's townhouse in Grosvenor Square. Lady Charlton had known the countess for some years, and they were on good terms still. Although they were not the insepa-rable pair they had been as young debutantes, Lady Grafton would have been much offended had her old bosom-bow failed to bring her daughter and her niece to the Grafton ball. In particular, the Countess was inter-ested in promoting the beautiful and wealthy heiress Miss Wells as a potential wife for her own favorite nephew, Lord Shelford, who, although of a good family, had not a penny to his name.

In the evening, Lady Charlton had sent her dresser, Collins, to assist Victorine with her toilette. Collins had dropped a hint to her ladyship that, in her opinion, Vic-torine's own abigail, Maud, was far too rural a chit to be solely entrusted with the task of putting the subtle fin-ishing touches on a girl aspiring to cut a dash at the most grand affair of her first ton season.

When Collins finally pronounced the young lady fin-ished at last, Victorine indeed looked astonishing, wear-ing a dress of light blue silk, with a spangled gauze overskirt, and a matching light blue gauze spangled scarf. In a thin necklet of sparkling diamonds, and a silver riband threaded through her yellow curls, she appeared as a very delightful young creature.

Helen Fraley fussed over her own young lady as best she was able, her hands full trying to make Pamela sit still until all the preparations for the evening were prop-erly complete. Still, it was an uphill battle.

"You let me do for you what I'm paid to do, Miss Pamela! I won't have you giving me trouble. I'll dress you just as good as that Collins and Maud dress Miss Victorine. You'll look well in London whether you like it or no, hear me? You've no cause to tell me none of these frills and furbelows matters, miss. For they do matter. I know it as well as I know my own name."

"Why do I allow you to bully me, Helen?"

"Somebody has to. You're so stubborn, anybody else can smell the stubbornness a mile off, and probably has better things to do with their mortal lives than tussle with you, I expect."

"A good answer. I am silenced, my failures of character being bandied about to my face even by my devoted abigail. Now, most stringent one, where shall I put these flowers?"

"They match your dress very nicely. Let's just put them in your hair, just so. And let's wear the Alençon spider-lace rose that your grandmother gave to your mother. You look very well, Miss Pamela. You really do. Your father would be proud of you, could he but be here to see you. And your mother, bless her soul, had she but lived to see you so pretty and all."

Thinking of her mother, whom she had adored, and of her father, whom she sorely missed, Pamela colored faintly. It was all very well, this round of balls and assemblies and picnics and rides—but she began to long for the companionship of her dear surviving parent, and the comforting familiarity of her home.

"Tell me, Helen," she said, trying to change the subject, "How is your own London social life proceeding? Will you prove to be a credit to your mother's ambitions for you?"

"Don't tease me, Miss, it's a hard business. If you wanted to be a real help to me, you might arrange for me to have a little more time off than one afternoon a week, and an evening a month. It's just not enough time to spend looking over the merchandise."

"Why, Helen? Whom have you met?"

"Never you mind. I'll tell you when I find a good one. Not until."

"With whose household does he work? Or is he a tradesman?"

"Well," said Helen with ill-concealed pride, "One of them works for your friend the Viscount St. Clare, and one of them works for another gentleman friend of yours, and I won't say who, and wild horses won't drag it out from me, and that's an end of it."

"Helen! Do you really have two young men dangling after you? You little flirt!"

"Nope. Just practical. Don't make sense only to meet one man. Have to look around a bit. Like buyin' muslin, you want to compare and contrast. Shop around."

"Well, I'm very impressed. Now that I know you have connections with aristocratic households, perhaps I could prevail upon you to do me a favor. The young man you're acquainted with who works for the Viscount—do you think you could ask about the fate of the horse that bolted on me? The sweet grey mare?"

"What do you need to know that for, Miss Pamela, if I may be so bold as to inquire?"

"That mare was a lovely, well-mannered animal—it wasn't her fault that she shied and bolted. I'd like to buy her, and take her home to Easton with me," replied Pamela, masterfully concealing her dissimulation.

"What an odd thing, Miss! Though, of course, you've always been crazy mad about your horses. Tell you what—I'll do the best I can. Now, you hear that sound? Lord Balmore and Mr. Bellfort are already here to take you to the Countess of Grafton's. Pinch your cheeks. There's a good girl—you look a rare sight!"

"Thank you, Helen. You needn't wait up for me—I'll put myself to bed."

"I'd be mad not to, Miss Pamela! I want to find out just what kind of a time you had—with whom you danced, who was there, everything! Do you really think I'm not interested in every little detail?"

"Very well, Helen. My social exploits *in toto* shall be entirely at your disposal."

Six

Judging by the jostling of carriages and chairs vying for position outside the Earl of Grafton's house, tonight's event was to be yet another sad squeeze. Of course, all decent affairs were required to be sad squeezes, or they were thought to be no success at all.

Lady Charlton and her charges, Miss Pamela Stone and Miss Victorine Wells, knew very well that this party would likely mark the acme of their season's ascent of the upper reaches of society. All three of them were thrilled to have been invited, and thrilled to be able to be part of the glittering affair.

Accompanied by their escorts, the ladies ascended the great staircase, and greeted their hostess. They tried to make their way to the ballroom, but it was a slow business in that crowd, and it took some minutes before the butler, himself an imposing figure in silver livery, was able to announce them.

They placed themselves in a corner with Sir Evan Wharton and Lady Wharton, and the girls began to amuse themselves by trying to locate the most notorious among the great crush of fashionables. The Prince Regent, of course, would not be attending, for he had come down with a slight case of influenza, but the Duke and Duchess of Richmond would likely make an appearance, and Lady

Sally Jersey had already arrived. They were trying to place a dazzling redhead who might or might not be the very latest of the Duke of Lancaster's mistresses when a tall man, dressed in a simple black coat and black silk breeches, caught Miss Wells's eye.

"Look!" said Victorine. "Isn't that John Whyte?"

"Where?"

"Over there, the one dancing with Belinda Falk-Duffield. She's fabulously wealthy. Sadly enough, she has the face of a cart-horse, but with all that money, who should care? Your precious Mr. Whyte seems to be finding her pleasant enough company. Look at him. He never looked so happy, even when he was with you, Pamela."

Miss Stone was not amused by this account, but her cousin, with classic lack of insight, failed to notice.

"Dangling after heiresses, now, is he?" observed Pamela tartly. "I'm surprised he didn't try to fix his interest with you, my dear Victorine. You're so much better-looking."

"Just between us, his brother St. Clare told me in strictest confidence that Mr. Whyte is not thought to be terribly intelligent."

Pamela barely forbore from smiting her cousin for repeating this little piece of slander, but managed to restrain herself. She was surprised how much she felt a quick rush of desire to defend Mr. Whyte, even though she was irked at him.

"I think your friend Lord St. Clare is perhaps jealous of his brother."

"Oh, no! Why should he be? St. Clare has everything and John Whyte nothing!"

Miss Pamela Stone felt her color rise, as she took offense at this additional inanity.

"You are wrong. Mr. Whyte possesses character, elegance, and grace," she pointed out. "In fact, in many ways I think he is the very model of a gentleman. You may not abuse him in my presence, cousin. He has been nothing but kind to both of us."

Pamela became aware of a strong surge of pained conscience. She really was to blame for their quarrel, and she really ought to make up with him. Victorine looked at her cousin with surprise.

"I'm sure I'm sorry, Pamela. I thought you were rather angry with him."

"Well . . . so I was. But it was over a private matter, upon which any two persons might reasonably disagree. It spoke nothing against his character. I still won't hear him abused, not by you, and not by Lord St. Clare either."

"Certainly." *What an odd fish my cousin is,* thought Victorine, *blowing hot and cold about that man.*

Mr. Charles Bellfort came over to claim Victorine's hand as the music began again, and Lord Balmore led off Lady Charlton, over her ladyship's protests that she must remain to chaperone her niece Pamela. Both Balmore and Pamela refused to allow her ladyship to hide behind this easy excuse, and Lord Balmore succeeded in drawing her away from Miss Stone into a lively country dance.

Lady Charlton looked very well on the dance floor, her niece realized. She wondered if Lord Balmore, a widower, might be paying court to the widowed Lady Charlton, so particular had been his attentions of late. An interesting development that would be, to be sure.

Pamela had turned toward an ornate gilded mirror to check on her headdress, antique figured lace gathered into a rose, surrounding several real rosebuds. As she turned back, a tall dark figure suddenly loomed up behind her. She gasped.

"Did I startle you?" inquired the Hon. John Whyte.

"Not at all, sir. I am not given to fits of fright as a general rule," said Pamela through her teeth.

"I see. Are you not dancing this evening, Miss Stone?"

"Not just at this moment, Mr. Whyte, as you see. Tell me, how do you do these days?" she inquired rather coldly. "It has been a long time since you have visited at Brook Street."

"I have been very well, thank you. I am sorry that I have been engaged in family business that took me away from London for a time. Now that we have met again, I should like to take this opportunity to inform you that, having listened well at our last meeting to your criticisms of my character, I have taken the same to heart. I wish you to know that I have now ceased entirely to indulge in any flights of fancy, thus enjoying a far more peaceful mind as a result."

"Indeed so?" she inquired with what she hoped was quelling hauteur.

"Yes, I felt sure you would feel happy for me."

Pamela was furious at this bit of sarcasm. She quickly launched a return volley, pretending an indifference toward him she was far from feeling.

"You are correct in your analysis. Hearing what you say, I am indeed happy for you. However, I must confess to some shock, Mr. Whyte," she replied lazily. With a false and languid smile, she inquired, "Can it really be that you are no longer seeing murderers and mischief-makers wishing to do me harm hiding behind each and every potted palm?

"If so, sir, I can imagine that such a change must leave

you suffering under the horrifying weight of a great deal of sudden leisure time. Having so rashly renounced your Gothic tendencies, pray, sir, what shall you do for entertainment?

"Now, Mr. Whyte, if you will excuse me, I see that my party is repairing to the supper hall."

Miss Pamela Stone made a great show of sweeping away haughtily from Mr. John Whyte. Inwardly she was upbraiding herself for having given in to her horrid temper, and having actually fanned the flames of dissension between them, rather than helping to extinguish them, as she had thought she ought to do. Her wretched mouth! But he had deliberately provoked her!

Nothing to be done about it anyway—and that odious Mr. Whyte behaved every bit as childishly as she herself had! "No more flights of fancy!" He could keep his caustic remarks to himself from now on. This was London, after all, and that insufferable, interfering man was *not* the only fish in the social ocean.

As he watched Miss Stone go, the Hon. John Whyte was upbraiding himself for having given in once again to his wretched temper. Still, that seemingly charming child had, he had luckily discovered, a wasp's tongue and he was well rid of her. To think he had entertained the notion of fixing his interest with her. Good riddance to the little alluring, provoking termagant!

Mr. Whyte was trying very hard to make his final escape from the Grafton ball, but to do so he had to pass through a hallway that was packed with guests.

There his heart sank as he saw Miss Stone again, in company of her aunt and Lord Balmore, Miss Wells, and

Charles Bellfort; there was no avoiding wending a path near to Pamela Stone if he wished to take his leave of the ball.

John Whyte thus had to push through the crowd as best he could manage. He was performing a slight, cold inclination of his head toward Miss Stone as he passed her when the crowd suddenly surged forth, sweeping Bellfort, Lord Balmore, Miss Wells, and Lady Charlton away from him, and pushing Miss Stone in the opposite direction, toward him, roughly depositing her against his chest, and shoving her for a moment directly beneath his chin.

There was a distinct tearing sound, and at the same time, John Whyte felt himself snagged soundly. In spite of himself, his sense of the ridiculous was aroused at having become pinned to the precise person he had been trying to avoid. He grinned wryly as he tried to extricate himself from whatever was attaching him to Miss Stone.

"Oh, no, don't move!" cried Pamela. "My lace is caught on your—what *is* it that it is caught on? I have no idea, I can't see, and I can't move. No, don't do that—please don't move! That lace rosette belonged to my grandmama! You'll tear it. It's spider-lace, and dreadfully delicate. Someone help us! To what could it be caught so firmly?"

"Your lace is caught on—that is, it is nearly wrapped around—my stick-pin."

"That is most assuredly *not* a stick-pin—it has long, sharp, horrid spokes!" she said indignantly, as she felt about in the general area trying to free herself.

"On the contrary, I assure you that it is an antique twelve-spoked diamond stick-pin."

"Rubbish. It's nothing like a stick-pin. You must be quite mad—I felt you were mad, all along."

Her mood then shifted swiftly, into a more disarming mood, nearer to that of a damsel-in-distress.

"Oh, please, Mr. Whyte, let's not brangle. I am completely caught, and if I move at all, my lace will be utterly ruined. Where is Aunt Charlton? Why are all these people pushing so? Why does no one stop to help us? Do they suppose we characteristically assume this sort of intimate positioning when in vestibules at private balls?"

"It is difficult to know what they assume. Ought we to inquire?"

Pamela, driven near to letting loose something like a growl, ignored this question, and said, "I still wish to know what wretched ornament has me snagged like a fish on a hook. Stick-pin, indeed!"

"Well, I can say with authority that it's not a barb—I suggest that those are more your province, ma'am."

At this, Pamela flushed beet-red.

Mr. Whyte continued, "I fear you must trust me and take my word of honor. Your spider lace is well and truly snarled in a spoked stick-pin."

"Oh, bother! Please, Mr. Whyte, this is not the time for us to be fencing about spoked or barbed stick-pins, or whatever it really is."

"Why ever not? It seems to me as good a time as any to fence about barbs and stick-pins. Or whatever it really is. I had to add 'whatever it really is' just in case I may be mistaken as to its true nature, as you have informed me I have a tendency to be. No doubt, next you will be blaming my poor twelve-spoked diamond stick-pin for having gored your grey mare that fatal day. Confess!"

Pamela made a choking noise.

"Oh, pray don't joke, Mr. Whyte. We are making the most terrible scene; you cannot wish to be the talk of the town. See? Everyone is staring at us. You must pretend that nothing is wrong."

"Nothing *is* wrong, Miss Stone. You are caught and are completely in my power."

"Don't tease me, you provoking man!"

"You are in my power, my child. Do let me demonstrate. If I move here—"

"Stop! Don't!"

"You see? You are forced to come with me! If I move in this direction—"

"I beg of you! Have mercy! The rose will tear!"

"I merely wished to demonstrate the situation so that you understand all the implications more fully."

Pamela suddenly lost a great part of her sense of humor and began a slow burn in response to this cavalier treatment, but, in fact, she could do nothing. She was tangled like a swordfish in a net. Who would come to rescue her?

"Mr. Whyte, how could you *dare* to wear a dangerously spoked ornament in such a crushing crowd?" said Miss Stone in an attempt to rebuke her oppressor.

"It is an heirloom."

"What is that to do with anything?"

"Heirlooms, however dangerously designed, are perfectly correct ornaments to sport at any social occasion of significance. Were you unaware of this? Further, I might as well ask how *you* dared wear a rose made of such perilously sheer spider-lace while attending an event you knew full well would be a frightful squeeze?"

She suppressed a rising peal of laughter, as Mr. Whyte continued inexorably on.

"Even more to the point, Miss Stone, how *can* you be so short? If you were to have striven to be just a little bit taller, by all the laws of physics, this would not have happened. Your stature alone must bear the full blame, I think."

"Oh! Odious man! Stop quizzing me and think of something to free us, won't you?"

"Ah, but that would require a flight of fancy, and I have been forced to give those up, at your own express command."

Miss Pamela Stone, whose reaction might understandably have gone either way to this piece of deliberate provocation, opted for a thoroughly amiable mode of response, and dissolved into a fit of nearly uncontrollable, musical laughter.

"Swine," she gasped, between paroxysms. "Hoist on my own petard, am I? Compassionless beast, you would have to rub my nose in it, wouldn't you?"

"I did nothing of the kind. I am far too well-bred to indulge myself in such a thing, however attractive the possibility. Be patient, my dear. Someone will soon take pity on us. Let us maneuver over there. I see some space."

Physical proximity was beginning to work its own wondrous magic on the previously brangling pair. Mr. Whyte had, naturally enough, never before held Miss Stone so close for so long a period. It was a very pleasant experience indeed. She smelled most delectably of roses.

Miss Stone, on her part, was imagining how very comforting it would be to be held close in the arms of this tall gentleman who smelled faintly of port and good tobacco.

She began to wonder what it would be like to be protected always by those strong, encircling arms. How swiftly the heart could rearrange its feelings, she reflected, lost in a sweet fog of contentment, and very much beginning to wish that no one would ever come to rescue them at all.

* * *

Mr. Whyte and Miss Stone were still standing closely entangled when Charles Bellfort appeared. In a flash he had comprehended their embarrassing predicament and taken steps to assist them. Most of the guests having now succeeded in making their way to the supper-room, the crowd had thinned out suddenly, giving Mr. Bellfort room to maneuver for the freedom of Pamela and John. However, the matter was by no means as simple as he had supposed, and Charles called Victorine Wells over to assist him.

"Your hands are more far nimble than mine, ma'am. Perhaps you can set these persons free. There is just a bit of lace there that is caught on the pin. . . . Do you see it? Yes, right there. Circling the spokes. It's caught up between them."

"I'll try. Stay still now. Be patient or it will tear. Just one more loop, I think. Very good. All done!"

"At last! Thank you, cousin!"

"Thank you very much, Miss Wells. I am in your debt."

"I don't know about you, John," said Mr. Bellfort, smoothing out his waistcoat, "But I've been standing around here for so long that I'm famished. Shall we not dine? May I take you in to supper, Miss Wells?"

"Certainly, Mr. Bellfort," she replied with pleasure and that couple disappeared.

This left Miss Stone and Mr. Whyte still standing near one another in the now empty vestibule. Mr. Whyte felt himself in an awkward situation. Should he leave the ball and go home, as he had intended, or try his hand with the fragrant though infuriating Miss Stone once more?

Miss Pamela Stone raised her chin toward him, mischief and challenge in her eyes. Looking at her so directly that her insides seemed to melt and quake at once, he spoke.

"I perceive that you, as well, may be in want of sustenance after such a trying experience as being entrapped by my errant heirloom stick-pin."

"Now that I am in a better position to see it, I own that it's handsome piece—however lethal."

"It belonged to my great-grandfather on my mother's side, Rupert Pembroke. It is virtually all I have left to show for that side of the family."

"A loss, sir, with which I can easily sympathize," said Pamela.

Mr. Whyte saw his opening, and chose to take it.

"Taking this opportunity to leave aside all the various barbs which have, in the past, entangled us to our mutual discomfort, will you not accept my arm to go in to dinner, Miss Stone?"

"That is kind of you, Mr. Whyte. I thank you; as it happens, I am very hungry indeed. But pray, in the interest of rediscovering mutual amity, let us agree to leave off all reference to barbs, pins, and scratches from this instant forward."

"My lips are sealed," said Mr. Whyte, though his lips were in fact quivering with amusement.

"Very good. So shall mine be."

"Ah, but then—how ever shall we dine?"

The young lady saw fit to prod the tall gentleman with her fan as punishment for his impertinence. With a overwhelming sense of relief and renewed pleasure, Miss Stone took Mr. Whyte's arm, and let him lead her to the supper room.

The two of them were once again in complete charity.

Seven

"I'm sure that I'm glad you had such a fine time to-night, Miss Pamela, but you'd best plan to sleep on past breakfast, or these late nights are going to put you quite out of looks. Your slippers already look just like those of them twelve dancing princesses."

"Don't they, though? I'm afraid their day is done, and they cost a small fortune. I admit that I am quite exhausted—after dinner, I think I must have danced continuously, and my ankles ache as if they had been broken. I shall be a happy to do just as you say, Helen, in the morning, and shall sleep as late as may be. I now know better than to contravene your advice in these matters, believe me."

"Oh, and Miss? About that grey mare we were speaking of earlier?"

"Yes?"

"You know, Sykes, Bellfort's coachman? He was by here tonight, and was enjoying a cup of tea in the servant's hall whilst the gentlemen were waiting for you ladies to be ready to leave to go to the ball. Happen was that he talked about the Viscount, and about that little grey mare of his that took off with you. Seems that his lordship kicked up a rare fuss about that horse when he came to look at her next day after you'd fallen. Said at first he'd have her put down."

"But why?"

"His lordship's coachman said that he'd she'd gotten a nasty cut on her hindquarter, and St. Clare went into a passion about it, since the accident had ruined her for driving."

"She did have a cut, then? You're certain?"

"Oh, yes, Miss! That was the whole problem! You see, that mare was one of the rare ones as could go well both under saddle and in harness, and she was one of a match-pair, and I suppose it had set his lordship back a pretty penny to buy them. But then when the mare got that wound, he knew as it wouldn't heal without scarring her, and Lord St. Clare would never let himself be seen driving around town with any but a perfect pair of horses."

"Certainly not. But St. Clare told me rather a different story of why he'd sold the horse—he said nothing about any wounds."

"Wound there was, though," remarked Helen, as she began to brush out Pamela's chestnut hair.

"St. Clare talked as if he were selling her off for having a bad temper—which I can promise you, she did not have. On the contrary, she was rather a slug—and a sweet slug, at that. But to think of his lordship wanting to put down a horse because of a cosmetic flaw? It is beyond all things!"

"Sykes said that the Lord St. Clare's coachman and the groom together pleaded for the beast to live, and appealed to his lordship's sense of economy—for he can be terrible tight-fisted about his stables. He saw their point, changed his mind, and then he sold off the pair of greys to a hackney jarvey on the very next day."

"Poor animals. I wish I could find them."

"Nothing to be done about it now. That's the way it is with these London fashionables—they won't bear with naught but perfection."

"It's still shameful. How did she come by the scratch, do they suppose?"

"Well! That's the mystery of it, you see. No one could say. Or would say."

"Unfortunate for the poor beasts to wind up pulling a hackney; it's too late now, however. Thank you for waiting up for me, Helen. Good night."

"Good night, miss."

Pamela lay in her bed awake for a few minutes after she put out her candle, mulling the story over in her mind, realizing that she owed the Hon. John Whyte an apology. His tale of the mare's injury clearly had not been exaggerated: there had been no briars, or thorns, or anything natural. It seemed that Mr. Whyte had been right—that the mare's wound had been deliberately inflicted. Why exactly one could not say, but it was a chilling thought.

Lord Balmore organized a drive to Richmond Hill, and the outing proved to be a great success. Charles Bellfort and John Whyte came, as did the three ladies from Brook Street. His lordship was able to walk with Lady Charlton, which had become a great object with him. He offered her his services as a confidant, and social counselor, which her ladyship, as a lone widow in London, greatly appreciated.

"For I am sure, your lordship, that I will become quite distracted if I cannot marry off my girl this season. She seems not to have taken as I thought she would—save with that Shelford, a gazetted fortune hunter, if ever I saw one."

"Shelford must needs consider money when he weds. It is a practical matter. Though his understanding is not strong, I do not think his character is deficient."

"I suppose not. I don't think that Celia Grafton would try to snare Victorine for her nephew if there were anything objectionable about him, to be sure. She's a perfectly straightforward woman, and not without a good heart."

"My own nephew Charles, you must have noticed, has a tendre for your daughter."

"Noticed? Indeed, Balmore, I have! Makes such a cake of himself over the girl, I feel quite sorry for him."

"He's no fortune hunter, you know. He has money of his own. He would be a suitable husband, don't you think?"

"I suppose. I was thinking that Charles Bellfort would do for my niece, though she seems to prefer Mr. John Whyte, rather against my better judgment."

"Why so?"

"You must be aware that, however much he may be a friend, he has no fortune, has he?"

"Very true."

"I can't like him living in her pocket. He should give way to someone more eligible."

"Perhaps he can work something out. He has mentioned his difficulties to me, and I have said I would lend him what help I can. His father, also, might be persuaded to settle some money on him."

"If Mr. Whyte can solve his financial problems, then it puts the whole matter in a different light."

"And what about Charles Bellfort, then? Won't you consider him?"

"At this point, I suppose I must. I confess I had hoped to snag a man with a title for Victorine, but now it doesn't seem possible, and perhaps it was a vain and foolish notion to entertain in the first place. Did Charles Bellfort ask you to speak to me today on his behalf?"

"No, it was my own idea. Thought to sound out the waters. Thought the two of them suit very well."

"Do you think so, indeed? Then your nephew has my permission to address her, if you think it would do, for I value your opinion very highly, Lord Balmore, as you must be aware. The thing of it is that I don't think she would accept."

"The best of good fellows, Charles. Don't she like him?"

"Yes, I rather think she does. She always speaks of him with affection, and I've observed them enjoying one another's company on many occasions. He might do very well for her, indeed, for he doesn't seem to mind her woolly-headedness. The problem is that Victorine may be incapable of recognizing Charles's good qualities. She's too romantic by half."

"Perhaps you shouldn't be so set on marrying her off till she's matured a bit, then. Perhaps she should acquire a bit of experience. She might make a better choice if she waits till she's not quite so green."

"You know, Balmore, I think you're very right. How lucky I am to have such a wise friend as you," she commented, tucking her hand more closely into his arm, and thus succeeding in bringing a blush to that gentleman's face, which the lady was not in a position to notice.

* * *

"It is a lovely view, isn't it, Mr. Whyte?"

"Yes. I like the way the river bends and winds here. So very green, all the trees near the water. It makes me wish I were a painter, so as to do it justice, and to be able to bring such a peaceful scene back home with me."

Pamela was silent for a moment, and then ventured to say what had long been on her mind.

"Mr. Whyte, I must tender you a profound apology."

"Why?"

"It's about that horse. The grey mare."

"Oh, heaven! I hesitate to enter into any discussion on *that* topic again, I can tell you."

"I can imagine so. However, the fact remains that only last night I discovered that I had been mistaken about what happened to that horse. It was just as you said. And, though it is hard for me as well to speak about it, it is probably even more painful for me to do so, since I am the one who was at fault, the one who was so foolish and prejudiced. I hope you will be good enough to admit, however, that any reasonable person would have found the truth a bit hard to swallow."

"I do admit it."

"You are very kind."

"I take it you have suffered no other unusual incidents, since that time?"

"No," she replied, with some surprise at his question, "None."

"I am glad to hear it. Let us resolve the matter in this fashion, then——that the injury did not occur naturally, that it was deliberately inflicted, but was, perhaps, intended not to injure you, but to injure the horse you happened to be riding. Or, rather, perhaps that it was aimed to injure St. Clare by means of his pricey grey mare—

perhaps by forcing him to break up and sell the pair of match-greys of which he had been so proud."

"That's a novel thought! It makes me feel much less vulnerable—and all because you have contrived to wrap up precisely the same event in clean linen."

"That is one of the prime virtues of creative perception—you see, you were quite right about my flights of fancy! I do have a distinct tendency to indulge my imagination, but sometimes it can be a very useful habit."

"As you have found a way to explain away my accident, and have done so in a way such that I don't have to fear that someone is still out there scheming to take my life, believe me, Mr. Whyte, in future I shall never regard your theories with anything but the most profound respect!"

"I shall hold you to that promise, my dear."

Eight

Acting with the blessings of Lady Charlton, conveyed to him by agency of his uncle Balmore, Charles Bellfort lost no further time in trying to fix his interest with Victorine Wells. He made it his business to discover everything she liked best, and saw that it was provided for her. He discovered everything that was not to her taste, and eliminated that from her experience. He never tried to take her riding, nor took her up in his high-perch phaeton (though he was a member of the Four Horse Club) but rather asked to drive with him in his spanking new barouche. He never took her to the theater, but he arranged for parties at Vauxhall; he avoided Somerset House like the plague, but suffered waiting endlessly for her as she shopped for hours in Bond Street. In short, in order to please her, Charles Bellfort became a slave of love.

Not that slavery was without its rewards, however— Miss Wells, under the strong spell of such devoted attachment, began to relax and to drop some of her more flighty ways and her more foolish preoccupations. She soon realized Mr. Bellfort for the kind and generous man that he was, and, encouraged by his acceptance of her just as she was, began to improve in her own understanding. He took the time to discuss with her even the silliest of novels, with the thought of improving her mind—and it did improve. No longer afraid of making a fool of herself, she began to have opinions of her own, ones that were not mere imitations of the overheard opinions of others.

Still, though he had succeeded masterfully in befriending Victorine, he somehow was unable to penetrate to the core of her heart. It seemed as if he must offer for her, but he was convinced she would turn him down, and so he held off, hoping that sooner or later he would find the key that would unlock for him the secret of her affections.

She came to know Charles Bellfort to be her dear friend, but knew nothing of his more profound feelings.

Having spent an increasing amount of time in Pamela Stone's company—at dinner parties, musicales, in Green Park, in Hyde Park, on drives to Richmond—the Hon. John Whyte had come to the conclusion that the time for reticent self-restraint had ceased.

As he had come to know with certainty her true character, he had, as a direct result, devoted much time to serious reflection upon his bachelor status. He had held discussions with Lord Balmore, and with Charles Bellfort, and they had given him much sage advice, which came to the following: pursue with vigor an improvement in your financial status, and pursue the young lady—fix your interest with her such that she returns your regard.

He was well aware that the occasionally volatile, but always captivating Miss Stone had engaged his affections. Not by nature a vain man, he did not feel completely certain of her feelings on the matter.

As had been the case from the very beginning, he was not at all sure what the honorable course of action toward her would be. He could not actually offer for her at this point. That being the case, what course must he pursue? For Mr. Whyte, the situation was not at all as simple as it ought to be.

He decided to put things to the touch, at least as far as he was able. Thus he was found walking along with Miss Pamela Stone just as he had been doing for some time, with Miss Stone's abigail, Helen Fraley, trailing along behind at a discreet distance.

Pamela noted that there was an extra bit of pressure that he pressed into the small hand he held in his, and an extra measure of warmth in his deep voice.

"We have known each other long enough," began Mr. Whyte, "that it can come as no surprise to you for me to wish to speak to you of my feelings."

Pamela said nothing, but her heart fluttered, and she favored her escort with an encouraging smile.

"I hope you will not consider it presumptuous in me to tell you that my feelings toward you are most warm and affectionate."

"You need not be so formal with me. Please, speak freely."

John Whyte hesitated for a moment, and searched first the sky then the ground with his eyes, as he tried to put his meaning into words.

Pamela tried to disguise her unease. Why was he hesitant? Surely he knew that she returned his regard. Did he not return hers? Had he merely been trifling with her? Was she to wear the willow for him? A million frightening possibilities loomed in her mind.

"There are obstacles, however."

Pamela's mind fairly cried aloud. Obstacles? What was he referring to?

"There are practical circumstances in my life—practical obstacles, I should say—that I feel I must resolve before I dare to seek to make any . . . any more formal addresses to you or to seek out your estimable father. I wish you to understand the depth of my feelings for you—if I do not presume too much by mentioning this—but I feel it is my duty to warn you off as well."

She could contain herself no longer.

"Warn me off? Pray, why?"

"I am, as you know, only a younger son. Technically, of course, I am my brother St. Clare's presumptive heir, and the second in line for the Cleremont earldom, after my brother.

"This will be the case, of course, only until Miles has a son. There is no reason to assume he will not, in time, produce an heir apparent—a son of his own. That being the case, I must admit to having no real expectations. Currently, as you know, I live very simply on a farming estate near Haverford. However, you may not know that I have no fortune of my own, and I have no estates or income of my own.

"For that reason alone, prior to making your acquaintance, I had entertained no serious thoughts of ever—of ever changing my domestic status."

Pamela blushed and smiled slightly, but made no comment.

"The thing is, because of my financial position—or lack of it, to be more to the point—I cannot in good conscience make a formal offer for you now. I only wish to God I could."

Here he took her hands, and had the sadness to see Pamela's eyes filling up with tears, while she fought to repress them.

"I would like to offer for you now. Please believe me. I can think of nothing so wonderful as to be able to ask you to do me the honor of becoming my wife."

Pamela's hands began to tremble as he held them.

"I cannot, in all integrity, do so. To seek to enter into an engagement with you now would be grossly unfair to you and grossly imprudent of me. What I earnestly request is that, if you value our friendship as I do—if I may ask so much of you—I ask that you have faith in me, and have trust in the strength of my regard. I shall do everything in my power to alter my situation so as to be able to make an honorable offer for your hand as soon as it is possible.

"Or perhaps there is no hope for me. Tell me truthfully, for I must know—do I presume too much?"

Pamela shook her head, so overcome with emotion that she could find no words to express her feelings.

"I am so glad. Please believe that I will speak again most seriously on this subject just as soon as I am able."

"Yes, of course."

"There is just one other thing I must, painfully, bring to your attention. We cannot consider ourselves an engaged couple, or behave in a manner that might lead others to believe that an engagement exists."

Pamela drew back, offended.

"Don't misunderstand me—my point is this: when other men express an interest in you, please be kind enough to give them your full attention. Should any one eligible offer for your hand—and I am certain there will be many other offers for you—you must consider yourself free to accept."

Pamela was ready to object strenuously.

"No, kindly don't deny me this. There are, I am persuaded, dozens of men who have far more to offer to you in terms of livelihood and consequence than I. I could not bear that you should not give your serious consideration to those other more eligible suitors who might do so much better for you than I could ever hope to do."

Her eyes blazed in answer, as she cried, "How shallow you must think me, sir. Rank and consequence mean nothing to me."

"Please, heed what I say: I am only too well aware that this is but your first season. It is unfair to seek any commitment from you at this time. I dare not ask and I do not ask that you cut yourself off from the society of eligible men."

"Do you so misunderstand my character?" she said, astonished.

"No, I think not. But, consider this: however much I care for you, at best I may be able to provide you with but a meager living, far less than that of a country curate. Marriage, as you are well aware, cannot be merely a matter of attachment. Particularly for females, the choice of husband will determine the entire course of their future lives. Therefore, please regard me as your most devoted friend, but, out of the regard I bear you, I ask that you do not fail to make the acquaintance of other men. Won't you accede to my request?"

"I have no desire to act in that way. But I shall do it if you wish it so, and because you wish it."

She paused for a moment.

"Now, Mr. Whyte—"

"John. Call me John, won't you?"

"I see I must. Having once been virtually pinned to you in full view of the ton for nearly half an hour, and having just now so very nearly received a proposal of marriage from you, I perceive it is our destined duty to deal with one another on a first-name basis."

He had to laugh, and said, "My duty is then my pleasure, Pamela."

"Very acceptable—now, we can say that there is at least one thing that is settled about our relationship."

"Just as you say, Pamela," he said in a low voice, sweeping her hand to his lips. "Just as you say."

Nine

"This won't do, Helen. It makes me look sallow and stupid. I hate these shoes, and I hate this hat, and these ribbons are hopeless, just hopeless. Haven't I anything else?"

"Are you in a fever, Miss Pamela? I disremember when you fussed over your clothes and your hair so much as you've started to do lately. Are you sure you're not coming down with influenza? Maud said there's influenza in Lady Stilton's household. You've been keeping town hours. Could've caught it at dinner t'other night."

"I'm *not* ill! I have been in London for quite some time now, and I'm trying to make an effort to make sure that my appearance is just as it should be. Everyone has already seen all of my outfits a hundred times, and I'm sure I look a perfect dowd!"

"You're going to an art exhibition, Miss! It's not like you're dressing for an assembly at Almack's! Are you feared that at Somerset House you'll be inspected by a Patroness?"

Helen Fraley's eyes narrowed as she thought the matter out, then widened suddenly as the truth came home to her.

"I know what it has it be. Oh, Miss, lovesick, are ye?" said Helen with a twinkle in her eye.

"Helen! Whatever can you mean?"

"Think I'm a dimwit like your coz', do ye now?"

"Certainly not. Oh, dear—what am I *saying?* Don't tempt me into incivility, Helen."

"Yep. You're lovesick, Miss, and may as well get used to people knowing about it."

"I am *not!*" she huffed.

"You are indeed. And I know full well who it is."

"No! Mr. Whyte is a kind friend, that is all."

"Don't try to pull the wool over my eyes. I seen how it is. He's a right one."

"He is, rather," said she wistfully, "Isn't he?"

"Told ye. Hasn't he offered for you, then? I thought he might have done. Can I wish you happy, Miss?"

"No, Helen, you don't understand. Recall that Mr. Whyte is but a younger son. He isn't able to offer for me. He has said as much."

"Oh, dear."

"But—we've an understanding that, should his lot improve, he is pledged to make an offer right away."

"There, then. I'm sure he'll do the right thing by ye. He's not the sort as to make promises and break them."

"He said that I must consider other suitors," she admitted grimly.

"Very proper in him, I'm sure. Looking out for your best interests. A good quality in a man."

"Good quality? Of course it's a good quality—he has many good qualities. How could I possibly think of marrying another man, just from crass monetary motives? That is what is painful, Helen. I can't bear the thought of parting from him—not having him to talk with, to be with. Do you understand what I mean, Helen?"

"It's as I supposed, Miss, isn't it? That'll be what's called love."

Pamela threw her arms around her abigail and wept for just a little while.

"This is it, then? But it hurts so much!"

"That it does, Miss. That it does."

Ten

Viscount and Viscountess St. Clare gave a small, select dinner party for a few of their most intimate friends. These included the Earl of Braithwaite, a noted Corinthian, and his spirited wife; the Earl and Countess of Grafton with her ladyship's nephew, Lord Shelton; Lord Balmore and his nephew, Charles Bellfort; the Hon. John Whyte, the Dowager Marchioness of Plimpton with her granddaughter, Miss Belinda Falk-Duffield, and her grand-nephew, Viscount Campden. Lady Charlton came with her daughter Victorine and Miss Pamela Stone.

Thus, it was a party composed of two feckless young heiresses, one plump-in-the-pocket bachelor, three young, well-bred unmarried gentlemen without a feather to fly with, two notorious loose-screws, a country lady lacking in fortune, one widow, one widower, two shockingly fast noblewomen, two high-in-the-instep ladies of a certain age, a noted Corinthian, and two dead bores. This mixture of persons was certain, realized Pamela when she perceived who was attending, to provide an interesting evening, particularly since several of the guests qualified in two or more categories. Miss Stone could hardly wait for the opportunity to bring this observation to the attention of Mr. Whyte, whom she could trust to share in her amusement.

Dinner itself went off without a hitch, save for the Marchioness's refusal to partake of any food whatsoever. She had, she loudly informed all the company, forsworn food for a whole week in order to purge her digestion of all impurities, and kept insisting that others would be well advised to follow her example. John Whyte and Pamela, seated far from one another almost as if by design, were able only to exchange speaking glances; her ladyship was well known in society for her eccentricities, so her conduct, though it would always be diverting, came as no surprise to anyone.

Following the removal of the final course, the ladies withdrew, and left the gentlemen to their liquor and cigars. The Earl of Braithwaite, the Earl of Grafton, Viscount Campden, Viscount St. Clare, and Lord Shelton, evidently well into their cups, became loudly and deeply involved in discussions of driving-pairs and driving-teams likely to be made available to the market due to their ill-fated owners having been towed deep into the River Tick.

Lord Balmore, Charles Bellfort, and John Whyte were on the other side of the room, discussing finances. Balmore was explaining that he was very familiar with the scandal that had attended the loss of Julia Pembroke's fortune, that which John's mother had brought to her marriage to the Earl of Cleremont, and that which should by rights have devolved upon her son John Whyte.

"It was the talk of the town at the time, my dear boy. A terrible scandal, and it wasn't only the Pembroke funds that were involved, not by any manner of means. There was, I must say, nothing suspicious about the fact that a fortune was lost, save for the execrable deed itself. It was a clear case of embezzlement by an employee of what had once been a most reputable bank, Carver, Williams, and Company of Berners Street. The man had managed to conceal his embezzlement for many years, due to his proficiency at forging documents that showed that funds were present that had, in fact, been sold off. Many, many people lost their life savings—and, a number of persons, sadly enough, took their lives rather than face an unaccustomed life of poverty. I believe the fellow responsible, a man named Fanshaw, went to the gallows for it. Small comfort for those who lost all that they had."

"It was not to be expected that I should suddenly discover myself the lost heir to a great fortune. Still, I had assumed that not all of mother's funds would have been invested at one firm only."

"It is a reasonable assumption, and one you should pursue."

"But in the meantime, leaving off these fanciful aspirations, what am I to do, sir? What is your advice at this point? I can't offer for a wife without having a living."

"Your father might set you up, mightn't he?" observed Charles Bellfort.

"I've never thought to ask him anything like that."

"I perceive you must try. There is, of course, as you mentioned always the possibility that there is something left of your mother's money. I think you should try to find her man of business, or her solicitor."

"The solicitors I've already spoken with, just last week. They say it is possible a small bit may remain, something invested in funds by a firm other than the one that went bankrupt, but it seems that they've lost touch with the person who was used to administer my mother's fortune. They have told me they will attempt to pursue this possibility, although papers pertaining to the details of the estate administration were lost in a fire—quite un-related—and it's been many years since anyone cared to inquire about it."

"That is very unfortunate. It seems that, with regard to your current difficulties, your best recourse is to re-quest assistance of your father. I can't see why Lord Cleremont should refuse you," said Charles Bellfort. "Even if he were legally to assign over to you the Mel-field income, it would be a very small thing for him, a very slight diminution, indeed, but one that would make the world of difference for you. I think you could very reasonably request it of him."

"Very proper," added Lord Balmore. "If you like, I can have a word with Cleremont myself. Have to go out that way myself one of these days. I'd be more than happy to put in a good word for you and your young lady."

"I hate to go begging to my father."

"One can understand that, I'm sure. But you would hate to lose the chance to marry Miss Stone, would you not?"

"Yes, I would—so I must swallow my pride, I perceive, Charles. Quite so. I thank you both. I shall do as you suggest."

Miss Pamela Stone was desperate for the gentlemen to rejoin them. She had been imprisoned in a long, plaintive discussion between Victorine and Belinda Falk-Duffield about the horrors of being an heiress in London. To her left, the Marchioness was prosing on about her alimentary tract to no one in particular, while Lady Charlton and Lady Grafton were reminiscing about their youth. The Countess of Braithwaite and Viscountess St. Clare were too far away for the subject of their conversation to be overheard by Pamela, but their shrill giggles penetrated the entire room, and began to give Pamela the headache.

At her wit's end, Miss Stone excused herself, and sought out the quiet refuge of the book room.

The book room was ill-lit, and its darkness soothing to her aching forehead. Finding no comfortable settle there to recline upon, Pamela chose to sit on an upholstered mahogany chair, facing its back, and lay her head down on her hands.

She had fallen into a blissful half-sleep when the door opened, and a figure came into the room, an entrance of which she was entirely unaware.

She was awakened by having her hand possessed and an arm thrust round her waist, and a tumult of words of ardent affection poured out upon her unwilling ears. Groggily, Pamela perceived she was being set upon by Viscount Campden, with whom she was barely acquainted.

"Say you will marry me, my sweet!" said he. "You can be assured of my eternal devotion, Belinda!"

"You're foxed, sir! I'm not Belinda."

"Are you not so? Then, I have erred, but in all honor, I shall ask you instead to marry me, Victorine!"

Viscount Campden succeeded in silencing Pamela's protestations by planting a long, unwanted kiss upon her lips. The library door opened once more, and the Hon. John Whyte, looking to find Pamela, entered within. When he saw the couple embracing, he began to excuse himself, then perceived the identity of the lady. He strode over to Lord Campden, dragged him away from her by the collar, and pushed him out the door.

"Impudent puppy! Be off, and never again so insult a young lady with your unwanted attentions!"

"Beg pardon. Mistaken identity. Bit of a *faux pas,* what?" Viscount Campden mumbled as he fled out the room.

Pamela held out both her hands to Mr. Whyte, who grasped them strongly.

"Oh, John, thank you! The poor wretch had no idea who I was . . . he thought he was proposing to Belinda, and when I said I wasn't she, he dubbed me Victorine, and proposed once more! If it hadn't been awful, it would have been funny."

"Put it out of your mind. These things can happen when a young gentleman contracts gambling debts, lets himself drink far too much, and comes drunken into company with heiresses. He begins to believe a quick marriage will put everything to rights."

"I am so glad you were here. I am so glad you came."

He lifted her chin up, and looked into her green eyes, with an intensity that seared her being.

"I am glad I came, as well, my dear," he said, in a strange, husky voice she had never heard him use before. "All my qualms be damned. I will not permit you to be held in the arms of any other gentleman than myself. I want you, lady, and I will have you, come what may. I will make you known to my father, and I will take you to wife. I take leave to inform you now, that I can wait for you no longer.

"I give you this to seal my pledge."

He took her in his arms and kissed her. They remained held in an embrace filled with a passion barely held in check.

The two lovers were locked thus when Lady St. Clare

opened the book room door, prepared to embark upon a *tête-à-tête* with tipsy Lord Braithwaite who was just behind her, holding on to her hand. She prevented Lord Braithwaite from entering, lest he, too, behold the ardent scene that was causing her ladyship to experience an intense distress. Distracted by her other intrigues in London, Lady St. Clare realized that she had failed to note the increasing intimacy between Miss Stone and Mr. Whyte. It was a tactical error she would soon amend.

How very remiss I have been, she thought to herself. *I had quite forgotten that this situation might require my close attention. Never mind. There's still time enough for divertissement.*

Watching from the shadows of the entranceway, Lady St. Clare made a solemn vow to remove her rival and to supplant Pamela in her brother-in-law's affections. A woman long used to getting whatever she wanted, she had no doubt that her wishes would be swiftly fulfilled. She might have lost a small battle, but, if she so desired, she would surely triumph in the war for Mr. Whyte.

Eleven

The next morning, Lady St. Clare's town-carriage with its great, gilded crest, drew up at the house on Brook Street. Lady St. Clare had come to deliver a formal invitation card to attend a grand ball at Haverford, and to induce the Brook Street ladies to spend several weeks at Haverford, as houseguests of the Earl of Cleremont.

Her ladyship was immediately shown up to the blue parlor, where she spent a few moments chatting easily with Lady Charlton. The two young ladies, Lady Charlton informed the Viscountess, were unfortunately not at home, but had gone off to Bond Street on a shopping expedition.

"Here is the thing, Lady Charlton. We will be hosting a small number of houseguests, perhaps forty or fifty, and we would be very happy if your party would join us."

"To stay at Haverford?"

"Yes. For a week or so before the party, and for some time afterward. You will find the company of our guests will be most congenial, and I'm sure you will all enjoy the country air. Really, Haverford is a most amusing place, and the season is nearing its end. Soon London will be thin of company, and dull in the extreme. You shall have to come to the country in any case, so it may just as well be to Haverford. Do say that you will come!"

Lady Charlton was overcome by such condescension. To spend time as houseguests at the seat of the Earl of Cleremont, and attend a grand ball at Haverford! Think of all the gentlemen Victorine and Pamela could meet! Never in her wildest dreams had her ladyship hoped to penetrate so far upward into Polite Society.

The Viscountess mistook Lady Charlton's stunned silence for hesitation to accept.

"You must accept, my dear Lady Charlton; I will not hear of your not coming," Lady St. Clare added silkily. "I first mentioned my desire that you visit us many weeks ago, you must remember, when we first met, so this invitation can come as no surprise to you, none at all. Since Haverford is an old family estate, it is a particularly beautiful place, and well worth the trip. It is filled with paintings I'm sure you will like to see. The grounds are fine as well—don't you think it will be good for the girls to go out into the country? Yes, there are so many things at Haverford that I wish you all to experience. I am sure you will give me that happiness, won't you?"

"So kind of you to extend such an invitation to us, your ladyship," said Lady Charlton. "But I wonder whether it is quite right to impose upon you in such a fashion."

"Yes, of course you must come. It will give both St. Clare and myself the most extreme pleasure, I assure you."

The Viscountess smiled another dazzling smile and waited.

"Certainly we shall come, then. We accept your very kind invitation with pleasure," said Lady Charlton, wondering if there would be enough time before they left to purchase the many additional items they would no doubt require.

"Good," said the Viscountess, rising and closing her reticule in a businesslike manner. "It is a settled thing. I shall send St. Clare's travelling carriage for you Tuesday week, and it will return you to London the following Tuesday—or perhaps the next, just as you wish. You will find it very well-sprung, I think. Oh—and of course I shall send another carriage for your staff and baggage. Everything will be taken care of, you must leave it all to me. You are safe in my hands. Good day, then, and I bid you a very pleasant journey."

Then, she was gone.

The following week, as promised, after they had spent several mad days of last-minute shopping, the Brook Street ladies were bundled into Lord St. Clare's travelling carriage for the journey to Haverford. The Viscount had caused two carriages to be sent for them—one brand new, luxurious, well-sprung travelling chaise for them to make the journey in comfort, and one to carry along for their baggage, and their abigails: Collins, Helen, and Maud.

It was all done in the very first style—with outriders, and liveried footmen and postilions, in fact, complete with every accoutrement of excellence. As she lay back on the deep plush squabs, even Lady Charlton had begun to be a little over-awed by such a display of opulent splendor.

Victorine, quite naturally, was in alt. His lordship St. Clare was showing them all such condescension! When, she wondered, would she be able to be alone with his lordship again, to express her gratitude to him directly? She was so much looking forward to spending more time with her devoted friend, Lord St. Clare, that Mr. Charles Bellfort, for all his constancy and good-humor, was quite eclipsed in her mind. As soon as Miss Wells stepped into that magical carriage, it was as if Charles Bellfort had ceased to exist.

Victorine was still in this fairy-tale mood as the black carriage with the St. Clare coat-of-arms emblazoned on it made its way through a tree-lined avenue to approach the great house of Haverford. It was a magnificent estate, and no expense had been spared to maintain the full glory of its magnificence. Great expanses of lawn swept out to either side of the gorgeous stone buildings. There were the beautifully kept gardens, outlined with level upon level of balustraded parapets.

To one side swept out the high yew hedges that outlined a great maze; to the other side were yew trees carefully trimmed over decades into the most fantastical shapes.

Three tall medieval towers stretched skyward; there were windows upon windows and wing after wing—as if the builder had started conservatively enough, with an immense stone castle, and then let himself run completely mad with addition upon addition in an incredible melange of styles. Even from the drive, it was easy to see the house was of gargantuan proportions—Victorine felt, for a moment, appalled—she would be lost within Haverford in an instant.

On Pamela's part, seeing the estate which seemed to her so impersonal and huge, she could not help but brace herself inwardly; she had resigned herself to being discomfited during her stay with the Viscount and his family, for she really did not care for such splendor. She was rather nervous about meeting Mr. Whyte's father for the first time, and hoped she would make a good impression upon him. Much depended upon her securing Lord Cleremont's good will, and his blessings upon their proposed union.

The things that she most looked forward to exploring were the fine galleries of art collected over several generations, as well as the present Earl's famous stables—said to house a magnificent string of hunters. It would certainly be possible to borrow a horse to ride over to Melfield, Mr. John Whyte's farming estate, as it was only a few miles away, most conveniently situated. In fact, their stay at Haverford meant that it would be easy to spend more time with John Whyte; this made the entire journey well worthwhile to Pamela.

Helen Fraley was sitting in the second carriage behind, and she was looking forward to her time at Haverford from her own personal perspective. Just at the end of her stay in London, after a good courtship, she had entered into a formal understanding with Peter Welish, John Whyte's man. Last night he had offered for her—she had told him she must think about it, but her heart told her all was well. There was only the question of her service, and his, but there, also, things seemed to be working out as well as could ever be hoped.

With a friendship growing between Mr. John Whyte and her mistress, perhaps she could marry Peter Welish and still continue in service to Miss Pamela—should Miss Stone become Mrs. Whyte, that is, as seemed to be in the wind. The two of them would suit, Helen thought to herself, just like me and Peter suit. Could anything be better?

* * *

At their long journey's end, having been handed down from their carriage, and greeted warmly by Lady St. Clare, Lady Charlton and Victorine and Pamela were quickly shown to their apartments. These turned out to be among the most beautiful suites Haverford had to offer. It was as if they had suddenly entered into a life of grandeur previously only existent in their wildest dreams.

None of the ladies' suites of room was particularly near to one another—indeed, the house was so enormous and the wings so oddly connected that it could not be otherwise. Lady St. Clare, showing them around, apologized for any inconvenience this might cause, but pointed out it was a common failing of great houses which had been improved in many different styles over many generations.

Victorine's suite was found to be the South Wing, and was a lovely room swathed in rosy silken draperies hanging down in great swirls, the valances hung as gigantic semi-circles of silk, with a dressing room to the side, and a room for her maid. The whole effect of the room was one of envelopment—when she disappeared into it, the room seemed so grand and Victorine so small, one could hardly nourish the hope that such a slight creature could ever find her way out again.

Pamela's apartment, again composed of a main bedchamber, dressing room, and room for her dresser, was around a different corner in a nook called the Old West Wing. It was blue and cool and aristocratic, with tall windows looking out over the grounds. A dignified residence, to be sure, but wintry rather than warm and accommodating. Pamela was certainly satisfied with the elegance of her surroundings, but it was not in her nature to feel at ease in such a grand setting as that of Haverford. It made her feel rather like a country mouse wandered into a king's palace by mistake.

Lady Charlton's room, in the Near West Wing, was even more exotic; part of the Apartments of State, fit for a Royal Duchess. The ceilings of her room were gilded to the hilt, and hung with great thick brocade drapes in an elegant shade of ochre and crimson. Every piece of intricately carved mahogany furniture was buffed till it shone; this suite alone had evidently been decorated at the cost of a king's ransom.

For all the ladies of Brook Street, it was as if reality had been left behind in London, and they had found themselves now living within a dream of elegance, opulence, and splendor far beyond anything they had ever known before.

Twelve

Several days passed uneventfully at Haverford. Lady Charlton, Miss Wells, and Miss Stone were treated to long, rather dull tours of the great house, wing by wing, tower by tower, and architectural style by style. They were taken on tours of the grounds, through the extensive park to the lake with its picturesque gazebo, and throughout the formal gardens and the maze. They, in company with the daily increasing number of other houseguests, went on visits to the attached abbey, viewed the various galleries and the paintings of the family's ancestors, and saw what was there to be seen from every view and angle.

By the end of four days, all three women had experienced a surfeit of Haverford's artistic, ornamental, architectural, and floral wonders. In a word, they were bored to tears. They longed for the good company of their gentlemen friends again. Somehow, the company of guests such as the all-too-easily-amorous Viscount Campden, Lord and Lady Braithwaite, Belinda Falk-Duffield and her titled valetudinarian forebear, quickly palled—even Victorine began to miss the quiet, kind companionship Charles Bellfort had always provided.

Neither Lord Balmore nor Mr. John Whyte had yet arrived in the neighborhood, although they were due to remain at Melfield during the time of the ball. Mr.

Charles Bellfort was to come to the country, too; however, all these gentlemen, it appeared, were still occupied in London on important affairs of management and politics.

Lord St. Clare, as well, was still in London, and Victorine's mood was not improved by his continued absence. She thought it shabby and remiss of him to have invited her to stay at his ancestral home, but not to be there to attend to her. She fell into the sullens.

The Earl of Cleremont, availing himself of a wide variety of flimsy pretexts, had managed to avoid making the acquaintance of any of his new houseguests, a circumstance Pamela Stone could not but regard with apprehension. John Whyte, by means of his man Peter Welish, had sent word that he would come as soon as he could contrive to do so.

Lady St. Clare, on the other hand, made her presence so all-pervasive as to be suffocating; she presided over a series of interminably dull dinners of the most crushingly formal kind. She had invited her usual set of dead bores and loose-screws of the first stare of fashion. The company was so unremittingly horrid, it seemed to Pamela almost as if her ladyship were particularly desirous of driving them all out of the house.

Two days before the ball, the greater part of the rest of the houseguests arrived, in a flurry of bandboxes, carriages, trunks, and servants. The arrival of the ladies and gentlemen of the ton made the general tone of the house become much more gay.

Pamela was perhaps most impressed by Haverford's evidently infinite absorptive capacity. Though carriages continued to arrive all through that day, and to discharge their elegant occupants, the great house never seemed to become full—it merely became relatively less void. In that immense mansion, there was a place for everyone, and everyone had his or her place, as if carefully placed on an operatic stage, or placed as dainty painted figurines in a Christmas *creche*.

John Whyte rode up to Haverford the morning before the ball, intending to meet with his father, ask his permission to make an offer for the hand of Miss Pamela Stone, make Pamela known to him, and only then, once his father had seen the jewel that she was, would he bring up the delicate matter of requesting that the Earl lend them financial support.

He intended to ask for very little, only the income from the Melfield rents. He believed that, with frugal handling of the Melfield assets, they might get along quite well. His inquiries into the handling of his mother's estate, and his inquiries after her family were still proving fruitless; there seemed to be nothing to be looked for in that quarter unless he could locate his mother's man of business.

On the other hand, if his father would assign him the money from Melfield, as Lord Balmore had suggested he might, John Whyte would be able to support a household in tolerable style, though by no means would his wife be able to enjoy the elegancies of life.

Having mulled the issue over at length and gone over his household accounts a hundred times, he believed that, with the Melfield income in his sole control, and by exercising stringent economies, he could put himself in a position to afford to marry Miss Pamela Stone within a year. He felt sure that his father would wish him to be suitably settled, and, he could, of course, continue to manage the earl's estates.

Resolute in the conviction that he had made the right choice, he was feeling more hopeful than he had in many weeks when Willby, the butler, greeted him at the door.

He was swiftly shown up to the library, the place where the reclusive, unconventional Earl of Cleremont spent most of his time. His father was really such a very odd man, John had to admit.

With advancing years, Lord Cleremont had nurtured an eccentric, almost freakish temperament. He insisted on spending most of his time hiding in his book room, rarely seeing the light of day thrown onto his mottled skin. He still kept his string of hunters, but that was just for show, as it had been many years since he had ridden them. Nevertheless, he had given orders that they were to be maintained in prime condition, ready for any guests who might come to enjoy them.

The Earl was reading when the door was opened to let his younger son come into the room. The Hon. John Whyte bowed to his father, formally, as was his habit. Suddenly, he felt as if he were a small boy again, being sent to the headmaster's room for a reprimand.

"Well, what is it?" his lordship snapped. Lord Cleremont had long ago renounced the genteel manners preferred by the ton in favor of manners consisting in arrogance and bombast, and these habits of conduct arose from a sense of consequential self-importance so vast as to be practically indistinguishable, in John Whyte's view, from sheer rude vulgarity. However, it was hardly John Whyte's right or in his power to seek to improve his father's character. He was as he was.

Lord Cleremont pointed his bony finger at a spindly chair, and John Whyte sat down.

"Father," he began with cordial formality, "I should like to ask of you to grant me the favor of some time."

"I'm granting you the favor of some time right now. Don't flummox me, and don't drive me mad with waiting—get on with it, boy. What is it you're after this time?"

The Hon. John Whyte took a breath, steeled himself, and begin again. His father's bizarre behavior made his presence a definite trial to endure. John began again.

"Father, I should like your permission to pay my addresses to a young lady."

The Earl of Cleremont made a snort of derision.

"Chasing skirts, now, is it, John? I had plenty of wenches in my time, I can tell you, and I heartily approve. It's just as well you're giving up that Puritanical streak of yours, and high time you started acting like a man instead of like a man-milliner.

"But here's my question—think you've got enough blunt to keep a high-flier? Can't see how you could, since I know how little you have, and I know how much the incognitas cost, and it's a bundle. The woman'll ruin you. No, leave that sort of thing to Miles. He's got pockets deep enough for those games. You don't. Just visit a fancy-house now and again; that'll serve your purposes and keep your pocket book intact. I'll leave you the names of the finest abbesses in London, if you like."

Mr. Whyte, aghast, tried to enlighten his parent.

"I'm afraid you misunderstand me. I wish to marry the young lady in question, Father."

"Marry? Marry a light-skirt? Pah! Don't be a fool."

"Attend my words, Father. As I said from the start, she's a young lady. She's a respectable young woman."

"Pah—they're no fun! But, blood will tell, of course—they're better for breeding. That's to be considered—it matters how the foals will turn out. Tell me, who is she, then?"

"Her name is Pamela Stone."

"Stone? Don't know 'em. What's her rank?"

"She's a—a gentleman's daughter."

"Just a gentleman's daughter? Could you not do better for yourself? I suppose not—you've got little enough to bring to a marriage yourself, save for the name with which I was good enough to endow you. Just how much will she bring as her dowry?"

"I don't know precisely, but—"

"I've been telling you for years, boy—you've got to *know precisely!* Ah, the Devil! I can see you've learned nothing from me. You're a younger son, and they've always got to marry for money—don't you know that?"

Mr. Whyte stifled his annoyance, as he had done so many times in the past, and tried to keep to the subject at hand.

"Well, Father, in her situation, I should think her likely to bring with her a hundred a year or so. Her family is from Lincolnshire."

"Lincolnshire! A hundred a year! Paltry—and a wench who's bred in the fens! Good God, John, if you'll accept a chit from Lincolnshire, why not try one from Yorkshire? Or from Cumbria? If your tastes run to poor northern gals, why not pick yourself a bride from Scotland? I'm sure they have lots of penniless brides there!"

"We can live cheaply, sir—"

"Going to have to, aren't you?"

"I wanted your blessing, first, Father. I'd like you to make her acquaintance. I'm sure you'd like her very well."

"Blessing? My blessing? That's a fine joke! All any of you wants is my blunt, and none of you paupers is going to get it. Except perhaps Miles. He's got so much bloody money of his own, he hardly needs to wish for my demise."

"Father, please let me make her known to you—"

"Don't take me for a ninnyhammer, young man. I know full well you've got no funds of your own, and who should know better how things are left? Don't try to gammon me! I had a letter from that soft-in-the-head Balmore just yesterday, whining about my giving you a wedding present of the Melfield rents. That's a good joke. You're talking about getting my blessings, but all you really want is my blunt. You're the spitting image of your mother, and you're every bit as bad as she was, God rest her avaricious soul!"

"Father "

"No! You hear me? The answer is no! I say I'll have none of your penniless Lincolnshire chit! Send her back to the fens, say I. You go marry yourself a girl with a decent fortune, as I've said many times before that you must, or I swear to you that I'll take away all that you've got now! Hear me, boy? I'll take back the farm! Throw you out on your ear! How shall you like that, eh, boy?"

"Melfield? But Father—"

"That's got you where it hurts, don't it, boy? I take back that farm, and you'll not have a pot to piss in, will you? Serve you right for having all these top-lofty notions in your head! You're not your own man, son, and you'd damn well better know your station for what it is, and come back to your senses!"

John Whyte's face was scarlet, but he held his tongue. Manifesting intense self-control, he managed to make a bow to his father.

"Very well. I bid you good day, Father."

"See here, boy—things could change! You marry that pretty wealthy chit St. Clare's gone fond on, or even marry that horse-faced heiress who's coming to the ball, if you're fool enough to like her better. You do that, you act with some kind of intelligence for a change, and I vow I'll sign over to you not just the income, but the deed to Melfield as a wedding gift! That would make a proper living for you and a proper bride!"

John Whyte had turned grey with rage. It took him a few moments to compose himself sufficiently to speak.

"I am afraid I am unable to accept your very considerate offer."

"If you won't marry an heiress, at least you'll have to leave that other chit alone, then. I won't have you carrying on with her under my roof; go against my wishes, and it'll be bellows to mend for you, my boy. You'll be out of that farm by night-fall, if I hear tell of any kind of carryings on of any kind, do you hear me? Have I made my position perfectly clear?"

His father filled his lungs for a final peal toward the door where John Whyte was headed, and his whole body trembled as he hurled the words at his younger son.

"Think it over, young fool! Think how well you should like bringing your pretty young bride to live and raise brats in the Marshalsea. Best just remember the Bible's words, Puritan! To him that hath shall be given!" he cursed loudly. "And to him that hath not—shall be taken away!"

The Earl of Cleremont cackled, guffawed, then dissolved into a fit of coughing. Jones, his lordship's devoted valet, stepped out from among the shadows of an arras, and tenderly wrapped a woolen shawl around his master's frail shoulders.

Thirteen

After his interview with his father, one which had gone far worse than he had ever dreamed possible, John Whyte exited from Haverford by a side door, hoping to ride away to Melfield unnoticed and nurse his wounds. It seemed as if every door to a tolerable future, and even to a tolerable present, had been soundly and unjustly shut upon him. He tried to work out alternatives, but his mind rebelled against it; one moment he would picture himself thrown out of Melfield, parted forever from the fields, the farms, the tenants he had lavished his time upon, and the next he would see himself toiling as the lowest kind of clerk-scribe, keeping accounts in the bowels of a banking house in the City.

In this mental state, that unhappy young man had the bittersweet fortune to come across the precise object of his blighted affections, Miss Pamela Stone. Pamela had spent the morning exploring a garden filled with carefully sculptured yew trees, and was now on the verge of returning to her apartments to take a rest.

For a moment, she nourished the horrid fear that her acknowledged lover was going to deal her the cut direct. He seemed not to acknowledge her at all, so white was his face, and so dejected he seemed. Then, he slowed his pace, seemed to recognize her, and to relent.

Mr. Whyte bowed distantly and took up a path next to her. However, he dared not look into her eyes.

"Good morning, Miss Stone," said he.

"Oh, no! What is the matter?" she inquired, with a lightness she was far from feeling. "Am I to be 'Miss Stone' again, then, *Mr. Whyte?* I am crushed; this *is* serious. But tell me, how have you been? It has been some time since I have seen you, or heard from you. I am glad you are come into the country at last."

Mr. John Whyte made no reply. Pamela Stone was nonplussed.

"Forgive me, but do I find you quite well today?" she ventured. "Have you fallen victim to the flu? Give me leave to say you do not look at all the thing, you know."

"No, I am not well. I am discomposed. You must forgive me, ma'am," he said, grimly. "I cannot speak with you today. I am not at liberty to discuss circumstances, at present."

Pamela was taken aback by his chilly, distant tone of voice, one that she had never previously heard used by him toward her. She blushed high scarlet, and stammered, "I-I do apologize, Mr. Whyte. I, of course, did not mean to be vulgarly inquisitive."

"Not at all; you see, I have had a bit of a shock. Believe me when I say I am not at present suited to be in company. I am not—I cannot be—master of myself at the moment."

He seemed about to bow and leave, then he relented, and turned back toward her.

Looking into his ravaged eyes, Pamela could not help but speak to him with great directness.

"John, please, tell me—what ever can have happened? Please let me—"

"Pamela, I—the servants are watching, they will report everything to their master, I cannot be seen with you like this—oh, damn! Damn the man's impudent, interfering ways!"

He stopped in mid-sentence, and cast his eyes down to the ground.

"Damn it all! Damn his servants! Damn everything! Shall I not even be allowed to say farewell?"

"Farewell?" Pamela gasped.

The Hon. John Whyte then took Pamela's hands in his, raised his gaze once more to look long and lovingly into her eyes.

When finally he spoke again, his words were formal, but his eyes were the eyes of the John she had come to know—and, she now knew, to love. His eyes revealed an ardor suffused with inexpressible pain, but his tone of voice was frigid and distant.

"Miss Stone, I hope that whatever happens from this day forward, you will always look upon me as your most obedient friend and servant. I have—I have held you in the greatest respect almost since the moment we met—the very greatest respect, and—and true affection. Unfortunately, I cannot say more at this time, and I—I am even constrained . . . this is so difficult for me to say, Pamela. You must have pity for me."

He could not go on. He waited, contained himself, and then continued to speak in a grave, formal manner, quite unlike any way in which he had ever behaved toward her before.

"Miss Stone, I am suffering under a grave kind of pressure, not to act toward you in any manner other than that of a distant friend. The precise circumstances constraining me can be made known to you later, but they do not signify. I have just now undergone a difficult—a very difficult experience.

"Please believe how saddened I am to have to meet you in this way. Please believe how very much I had hoped to be able to say—other words to you. But I cannot. I cannot marry you, Miss Stone. I may not. Nor can I befriend you closely, as it has been my pleasure to do in the past. It lies not within my power. There is no more to be said. Farewell, my dear Miss Stone. I do love you so very much. May God bless you."

He bowed formally, kissed her hand, and strode off toward the stables.

Pamela was so shocked she had to seek out the support of a stone bench in a corner of the garden where she could remain unobserved. She soon broke into an uncharacteristic round of tears.

Fourteen

Viscountess St. Clare had been watching this poignant scene from an upstairs window. Although she couldn't hear what it was about, she was able to make an intelligent guess.

It seemed to her that Miss Stone and Mr. Whyte had quarreled, and Mr. Whyte had left Miss Stone in the lurch—which was, Lady St. Clare thought, just as it should be. It was certainly the right thing to have arranged for a series of intimate conversations between herself and her father-in-law, with regard to this unsuitable upstart John had got himself entangled with, this wretched chit, Pamela Stone. It seemed that their little talks had quickly borne desirable fruits.

"I am happy to see that girl on her knees, weeping," Lady St. Clare thought. "She is far too fond of herself—thinks she's better than the rest of us women. But she weeps like the rest of us, and can bleed like the rest of us, too. I am glad to see thus revealed this paragon's feet of clay.

"Tomorrow night we shall see what will come of it all. Perhaps I shall dance an intimate waltz with the now-unencumbered Mr. John Whyte. Perhaps, then, after we have danced, we two, the tall gentleman and myself, shall accomplish even more.

"After all, *pourquois pas?* Everything is strongly in my favor."

Lady Charlton chanced upon her niece sitting in the topiary tree garden some few minutes later, when Pamela had only partially recovered herself. Pamela saw fit to tell her aunt what had passed between herself and the Hon. John Whyte, and Lady Charlton tried to console her niece as best she could.

"Now, now, dear, it's clear what's happened. He's done his home accounts, he's found he can't afford to marry, and he's leaving you free to do better by yourself."

"I don't want to do better by myself!"

"Now you listen to me, young lady. These romantical notions in novels are all well and good when they're bound up in three volumes, but when it comes to having funds to feed and clothe and put a roof over a houseful of young ones, it's no time for being romantic."

Lady Charlton continued inexorably on, "You're still young, so you may not know how hard it can be, but I've seen it—even with my poor sister Kate who married beneath her for love, God rest her soul. The moral of the story is that life is no novel: if you don't have the blunt, your children will have no life, no life at all.

"Kate's six dead children can attest to that—and she herself, a sweet-faced, sweet-tempered girl who is with us on this earth no longer. That marriage ruined her—and the man whom she loved so well. So, do not let yourself be romantical. Be practical. Trust me."

"Oh, can it be so?"

"Now you sound like your cousin Victorine. She may be my daughter, and well-loved she is by me, but I know the limits of her understanding. Your powers of understanding I had supposed to be much greater. Yes, young ma'am, what I say is true:

"Now, some other people in the ranks of the ton may consider you as having but a paltry fortune—but, you have the great *good* fortune to be no wealthy cit's daughter, but a true gentleman's daughter, raised as a gentleman's daughter should be.

"And it would be wrong to pass any lesser station in life on to your offspring, no matter how close an attachment you may have made with Mr. Whyte, no matter what your expectations of him may have been. You can't just follow your love into poverty; I won't allow it, and I can assure you that your father won't allow it. Have you considered his feelings in all of this? How he would feel to have his daughter married, without a feather to fly with?"

"Oh, Auntie—"

"Don't you 'oh, Auntie' me. That young man of yours has a good head on his shoulders, and he's pulling out at the right time, just as a gentleman ought. He's letting you know that he can't make a home for you, whatever his reasons may be for it; he's convinced of it, and, in all honor, he's withdrawing from the lists. Apparently he knows you'll be better off marrying someone else. So, if you love him, pay attention to his wishes, that's what I say."

"Oh, no, no."

"Twaddle! It feels like the end of the world, right now, but I assure you that it's not. You'll get over it, for all it doesn't seem that way at the moment. First love, calf-love, that's what they say."

"Oh, but Auntie—"

"Not another word, you foolish seventeen-year-old

child. You're just out of the schoolroom! This is just your first season! Relax, give your life a chance to happen a bit more, that's all I'm asking. Not asking, I should say—I demand it of you, as your chaperone, as the one your father entrusted with the care of you. The Haverford ball is but tomorrow night. We'll find someone nice for you to dance with, my girl. Balmore will be here by then, and I'll seek his advice; he's a lovely, practical man. Dry your tears—we'll find you an eligible *parti*. Have patience, child. Wait until tomorrow, and see."

Fifteen

The night of the ball arrived at last. A small fortune in candles was burning brightly in all the main halls of Haverford; another small fortune in fresh-cut flowers decorated the finely painted vases in the front hall, the golden damask-draped alcoves of the grand ballroom, and the intricately carved mahogany side tables that graced the various parlors through which the Earl's guests would pass.

For weeks, maids had been set to polishing the heirloom silver till their fingers ached from the effort; they had labored at buffing the wood till it held an almost reflective brilliance. In the end, the staff had abolished all grime, tarnish, and dirt, till not a speck of dust could be seen, even in the most remote corners of the grand mansion.

On that night, tall, bewigged footmen were plentiful and ubiquitous, found standing at attention wherever one looked, decked out in the Earl of Cleremont's most splendid livery; the old man, miserly in so many ways, was nevertheless a great believer in keeping up appearances; this was the reasoning behind the funds he still poured into keeping up his stables and his hunters. Lord Cleremont rarely entertained, but when he chose to do so, did so in the grand manner.

The front drive was a commotion of carriages letting out their occupants, great ladies in plumed turbans being gently handed down out of their conveyances. Horses were being taken off to the stables, elegant guests being escorted through the entranceway. Wraps and canes were quickly whisked away by the numerous, efficient, nearly invisible servants.

After making their entrance through the main hall, the ball guests ascended the sweeping curved grand staircase, and were ushered toward the main series of rooms; as the ladies and gentlemen filed in beneath the gorgeous gilded ceiling, their arrivals were punctuated by the stentorian announcements of Mr. Willby.

The Earl of Cleremont had declared he would suffer through no private dinner prior to the ball, and indeed, his lordship himself did not even bother to come to greet his guests as they arrived. Lord Cleremont's heir and his daughter-in-law performed that office in his stead, standing at the top of the long receiving line at the head of the sweeping main staircase.

Those who knew the old gentlemen well were not surprised either by his absence or his denial of the usual intimate dinner, for Cleremont's social eccentricities were legion. They knew that a full range of refreshments would be offered now and throughout the evening, and that, even if his lordship did not deign to grace the company with his presence for more than a few minutes, the opportunities for dancing at a Haverford ball would be many, and that the late supper to follow would be well-prepared and well-served, and the food plentiful and delicious. With or without the attendant presence of Lord Cleremont, the ball would be a great success.

The ballroom was awash in laughter and conversation as young men made their way from lady to lady, asking for a place to be saved for them on the young ladies' schedule of dances. The swishing of so many fans was almost sufficient to cause small swirling breezes to sweep over the dance floor; at the beginning, everyone seemed transfixed, waiting for the musicians to strike up a tune.

Pamela, somewhat to the surprise of Helen Fraley, had dressed with extreme care for the Haverford ball. She allowed her abigail full rein for her talents, unprotesting. Thomas Stone had insisted that she purchase at least one ball gown from the divine Madame Fanchon, and it was this one that Helen had selected for Pamela to wear this evening.

As Pamela ascended the grand staircase, she had the satisfaction of believing herself to present an excellent appearance. Her gown was a bit sophisticated for a debutante, though it had been bought largely with the future in mind. It was made of mint-green silk with an overskirt of silver gauze, and had been trimmed with seed pearls. The bodice was cut quite low, emphasizing her soft curves, and it fitted her beautifully. She wore her mother's triple set of pearls.

Lady Charlton was also in the best of looks; she seemed, week by week, to be looking less like an aging chaperone, and more like a handsome, modish matron. Lord Balmore's continued attentions had resulted in her ladyship completely redoing her toilette. For the Haverford ball, Lady Charlton was wearing a gown of pale gold crepe decorated with delicate lace trimming; she had doffed her turban and feathers in favor of a stunning diamond tiara, and wore it with its matching bracelets, necklace, earrings, and ring. She appeared to great advantage, and the look of admiration on Lord Balmore's face when he greeted her and escorted her up the staircase made all her daring well worthwhile.

Miss Victorine Wells was looking pretty in a very pale yellow gown of silk, with a low neck ornamented by a tiny lace border; its puffed sleeves were divided into smaller puffs by several ribands of silk. Though outwardly appearing very much the thing, inwardly Victorine felt unsettled and unsatisfied.

Lord St. Clare and his wife had been perfectly civil to her when they were received by them at the head of the Grand Staircase, but Victorine had received none of the usual distinguishing friendliness she had come to expect from the Viscount and his wife.

As they had now become houseguests, Victorine began to wonder if she had offended them in some way. She had seen nothing of his lordship since she arrived, and from Lord St. Clare in particular, this neglectful distancing was unutterably painful to her. Once she knew that the receiving line had broken up, her eyes kept sweeping around the ballroom, searching unavailingly for Lord St. Clare, waiting for him to come to her.

Pamela noticed nothing of her cousin's unease, for she herself was searching anxiously for a sign of Mr. Whyte. She was happy to have made the effort to show herself off to best advantage. It was likely, she thought, that tonight she would finally make the acquaintance of the Earl of Cleremont, the person she now believed responsible for quashing her hopes of marriage to his lordship's younger son.

She noticed Mr. Whyte's arrival as soon as it occurred. He was wearing the requisite silk stockings, and black knee-breeches; he had chosen to wear a white waistcoat, and a severe but beautifully cut black coat. She also noticed that, beyond bowing to her in a correct and civil manner, he made no further attempt to engage her in any way. John

Whyte remained with his own bachelor party, comprised of himself, Charles Bellfort, and Lord Balmore.

Poor Pamela felt completely mortified by Mr. Whyte's conduct. It seemed as if that gentleman wished to avoid her company altogether. He made no approach to secure her hand for a dance. Once, when their eyes chanced to meet, Mr. Whyte bowed again, almost imperceptibly, then looked away quickly, as if wounded by the touch of her gaze.

Soon, Lord Shelton came by to apply for Pamela's hand for a country dance, as did the faithful Mr. Bellfort, and a few other gentlemen as well, but anyone who knew Pamela and John must be aware that Mr. Whyte was pointedly avoiding her presence. It was humiliating in the extreme. How wrong, it seemed to her, to be so completely deprived of Mr. Whyte's company, and being even denied commerce with him as a friend. What could have happened that he felt he must distance himself from her so thoroughly? She wished she could leave the ball at once.

Victorine also was disconsolate. She thought her choice of partners for the ball paltry; she wanted a word in private with Lord St. Clare, and nothing less would do for her. Mr. Bellfort and Mr. Whyte had asked to dance with her, as did many another young man, but their attentions could not satisfy the hunger that had suddenly surged forth within her once again. Viscount St. Clare had not yet appeared to claim her, and Victorine felt utterly bereft.

Victorine had increasingly begun to panic at the Viscount's cool behavior toward her—was there really to be no further contact after those few stolen moments in the park? She could not bear it. St. Clare was surely holding back from her for propriety's sake, from a desire to protect her reputation. Must he continue to do so?

Overcome by a kind of agitated passion, Victorine made up her mind in that moment that she wanted the Viscount, and that she would have him.

I am not a child anymore—I have felt, with St. Clare on that drive weeks ago, all that a woman can feel toward a man. I don't give a fig for propriety—and my reputation be damned! I will see him; I will see him tonight; I must!

Had the Viscount St. Clare been made aware of the nature of the thoughts passing through the mind of his next intended, he, of course, could not have been more pleased. He had worked her up into precisely the frenzy he needed to accomplish the task contemplated some weeks ago. Recompense would no doubt be his, well before the next dawn broke.

The Haverford ball was soon under way in its full glory; the personal difficulties of the various guests seemed for a time quite swept up into the strains of the music, and thus were banished out of mind, for the nonce at least. The pleasure of dancing itself was enough to put one's mind in a lighter mood.

Pamela Stone, during one of the brief times when she had not been asked to dance, was forced to enjoy the bitterness of seeing the man she had only recently entertained thoughts of marrying waltzing first with the rich Belinda Falk-Duffield, and then dancing the quadrille with Miss Victorine Wells, her own wealthy, dazzlingly lovely cousin.

He is specializing in heiresses again tonight, isn't he? Perhaps that's the Earl's idea, and it might really be for the best. Either one of them is a better choice as a wife for him than I am, Pamela thought to herself ruefully.

How can I compete with them? What could I bring to a marriage with him but a sharp tongue, and a lack of fortune? He cannot afford to marry me. He must think of his own future—and he would be better off if he married either one of them, Belinda or Victorine.

She was beginning to feel ever more despondent, when Mr. Bellfort approached her to claim his dance. He made a short bow, then looked at Pamela with some gravity. He took her hand for the set, and they settled into their places.

"I perceive that you are not quite yourself this evening, Miss Stone."

"No, I must admit that I am not."

"May I be of help?"

"No, Mr. Bellfort, I think that there is nothing you can do, unless you could contrive to transform me into a stunningly beautiful heiress like Victorine. Or into a homely heiress like Belinda Falk-Duffield. Either would suffice."

She looked over feelingly toward Mr. Whyte, who was now smiling amiably toward her cousin as he handed over a glass of ratafia he had fetched particularly for Miss Wells. *Why did he not come to me?* Pamela asked herself. *Why had he not come at least to explain his change of heart?*

"I see that Mr. Whyte is now with your lovely cousin, Miss Wells. Don't tell me that that's the quarter the wind's in, Miss Stone, for I don't believe it. It is a shame that younger sons must bear so many burdens; I feel sorry for John if he feels forced to pursue a match with Miss Wells for her fortune alone. I know John well: I do not think that he and your cousin would suit."

"No, I feel sure they would not. But it would be thought a good match by the world, wouldn't it? He would improve his financial position, and she her social position, by virtue of marrying the heir presumptive to a Viscountcy, and the second in line to an Earldom. It would do well enough from the point of view of society, wouldn't it?"

"I suppose. Not a brilliant match for Victorine, however, so it probably won't fadge. I don't think you need worry about John falling in love with your cousin, however attentive he may seem to her this evening. Likely there is something else going on of which we both are unaware.

"Miss Stone, please allow me to take you into my confidence tonight. By now, we know each other well enough that I feel I can reveal to you how deeply I can sympathize with your distress. Like you, I have been nurturing hopes of attracting the attention of a person toward whom I have tolerably strong feelings; however, my match as well is likely to be deemed unsuitable by the person most deeply concerned."

"How can that be?"

"For me, there are reasons other than those creating obstacles in your case. I know that John Whyte holds you in the greatest regard, and I know the character of John's father is likely to be the source of your own difficulties.

"But the match I myself have wished for—and still wish for—is unsuitable not because of any disparity in rank or fortune, but because the object of my interest was—and is—Miss Victorine Wells. I am hopelessly devoted to her, and I was from the very first instant of knowing her.

"The obstacle for me is this: my treasured Victorine is an exquisite, unusual, gentle being, a diamond of the first water, and I myself am but a short, squat man. I am not good enough for her, you must allow. I am not dashing, not handsome, not daring, not brave. I possess none of the romantic qualities which might fix my interest with one such as Victorine.

"That being the case, what I most wish for cannot come to pass. Even so, for a while I nurtured hopes that, in time, Miss Wells might come to notice me. But, as you can see, it has come to nothing. She counts me as her good and faithful friend, but as nothing more. Though I have done my best over these past weeks, I have been unable to attach her. In fact, I am quite invisible."

"So sad, is it not? That the object of one's honest longing may be unobtainable," said Pamela grimly.

"Indeed. It is unfair that the heart chooses its own objects of love, regardless of possibility and impossibility, suitability or unsuitability, or any of the practical things."

"Yes; we are entrapped by our higher feelings."

"That is the bittersweet nature of life: it is so difficult to find the person one loves above all others. Having had the rare good fortune to find that person may not suffice—one may merely find one's love, yet not have them return one's regard. Still, by our heart's desires we are bound forever; we may end by being required to treat as mere friends those persons we most wish to cherish tenderly. And find our ourselves forever treated as mere companions, mere acquaintances," added Mr. Bellfort.

"If even that much happiness is vouchsafed to one," said Miss Stone bitterly, and her lips tightened into a thin line betokening regret.

Sixteen

In a distant corner of the great house of Haverford, Darcher, Viscount St. Clare's valet, was tidying up the Red Room. He was busying himself going from place to place, dusting here and rearranging there, humming along with the ball music far in the distance. As he worked, he checked to make sure that everything was ready for his lordship St. Clare, who was always extremely fussy about preparations for his evening entertainments.

Everything had to be spotless; everything that might be needed had to be in place; everything his lordship might possibly want had to have been anticipated and procured well in advance, or there would be hell to pay for it. His lordship could not abide slackers.

The Red Room was a smallish room in the farthest corner of the South Tower, extremely secluded, hung with several layers of thick scarlet and gold brocade draperies. The ceiling was painted with satyrs cavorting amidst a sumptuous feast, a scene bordered with an almost sickeningly intricate line of gilding that edged the entire room.

There was, as well, in the Red Room, near its center, a priceless carved mahogany table, with clawed dragon feet. On the evening of the ball it was set with a sterling silver tray bearing two glasses, two bottles of champagne in a silver bucket, a pair of small gilt sherry glasses, and a cut-glass decanter filled with an insidiously dark liquid.

On the far wall were several large, ornately carved gilt-edged mirrors, one partially hidden behind the first layer of gold and red brocade hangings. There was even a spy-hole, carefully hidden in the wall, remnants left over from the part Haverford had played in an earlier bit of English history.

The largest piece of furniture, which dominated the room, was an enormous carved four-poster bed hung with scarlet damask draperies, laid over with a pile of silk-covered cushions, oriental-style. It was not immediately visible to an entering guest.

As he worked, Darcher found himself almost giddy with pleasure—it had been almost a year since the Red Room had last been properly put to use. He was proud that he was sure to be allowed to take some part in this evening's entertainment. And on the night of the Haverford ball, no less! A very special occasion for everyone.

Darcher had always found these special evenings in the Red Room most entertaining. Even in the times of his lordship's father, the nights of intimate entertainments in the Red Room had always proven to be highly memorable events. Yes, it all brought back the very pleasantest of memories! It was a fine thing to be young!

Miss Victorine Wells was in the grand salon, enjoying a fit of what appeared to be the sullens, and her mother was trying to coax her into a better mood. Nothing seemed to please the foolish child tonight. She had been dismissive, if not rude, to the majority of her dance partners, and she kept looking around the room as if she were expecting someone who did not appear.

Lady Charlton was beginning to become exasperated

with her daughter. Why couldn't Victorine just settle for one of her suitors, allow him to fix his interest with her, and be done with it? She still seemed to be making no progress at all, and the season was as good as gone. Mr. Bellfort clearly adored her; why didn't he offer for her? Why shouldn't she accept him? Her ladyship was of the opinion that enough was enough.

"Victorine, child, don't keep that look on your face," she chided her daughter. "It does you no compliment. Why can't you make yourself pleasant to the gentlemen this evening? You have almost ignored poor Charles Bellfort, whom you must be aware is devoted to you."

"Oh, Mama. I know that Charles is a dear man, but, please, don't talk to me tonight about suitors and gentlemen and propriety. I have the headache—can't you perceive that I am out of sorts? Don't fuss at me so, Mama! Why don't you have Charles Bellfort fetch you a glass of ratafia or of wine? I'm sure it will improve your own mood."

"How can you be so uncivil to me, daughter?" replied her mother, with unaccustomed warmth.

"Forgive me, Mama. I'm very nervous this evening. You require better company than I can provide. Where is Lord Balmore?"

"He was here but a moment ago. He seems to have gone off; it is most unlike him. I rather think I shall go off myself to seek refreshment. Stay here, and I shall return directly. I am not pleased with your manners this evening, Victorine. Try for some conduct, will you?"

"I am sorry, Mother," she replied, suddenly repentant. "I shall stay right here."

Almost as soon as Lady Charlton had disappeared to seek out a servant bearing champagne, Lord St. Clare manifested next to Miss Wells, just as if out of thin air. His glossy black curls were brushed into a fashionable Brutus, and his evening-dress was of the very first stare. He towered over her as he silently approached her from the rear.

His lordship stepped behind Victorine and ran a finger down the nape of her neck. She gasped with shock. St. Clare took no notice, but began twirling a curl around his finger and tugging on it, almost painfully—and he did so with such subtle movements that no one but his lordship and Victorine was aware of what was occurring.

Victorine blushed as she recognized his lordship's touch, but said nothing; she was proud that he had finally approached her, and proud that his hands were upon her again at long last, however publicly, however slightly, however subtly. The moment she had been dreaming about had finally come to pass: her heart started pounding deeply and rapidly in her chest.

St. Clare made as if he was looking far over on the other side of the ballroom, but his lips were almost touching Victorine's ear as he whispered to her, "My little love! I cannot bear it! I have tried all this time, all of these weeks to suppress my love for you and my devotion to you, but it will not do. Trying to discipline myself, I have failed utterly all this long time, and I can live without you no longer!"

"Oh, St. Clare," Victorine murmured, pressing closer to him. "I have missed you so very much."

"Come to me tonight, my love."

"Come to you? But Lord St. Clare, how can I?" she said, astonished.

"Don't you desire to?"

Victorine tried to look him full in the eyes, but St. Clare made her turn her face away, as if they were both watching the dancing.

She understood that he wished to behave circumspectly, and continued on, "Of course I want to, my love. But—how can we?"

"This is my house. I can accomplish anything here."

"It is your father's house still, is it not?"

"Yes, but, my dear— my father and I are of one mind. It has always been so. Trust me. I shall tuck you away, safe in this house, in my arms, like a precious family heirloom."

"Oh, your lordship! I wish that I could, but I mustn't."

"Say no more—you are putting a knife through the very chambers of my heart."

He moved his lips till she could feel his breath warming her skin.

"Victorine, say only that you will meet me after midnight. Just let me feast my eyes on you once more—that is all that I ask. First, you must be presented to my father, and then, my man Darcher will come for you to escort you to the eastern chamber it is called the Bride's Room. Is it not apt? We will have a late supper of oysters and my most excellent champagne. And we will talk—talk of our future. Our future together. I wish to be—your husband."

"Our future? Oh, my dearest, my dearest love! I had no thought of that! To be your wife, then? Of course I shall come!"

"I knew you would be pleased." His lordship Viscount St. Clare leaned down, and planted a long kiss on the tender tips of Victorine's fingers. "Till then, my love."

"Oh, yes, your lordship. Till then. I cannot wait."

"Nor can I, I do assure you."

St. Clare bowed, and was gone.

* * *

Finding the Haverford ball a sad crush—too many people, and not nearly enough air—Pamela decided to escape onto a rear verandah. She leaned for a moment against the balustraded parapet, her head tipped down toward the ground. She was masked in shadows, and was listening only vaguely to the sound of conversation and music behind her.

None of this, at the moment, seemed to have anything to do with her, Pamela Stone. Yesterday, she seemed to belong to this world and to events such as these—but today, suddenly and rudely bereft of the company of her dear friend John Whyte—she discovered that, in John's absence, she cared not a fig for any of it.

Well, it was over and done with. All there was left to do now was to come to terms with it. *How long would this state of mind last?* she wondered. *How long does it take for a heart once again to become whole?*

Pamela felt tears welling up, and she decided to go walk in the garden, embarrassed lest someone discover her distress. It was a pleasant night, and the feel of open air on her skin was soft and soothing to her as well.

The thin gauze of her ball gown swished softly against its silken underskirt. The Fanchon gown had cost so much to purchase, a lovely, delicate green that set off her eyes perfectly—and tonight, she realized she had no taste for it at all. Indeed, why should she?

She could have been dressed in rags and not cared one whit. It all seemed like vanity, everything seemed like vanity—vainness, emptiness. All that signified in human life was true affection, and true love—and that was what Pamela knew she would be deprived of, merely by pecuniary considerations, based on the circumstances of her birth and John's birth. It seemed so unfair, and yet it was incontrovertibly the case.

She was so lost in these thoughts that, as she stepped around a fir tree into deeper shadow, she did not perceive someone else rapidly proceeding toward the house from the opposite direction. The two collided, and for more than a moment she was terrified, for it was a great, tall man who had run into her, and suddenly the man's arms were around her. Of a sudden she realized the strong arms were not there to take advantage of her, but were there to steady her, to support her, and that the arms were those of the Honorable John Whyte.

"John! Oh, God, how you frightened me!"

She could not help herself, his name escaped her lips before her brain could put a stop to it—and her tears fell naturally and freely from her eyes.

John Whyte said nothing in reply, but held her head against his shoulder as she wept, running his fingers through her hair. They were still in shadow, no one could see them: for the moment they were safe, away from the inquisitive eyes of the earl's servants.

"Pamela. My dearest," said he as he crushed her to him.

"John, John—what is wrong? What happened to you yesterday? You were so cold to me. It was so unlike you. And tonight you tried to avoid seeing me—purposely, did you not?"

"I did try to avoid you. Only because I could not bear the pain of seeing you in another man's arms and not my own."

"What, then, is wrong?"

"Everything is wrong, Pamela. I cannot be your husband, just as I said. I cannot marry you because I can offer you even less than I could before. I can offer you not even the vaguest semblance of gentility; I can offer you nothing. Less than nothing."

"If I have no future with you, then there the present as well ceases to exist for me. Don't you know that? I cannot live without you, John."

"You must live without me; you shall, my dearest light, and you must. You cannot be married to a pauper—and that is what my father has in mind for me if I do not do his bidding. There is no hope for me, not at all. I will not let you be married to a pauper. How could you think I would let you share such a fate? What a shabby end *that* would be to thrust upon one's beloved!"

"I don't understand! What will become of us?"

"I cannot say, dear love. It is over for us, and it must be. I am happy merely to have stumbled onto a chance to hold you in my arms at least once in my miserable, benighted life."

"But what has happened? Why do you speak of becoming a pauper? How can you have less now than you had a week ago? Have you had some terrible loss on 'Change?"

"No, it isn't that. Yesterday—when last I saw you—I had just that very moment come from an interview with my father. I had just asked his permission to pay my addresses to you."

"John!"

"Don't smile at me in that delicious manner, my dear Pamela. There is nothing to smile about at all. Father denied me his permission."

"I smile because I am happy that you consider me a suitable wife."

"My dear sweet goose! 'A suitable wife,' indeed. You know full well that I have loved you since the day we rode together in the Park, and my respect and affection have only increased since then."

"With only brief interludes of odious misunderstanding!" she said, not trying to hide her upturned lips.

"Don't jest about that, love, and please, don't look at me in that enticing way, for it is no use. There is to be no happy ending to our fairy-tale romance. As I said, my father refused to allow me to wed you."

"Has he the power to do so? Surely not?"

"Legally, of course, he cannot prevent me from marrying as I please. But he does have power over me. A great power."

"What power is that?"

"Melfield, the farming estate upon which I live and which provides what little income I have, does not belong to me."

Pamela's face paled with sudden comprehension.

"Melfield does not belong to me. It belongs to Father. I live there on his sufferance. If he were to turn me out—I would be indeed penniless."

"A father could not do such a thing to a son!" Pamela replied with a blaze of indignation. "Is he mad?"

"Perhaps. But the point is that Father could do so, and would do so, and will do so. I confess, I had expected that he would not treat me quite so meanly. I had thought that, once I asked for his blessing on my marriage, that he would at the very least permit me to continue living as I have done at Melfield. I was fool enough to nurture the hope that I would be permitted to keep the rents from the surrounding cottages. I thought that, with severe economies and good farm management, we two might make a life for ourselves. A simple one, to be sure, but a life together. A good life.

"However, I was wrong. Father explained his position to me very clearly—in no uncertain terms, that if I married you, a young lady without any great fortune, he would throw me to the wolves."

"I can't believe it."

"I can, now. I believe my father hates me, or so it seems from his behavior toward me. I knew Miles was his favorite, but I had no idea that Father had such disdain for my feelings as to threaten to cast me out of my home merely for failing to dangle after an heiress."

"That is what he asked of you?"

"Precisely. He said that if I married you, a mere gentleman's daughter, he would cast me out of the family, and throw me out of Melfield. He also said that if I married a more suitable wife—he mentioned Miss Wells and Miss Falk-Duffield, of course—that he would give me Melfield as a wedding gift."

"Oh, John. Dreadful! I don't suppose it likely he will relent?"

"He will never relent. It is not in his character. So there it is. Now you know the cause of my anger, and the cause of my shameful neglect of you this evening, and my conduct toward you yesterday. I had not wanted to explain it to you, so mortified was I at my father's behavior, and I feared to even speak to you in the ballroom lest father make one of his sudden appearances as a host and see us together.

"Believe me, it cost my character a great deal to be so circumspect. However, it seemed the prudent course for the moment, until I shall have worked out some other solution to the problem—if solution there be, for I can see none.

"But just now, here, when I felt you once again against me—what could I do except do what I did, and crush you in my arms? At least I had to seize the chance that fate gave to me—to let me tell you that I truly love you, that

I cherish you, and it has been my dearest wish to make you my wife."

"John," whispered Pamela as she pressed closer against him.

"But it would hardly be an act of love to make you the wife of a pauper, would it? Worse even than being the wife of a mere gentleman-farmer! I had thought that future to be bad enough—supporting a wife merely on the income from the Melfield tenants. But with no house? No estate? No income whatsoever? Marrying on such terms, I might as well lead you straight from the altar to the poorhouse."

Pamela shivered, whispering, "I can't think of it. I can't bear to think of it. Not now. We'll talk again tomorrow."

The tall man bent down, cupped her chin in his hand, and began to kiss her once more. She responded, then let her gaze fall toward the ground.

"Ah, Mr. Whyte, I am afraid now as I have never been afraid before. 'Come love, let us kiss, and part?' Like John Donne? Is that what this kiss is a prelude to? Parting?"

"I fear so."

"No, I refuse! We shan't kiss and part."

"Shan't we?"

"We will find a way. We must."

He wrapped his arm around her small waist and pulled her even closer to him, saying, "Very well, my small, brave wonder."

Hidden in the deep shadows of the fir tree, two shadowy forms entwined, seeming almost to entirely enfold one another. The night was moonless, so it was difficult to tell what was real and what merely the play of light against shadow.

Seventeen

Past midnight, the Right Honorable Bertram Francis Whyte, Seventh Earl of Cleremont, Tenth Baron Haverford, condescended to make his annual appearance at the grand Haverford ball. As he entered the main salon, those guests who had not yet made his acquaintance were interested to observe that Lord Cleremont was a tall man with a great shock of white hair framing a face that, though weathered with lines, was still very handsome indeed.

A brief appearance at the ball was all Lord Cleremont intended to make—he cared little for the opinions of others and felt no weighty social obligation incumbent upon him to show interest in conversing with his guests. He had provided the hall, the musicians, the repast, and the company—that was, in his opinion, more than enough. Further, it was his ball, after all, so it was unsurprising that he should do whatever he wished at it.

His lordship was quite used to doing whatever he wished. It was what his father had taught him to do and what he had tried to pass on to his son and heir, Miles. Aristocracy had many privileges, and it was part of more profound responsibilities of a member of the nobility, he thought, to take an active part in availing oneself of the privileges of rank.

So Lord Cleremont did just as he wished, thinking

nothing of the opinion of others, and taught his heir the same manners. Cleremont came to his balls whenever he pleased and left whenever he pleased; he had no care for the opinions of the rest of society, for he was above them. In this manner he had lived his entire life.

The Earl of Cleremont's appearance in the main ballroom caused some stir—it always did. People began to line up to be presented to his lordship or otherwise to pay their respects.

Lord and Lady St. Clare saw to it that those who had been invited to stay at Haverford met Lord Cleremont first. The Brook Street ladies were thus among the very first to be presented to the Earl of Cleremont.

The Earl seemed very pleased with the fetching Miss Wells; his son John thought his father gave her an almost lascivious glance—but perhaps it was merely her fortune that was giving his father such apparent pleasure. His lordship was blandly polite to Lady Charlton; he gave poor Miss Pamela Stone the chilliest reception imaginable.

The Earl found it difficult to believe that it was this poor little dab of a girl that his fool son John had conceived a *tendre* for. What nonsense—as if marriage was a matter for the heart rather than the head! He offered Pamela no more than a slight, frigid inclination of his head, and, then turned away to engage in polite conversation the next person presented to him.

After the dead silence between them had fallen, Pamela withdrew the hand she had foolishly extended to the Earl, and passed on, humiliated again. She felt that the very worst of the evening must be over, and that, having met his lordship, she could now leave the ball in good conscience and withdraw to her bedchamber. She found herself well on the way to developing the headache, and she longed for the sweet relief of sleep.

Pamela looked around for Victorine to accompany her, but her cousin seemed to have disappeared entirely, as had her aunt, Lady Charlton, which was odd in itself. They had both been presented to his lordship just before she had, so Pamela had to assume that they had gone off together. In any case, Pamela thought that she had best escape while she could.

Pamela caught John Whyte's eye and nodded him a wordless goodbye. He smiled and bowed slightly—but he was still standing near his father, who was prosing on loudly to his two sons about the many good qualities of Miss Wells, so she could do no more than that. She looked around to bid good night to Lord Balmore and Charles Bellfort, but could not find them either. She made her way out of the salon, happy to be leaving the ball at last.

Below stairs, far from the sparkling champagne and chandeliers, another kind of drama was playing itself out. Young Maud, Victorine's abigail, had been caught in a closet in the arms of Darcher, Lord St. Clare's valet. Mrs. Fawkes, the head cook, was demanding that they both be turned out of doors, while Mr. Willby, the top-lofty butler, insisted merely that Maud must go—and must go tonight, before the moral tone of the entire household was compromised.

Maud, of course, was in tears, and Helen Fraley, her best friend, was sticking by her faithfully—much good it would do anyone.

"Mrs. Fawkes, it's not true, mum!" Maud was wailing. "He pushed me in there—he forced me in. I'm a good girl, I am!"

"It is of no moment who did what to whom. His lordship is hardly going to let Darcher leave his service for the crime of kissing a servant girl in the closet," opined Willby. "The household is upset; that is what is unacceptable. The girl is loose, and she is flighty. She must go, and she must go tonight."

"Gawd, Mr. Willby, you can't let me go without a character!"

"Why not?"

"I want to see Miss Victorine. She'll help me."

"You'll see no one."

"You can't put me alone on a coach to London in the middle of the night. It ain't decent! It ain't fair! What'll become of me?" she wailed, knowing it would be the end of her.

"You'll be on that stagecoach and all the worse for you if you don't, baggage."

"That's not fair!" interrupted Helen Fraley. "You can't do that. She's not in your employ, Mr. Willby, is she?"

"She most certainly is not. Perhaps you, Helen Fraley, should accompany your friend on her return to London, if you feel so strongly about her safety?" commented Willby acidly.

Before Helen could retort, Peter Welish was at her side, pinching her elbow, and whispering, "Helen, don't make a fuss. Let her go." He had come over to deliver a book of accounts to the Earl, and had stolen a few moments to speak with her.

"But it's wrong!" hissed Helen to Peter.

"Let it go, I tell you," and he steered her out of the room, and made her hush till they were out of earshot of the rest of the servants.

"How can you let them do that, Peter?" she asked, outraged.

"I let them do that cuz they're stronger than me, and stronger than you, too. Talk to your mistress if you want. Don't make trouble down here, or they'll let the same thing happen to you one day."

"How can they do that, Peter?"

"How? Don't matter a bit how. It's their house, Helen, and they run it the way they like. Always have, always will. Get on, now, go back up to your mistress. You can talk about it to Miss Pamela, I warrant, and maybe some help will come for Maud by way of one of your Quality—but you watch your step with the upper servants in this house. They're just as havey-cavey as their masters, mark my words. You just be careful, hear me?"

Pamela came upon Lady Charlton walking through the Main Gallery in an extremely tipsy state for a lady of quality, and had to assist her in reaching her bedchamber and her maid. The unexpectedly early departure of Lord Balmore from the Haverford ball had no doubt affected her ladyship adversely.

"You don't suppose he is angry with me, do you?"

"Why would you think that, Aunt Charlton? I thought he had expected that he might be called back to London suddenly."

"He did mention that—you don't think he was merely trying to find an excuse to leave me?"

"Now that is being foolish beyond permission, Aunt."

"It was that dreadful Edwina Braithwaite who gave me the notion. Talked about Balmore's keeping some opera dancer or other who's twenty years younger than I am. I vow, I felt so old! So helpless! I know Edwina only brought it up to be catty—she's that kind of girl, beautiful but venomous—and then, I lost confidence in myself. She said she thought he'd had enough of the country air, and then, in that horrid winking way of hers, gave me to understand that she thought he'd gone back to London to have a spot of fun with his precious little barque of frailty!" wailed Lady Charlton.

"Hush, Aunt! Whatever his connections in London may be, he certainly wouldn't leave your side for such a dubious reason. He's a great gentleman. Don't let Lady Braithwaite get your goat. You know full well she says things like that on purpose, just to stir up trouble. Hush, now."

Collins, her ladyship's dresser scratched on the door, and appeared, carrying her ladyship's nightgown and a lace cap.

"I will see you put to bed. Collins, would you take her ladyship's gown, and pull the bell for some lemonade."

"It's after midnight, Miss! Shouldn't her ladyship rather enjoy a glass of hot milk?"

"My head hurts," remarked her ladyship. "Collins, do bring some lemonade. The very thought of hot milk makes me shudder."

"Too much champagne, Aunt."

The upstairs maid appeared, and Collins left with her, to put away her ladyship's ballgown properly. Lady Charlton, with Pamela's help, threw on her lace night-dress. Her niece bid her sit at her dressing table and began to brush her hair.

"Yes. I'm afraid I overindulged. I should know better, shouldn't I? I was so very disappointed by Balmore's leaving, don't you see, Pamela? I've grown to trust him, and to depend upon his company, and now that he's had to go back to town, I feel quite bereft and out of sorts. I do hope he returns quickly. He did dance with me, however. Twice," her ladyship sighed.

"You must know that he dotes on you, Aunt Charlton. I am fully persuaded he will return as soon as ever he may."

There was a knock on the door, as the upstairs maid appeared bearing the glass of lemonade. Pamela took it from her, and desired Collins to retire for the night.

"Drink this, and just go to sleep, Aunt Charlton. Everything will be fine, very soon; just you wait and see."

"All right, dear, and thank you for being so kind. Is Victorine quite alright? She was so nervous and wretched earlier on in the evening. I don't know what I'm going to do with her. Why can't she accept Charles Bellfort? Why hasn't he asked her?" with a rising edge of hysteria in her voice.

"Don't let yourself get excited. Go to sleep. Victorine has already retired, I am told. She's safe in her room, and you will deal much better with her in the morning, after both she and you have had a good night's sleep."

Having reassured her aunt as best she could about her daughter and her friend Lord Balmore, Pamela Stone wended her way through the warren of corridors back to her own bedchamber once more.

"His lordship St. Clare should have issued us maps along with his invitations," Pamela sighed to herself as she walked along the dark, drafty, interminable halls. "I've never seen a house laid out in a more peculiar pattern."

Pamela, as she walked alone through the house, was inclined to dwell more and more on her own predicament.

Seeing no obvious solution to her difficulties, she became increasingly blue-devilled.

On entering her room, she saw her abigail still waiting up to put her to bed. She was very happy to see Helen's friendly face, though her own wore a grave expression.

"There now, Miss Pamela. Did you have a nice time at the ball?"

"No, Helen. I confess I did not. I tell you plainly, I'm ready to go home to Father."

"Yes, Miss, I know what you feel like. I don't like this household, I can tell you. There's havey-cavey work here. More than anyone knows," Helen said in hushed tones.

"Whatever do you mean?"

"I mean, that's what Peter told me."

"Who's Peter?"

Helen blushed. "He's my young man. I've mentioned him once before, but now we've an understanding."

"Helen! I did not know! How lovely for you! Does that mean that I am to lose you, then?"

"Perhaps not, Miss," said Helen with a sly look. "Peter is in service to someone you know—Mr. John Whyte."

Pamela's face fell. She steeled herself to conceal her depression and turned away.

"Miss, what's the matter? I thought all was going well for the two of you."

"I can't speak about it, Helen. I can't. I'm sorry."

Helen raised her eyebrows at Miss Pamela's unusual reticence, but bobbed a curtsey, her feelings hurt that Miss Pamela was choosing not to confide in her.

Helen Fraley, recognizing her mistress to be in low spirits, decided that the story about her friend Maud's dismissal could certainly wait until morning. *Poor Miss*

Pamela, she thought. *What can have happened that she should be so upset about Mr. Whyte?*

Helen tiptoed carefully out of the room as she saw Pamela falling into a deep sleep.

Victorine had kissed her mother good night, pretending to be tired and bored with dancing and wishful only to retire early. Her mother, unhappy at the Lord Balmore's recall to London, her unhappiness having been assuaged by copious amounts of champagne liberally supplied to her by a footman at the express orders of the Viscountess, had failed to notice that her daughter had retired from the grand Haverford ball.

Victorine, upon exiting the ballroom, was unsure where her assignation with St. Clare was to be. She had started walking down a long corridor in the general direction of her bedchamber when Darcher caught up to her.

"There you are, miss," he whispered. "You must follow me."

"Did his lordship send you?"

"But, of course."

What a flat this one is, Darcher thought to himself, *though a true jewel of a girl, a great beauty. His lordship surely has the most magnificent taste in females.*

Victorine's heart beat wildly at the realization that her dream was coming true at last. She could hardly contain her excitement as she followed Darcher, who was carrying a branch of candles, through gallery after gallery and staircase upon staircase. She felt like a princess in a fairy tale, feeling that every step was taking her closer and closer to the fulfillment of her heart's true love.

Victorine was aware that Haverford was a household

of upwards of fifty bedchambers, and she did not bother at all to mark the way she was being led. The pair had been walking for what seemed an eternity when the valet finally stopped before a great oaken door.

He pointed out the way for Victorine, having opened the door for her, and bowed formally.

"The Bridal Room, Mademoiselle," he pronounced in the most formal tones imaginable, while inwardly beside himself with amusement.

"The Bridal Room?" Victorine gushed with delight. "Oh! What a lovely name! How terribly romantic!"

Pretty little idiot, he thought to himself. *She's swallowed all the hums his lordship's thrown at her. Perfect! It was to be a rare evening at Haverford, to be sure.*

"Thank you so much," murmured Victorine. As she entered the elegant room hung with layer upon layer of thick blood-red and gold brocade hangings, her breath was quite taken away.

The room was unlike anything she had ever seen. There was a table in the center set with what seemed to be pure gold cutlery, and precious crystal glassware. There was a most alluring arrangement of flowers in a central bowl, pervading the air with the sweetest scent imaginable.

There was a rustle from one corner, and Victorine jumped, dreadfully startled.

"Pleeze, do not be afraid, Mademoiselle," said a small, dark middle-aged woman with a marked French accent. "I am Madame Darcher, wife of his lordship's valet, who escorted you here. His lordship asked me to see to any of your needs. He regrets that, busy as he is with his many other guests, he will be delayed for a few moments, and sends you his compliments."

"Oh. Thank you."

"I have also brought with me this," said the maid, proffering a glass of milk on a silver tray. "His lordship was most anxious that you have some restorative, thinking that after the ball you may be fatigued."

"Oh, no thank you; I don't really care for anything."

"But Mademoiselle, you are obliged to do so. His lordship most specifically expressed it. Lord St. Clare will be most seriously displeased if his wishes are not carried out in full. I am sure you appreciate that his lordship is a man of—how shall I put it?—the very strongest will. Oh, no, his lordship will be most displeased with me if you do not take it. Please, I beg of you. It is such a small request, and will be so good for you."

"Very well," said Victorine, and she drained the glass completely. Madame Darcher looked on with complete satisfaction, knowing she was performing her job well.

Victorine remained standing for a moment, not knowing what to do next, and wondering why a servant would make such a fuss about drinking a glass of milk. Then, she blinked her lovely blue eyes, and suddenly yawned.

"If Mademoiselle still feels fatigued after the long ball, behind here," and she pulled open some drapes, "there is a settle upon which one might recline and refresh oneself."

"Oh, my! There is no need for it, I'm sure."

Her eyes could not seem to focus very well. A settle, did the woman say? It looked more like a four-poster bed.

No, there was a settle, in the room, just as the woman had said. However, next to it, her eyes did indeed distinguish a bed. A very large bed. Looking over at the four-poster, Victorine was taken aback. She had not realized that she had come into a bedchamber. This would not do.

Of a sudden her precarious and unprotected state was

brought home to her in a very real way; she began to realize what a very dangerous step it was that she had taken. Never, of course, in her entire life had she been alone, unchaperoned, in a room with a man who was not a close family member. Much less a room with a bed, in it!

Good god! Victorine's heart began pumping with fear rather than desire, and she began to rise up, and tried to make for the door.

At just that time when she was beginning to feel profoundly afraid, the feeling was replaced by a persistent drowsiness. She sought a chair upon which to sink back down, while she reconsidered her behavior and her situation.

Certainly, she ought not meet the Viscount. In fact, it was a very foolish thing she was doing, and she really ought to go right back to her room.

She should leave this room immediately, except for just one factor—that she began to have an almost overpowering desire to take a nap. Just a short one. It was a long way back to her own room, after all. Better to take a little rest first.

In fact, she began to realize, the idea of lying down on a nice soft bed would be very comfortable indeed. The whole room began to take on a kind of softness that seemed very comforting to Victorine. She might just wait and see the Viscount for a little while, after all. Nothing untoward could happen in such a nice, soft, comfortable room. Everything suddenly was seeming so very friendly, she wasn't afraid any longer, not at all.

"His lordship will be along directly?" she asked, a little lazily.

"Yes, Mademoiselle," replied Madame Darcher with a knowing grin. "Will that be all?"

"Yes, thank you."

Once Madame Darcher had been dismissed and left the room, Victorine could not help but part the red damask curtains, and lie down for just a moment on the bed. A delicious drowsiness was descending on her, and her mind was beginning to turn its thoughts back, dreamlike, toward the desirable consummation of true love.

Lord St. Clare had been occupied with friends in the ballroom until he saw Victorine leave. He looked at his watch, left the ballroom, and went into the hall looking for Willby.

"Ah, there you are, Willby. I trust everything went as anticipated?"

"Yes, your lordship."

"Very good. What time do you suppose all will be prepared in the Red Room?"

"Madame Darcher has just reported back to me. She believes a half an hour should suffice."

"Excellent, Willby. Excellent. I shall be with Viscount Campden, playing cards. Don't hesitate to interrupt us; I need to be informed immediately when the proper time arrives."

"Certainly, your lordship."

Eighteen

"How has your evening been, Charles?" inquired John Whyte of Mr. Charles Bellfort, as they sat down in the relative privacy of a corner of the salon set up as a card room. "Mine has been unspeakably boring, and hideously tedious. Can you convince me that you have spent a less repulsive evening than have I?"

"On the contrary—I should characterize *my* evening as hideously boring and unspeakably tedious. Why, you may ask? This evening, the incomparably beautiful love of my life saw fit to treat me as if I were even less meaningful to her than a marble baluster. I would have good reason for suicide, were I so inclined."

"But you are not."

"No," he sighed with regret, "I am not. Sometimes I wish I were."

"Shall we go home to Melfield then, and drown our sorrows?"

"Yes. There's no amusement in remaining here watching poor young Campden lose yet another fortune."

"Sometimes I wish I were a gull-catcher. It seems a very stable way of earning one's living—there are always so very many pigeons ready to be plucked," said John Whyte.

"I thought Campden was already too far gone into the

River Tick to be worth the attention of any Captain Sharp."

"True. But the scamp seems to be attracting Miss Falk-Duffield's attention very admirably, and no doubt he's playing tonight—and losing—on just those expectations."

"I wish him joy. And her, poor thing. No doubt she is aware that she is courted not for her face, but for her funds."

"Ah! That reminds me—I must take leave of Father."

"I'll ride on ahead and meet you at Melfield then, shall I?"

In anticipation of his departure, John Whyte made his way through the groups of guests to approach his father; he gritted his teeth, bit back the words that he wished he might utter, and managed to bow to Lord Cleremont most respectfully.

"Sir?"

"Yes?"

"I shall take my leave of you for tonight, sir."

"Very well, John. I was happy to note that you have complied with my wishes."

"I beg your pardon, sir?"

"I noted you dancing twice this evening with young ladies of proper fortune, Miss Falk-Duffield and the Ramsden chit. You also spent a deal of time with the divine Miss Wells. Good boy. Thirty thousand pounds, hasn't she?"

The Hon. John Whyte stiffened slightly.

"I believe her portion is thought to be considerable, sir."

"And she is a diamond of the first water as well."

"Yes, she is that. She is very beautiful, sir."

"So, you see, although I was admittedly harsh with you yesterday, it was a harshness born of love. It was anger born of my need to see my son well settled. It was merely the act of a father exercising his paternal influence in order to prevent his son from making an imprudent marriage, and in order to assure his son's future happiness. I was thinking of you, my boy, only of you. I had only your welfare in mind."

"I am sure you were of that opinion, sir," John replied frostily.

"A handsome fortune and an exquisite face! Really, John—what more could one want in a wife?"

John Whyte could thing of many things, sense being foremost among them, but he forbore to speak.

"St. Clare and his wife were right, don't you see?"

"I do not entirely comprehend your meaning. What have my brother St. Clare and his wife to do with this?"

"It was their idea, you see. Dear Marguerite most fortunately—and quite properly, I might add—pointed out to me on the very day their party arrived at Haverford that she felt your attentions to that Stone girl were becoming marked. She pointed out that marriage with that chit would be a most unsuitable for you. Miles let me know that Miss Wells, on the other hand, would be just the wife you require. Lovely, compliant, and with an enormous dowry. He spoke with me at length about it just before I saw you."

He went on, oblivious to his son's swiftly repressed reaction of wrath, "I quite agreed with Miles—and I think he showed great perspicacity. I also appreciated his sense of duty to the family in letting me know the lay of the land. Put a stop to it just in time, I see."

Damn Miles, John thought to himself. *Damn his eyes!*

"I, myself, have noticed that your behavior tonight at the ball has been everything I could have wished for. I am very pleased with you, John, for once. Your attentiveness to Miss Wells—not to mention the Falk-Duffield chit, though she is such an antidote—was very proper; I am glad to see you have come to your senses and relinquished your attachment to that Stone girl, who could never do you any good.

"I think you need have no fear of Miss Wells spurning an offer from you, for your breeding is superior to her own, and her fortune was acquired through trade, I am given to understand. Some sort of nabob's money or other. Tainted, but at least not made in City trade, thank God. I trust that you will waste no time in attaching this child's affections. It is very good luck for you, I must say. I had not thought you had it in you to do so well for yourself—you were always such a sad sober-sides. I bid you good evening, John."

"Sir."

As John Whyte bowed to take his leave, he was glad his face was hidden from his father's view. So Miles and Marguerite had brought their tales to the old man? What was their meaning? Was Miles interfering merely to amuse himself? Damn the man! Drat that interfering wife of his as well!

John delayed his plans to ride home to Melfield just long enough to partake of a large glass of strong brandy, which he took out onto the verandah. He absentmindedly gazed over the grounds of his father's estate and wondered why he, of all persons, should have been cursed with both a father and a brother whose behavior and manner were intolerable to him.

Why also had he been cursed with having no means? His mother had left her fortune to him alone—Miles, of course, being expected to inherit the earldom—but long before the time John had reached his majority, what should have been his inheritance had simply ceased to exist. Embezzled away. It was not such an unusual occurrence, he had to suppose—but why had it to happen thus? The whole of a large fortune—gone without a trace.

Gone, as was his family—either gone into death, like his mother, or gone away from him in alienation. His father, his mother, his brother—the only family he had ever known. He felt most sorry for his poor gentle mother, and sorry for what she must have had to suffer, for surely her husband had not loved her. She could not possibly have had a happy life.

I will not suffer a fate like hers, John swore to himself. *I will marry for love or I will not marry at all.*

As John Whyte was indulging in these sober reflections, Marguerite, Lady St. Clare, was watching him just from within the ballroom.

She was dressed to perfection in a gown of ruby gauze, with a matching overskirt. It was cut down over her ample bodice most revealingly, it was damped down to show off her figure; a necklace of matched ruby pendants disappeared into her cleavage in the most (she thought) irresistible fashion imaginable.

She wore her hair piled high upon her head, a ruby diadem crowning her raven-black curls which tumbled this way and that, with an apparent naturalness that belied the long time it had taken her dresser to achieve the effect.

Nevertheless, Lady St. Clare looked ravishingly attractive.

Watching him, her ladyship tried to guess the reasons behind the Hon. John Whyte's evident low spirits. She had witnessed his argument with that dreadful Stone chit, that had ended with the stupid wench in tears. She approved of her husband's plan to fob off Victorine Wells after he had done with her by marrying her off to his strait-laced younger brother, and she had heard a bit of the Earl's most recent lecture along similar lines. His marriage to that pretty idiot could hardly alter her own plans for the tall gentleman.

A light smile of pleasurable anticipation lit her features. John was so attractive—it might be pleasant for him to sire on her a child. If she had a child by a lover such as John Whyte, Miles certainly wouldn't care. Why should he? She had made no fuss about any of his numerous love-children, and indeed, why should she?

She was the wife, she was Marguerite Perigord de la Tour, the Viscountess St. Clare, not some well-paid highflier. The rules of the game were the rules of the game—and in her circles, they sufficed. The child, who would doubtless be a boy, could inherit the earldom—that would be amusing! Same blood-lines, after all! What a tremendous lark it would be! And what fun she would have while carrying it off!

On this note, Lady St. Clare drew close to Mr. John Whyte. She was so close she could smell the scent of tobacco on him.

John Whyte knew the approach of his sister-in-law by the cloud of musk-rose which preceded her. He disliked the smell intensely and even more did he dislike it when she sidled up to him, stroked his cheek with her fan,

smiled her vicious little smile, and ran her hand possessively down his shirt-front.

He backed away instinctively, bowing politely to her
with cold civility, saying, "Good evening, ma'am."

"John. Why do you never call me Marguerite? It hurts
my feelings so terribly, John. Brother of my husband, dear
member of my family."

Had John Whyte's situation been less complex, he
would have thrown the hussy off and left her presence.
Things with his family being at the turn they were, he
felt that he must escape from her ladyship's clutches with
perfect civility, without causing her to go back to her
husband and create a scandal.

It seemed not unreasonable that her complaints would
result in Miles visiting the Earl, and having his father's
wrath once again hurled down upon his head. He could
not afford to be thrown out of Melfield until he had con-
structed some alternative. Thus, despite his better in-
stincts and despite the pain it caused him, he held his
tongue, and tried to maintain a cold, composed civility
toward the jade.

This forbearance only gave the woman more incentive
to reveal herself.

"Do you find me attractive, John?" said she, still
touching him.

He inclined his head, although he was, in fact more
than slightly revolted by her. Had she been drinking? She
was actually making advances to him under the roof of
her husband's house—his father's house! Curse all the
French and their damnably decadent ways!

She brought her face close to his. Her lips were red
and full, but he detected about her a faint smell of a
anise-based liqueur.

"Kiss me, John," she whispered huskily.

John gritted his teeth and said nothing, his patience nearly tried beyond endurance.

She raised an eyebrow, questioningly, and baited him, "So, John. Are you not a man, then?"

John Whyte burned with fury. He longed to tell her how appalled he was by her continental, libertine ways. But he chose not to. He looked down the bosom of her dress and let his eyes rest there in a deliberately insolent manner.

"Were you ever to be granted the opportunity, I'm sure you would find that I am a man indeed, ma'am."

Lady St. Clare felt her heart quicken in response to his lascivious glance. God, she could hardly wait to have him to herself!

His gaze then shifted to her eyes, and stared her down with a directness that made her feel the full weight of his strength and character. This too, she found, pleased her deeply.

He spoke, using a low, whispering, surly tone.

"I am a man, Marguerite, but I am an honorable one. You are the wife of my brother. Beautiful though you be, how should I carry on a dalliance with you?"

Anger rose in her, as it always did when she did not have her own way at once.

"But these things are done all the time, John. It is done all the time in our circles. Surely you must know that. You cannot be such a naif!"

"I choose not to behave in such a manner," he replied coldly.

Lady St. Clare's eyes became wild with a mixture of rage and passion.

"Kiss me, John. Kiss me here and kiss me now," she

said, her eyes narrowing with malice, her voice a low hiss like a serpent's.

"I will not."

"Oh, yes, you will, my dearest love. Kiss me, or else I will scream out to all the assembled guests that you are taking advantage of me. Think how your pretty little Miss Stone would like to hear that. Think about it—it is your good name, John, that will be lost—not mine."

John Whyte laughed a harsh laugh.

"I feel sure you haven't a good name to lose, my dear."

He took this lovely snake into his arms, and crushed the breath out of her, kissing her savagely. Letting his anger against his brother and his wife and his wretched father and all his constricting circumstances release itself in action, he began to fondle his sister-in-law with neither gentleness nor discretion, as any drunken wastrel would have done to the lowest-born lady of the night. Then he threw her off, and strode away from the verandah toward the stables, wiping the dreadful taste of her from his lips, and cursing the day he had ever been born.

Nineteen

"My dearest love? Are you within?" called the Viscount, as he opened the great oak door and let himself into the Red Room. He walked across the thick carpeting, as swift and quiet as a cat.

Victorine sat up the great bed and clapped her hands together with delight, saying, "Oh, St. Clare! You've come at last!" Miss Wells was smiling brightly, feeling relaxed and entirely at her ease. She ran a hand anxiously through her blond curls, as if to repair their tumbling disarray.

St. Clare smiled back at the girl with a deep and genuine satisfaction. Crossing over to her, he sat on the edge of the bed, taking her small hands in his, and pressing them to his heart. He noted that there was a marked languor about her, and that the pupils of her lovely blue eyes were dark and wide and over-bright. Bringing her soft hands to his lips, he kissed each one of her fingers, murmuring, "Dear child! My very dearest child!" Victorine blushed sweetly in response.

"I'm so glad you're here, St. Clare! When I first came in, I felt alone, and I was rather afraid, and I felt I was not doing quite the right thing by having come here so late to meet with you. Now that you are with me, I feel so relieved, and so very happy to see you."

"I am relieved as well, Victorine, my dove, and I also am so very happy that you have come to me. You have pleased me very much."

"Have I really? I'm so glad!"

St. Clare made a signal, and Darcher suddenly appeared bearing two sparkling glasses of champagne, which he placed on the center table. The Viscount took Victorine by the hand, gently, and brought her to the table. He sat down himself, and bade the young girl to seat herself on his lap. She did so, most willingly, and he embraced her. Her fantasy now complete, Victorine sighed with profound contentment. St. Clare tipped her chin up as he spoke to her.

"Victorine, my dearest, my heart's love," said Lord St. Clare, "I have ordered the very finest champagne in order that we celebrate this extremely auspicious occasion. Let us drink to our mutual affection."

"Oh, but Mama does not allow me to drink champagne!"

The Viscount laughed lightly and shook his head.

"In that regard, you need seek your esteemed Mama's permission no longer, I think, Victorine. Come, come, my child—the drink will relax you. Champagne is a celestial drink, one conceived to suit lovers' purposes alone."

Responding to him instantly, Victorine drained her glass completely.

"Oh, St. Clare! The bubbles make me want to sneeze!"

"That is because you have not as yet developed the taste for it. That will come, in time, and with experience. Let us drink again, my angel! We can drink to celebrate our future marriage!"

"M-marriage?" gasped Victorine. "Oh, St. Clare! I had not thought to hope that we could be married!"

"But I did hope so. I have thought about it, long and hard, my dear, ever since that first day in Hyde Park. I thought about my need for you, and my love for you, and my deep desire never to be parted from you. Having consulted my legal advisors, I now believe I may obtain a divorce from my wife, and thus I will be able to wed you at once. Should you not wish to become my Viscountess and the mother of my children? I have no children and no heir at present, you must remember. Shall you wish to wed me, my Victorine? Is not our marriage an event worthy of celebration?"

"Yes, yes, my dear St. Clare!" cried Victorine, throwing her arms around his neck gratefully. "We must drink to our happiness! Of course we must do so! We are so lucky, we two!"

"Indeed. And now, here is one more glass, if you please."

Victorine looked puzzled. "Do you truly desire me to drink yet another glass?"

"I do, my dear. Very much so." Lord St. Clare snapped his fingers once more to Darcher, who appeared out of the shadows and refilled the glasses yet again. "Champagne is truly nectar, my pet. Share this nectar with he who adores you most. It will do you a world of good, I assure you."

Victorine hesitated for but a moment, and then complied. The Viscount begin to nibble the nape of her long, white neck, and Victorine threw back her head and giggled.

"It tickles so when you do that, your lordship."

"Does it, my dear?" asked Lord St. Clare, kissing her shoulders, her breastbone, and then burying his face in her sweet bosom. "How soft you are! How young! How I have longed for you all these weeks!"

"Oh, St. Clare, I'm afraid that the champagne has quite gone to my head. I feel so very giddy! I feel I might fly! I feel I might do anything!"

"Why, then, fly away, my white bird, and do as your heart bids you. And let us each have another glass apiece."

"Oh, yes! Let's do, it's such fun!"

Their glasses filled to the brim once more, the Viscount showed Victorine how the two of them might entwine their wrists, and drink in that manner, close to one another. Suddenly, Victorine's breath began to come stronger and faster; she trembled with a sudden though inchoate understanding, as her natural passion began welling up within her, pushing to the fore. Lord St. Clare, noticing with pleasure this spring's awakening, sought to take advantage of the moment. He pushed her back away from him, then lifted her up in his arms and carried her to the chaise-longue, where he set her down as tenderly as ever could be.

He parted her skirts with one hand as he held her tightly with the other, kissing her strongly on her cherry-ripe lips. Softly, he moaned to her, as if anticipating his ultimate satisfaction, and then, his voice grown husky, he whispered her name.

"Victorine . . . Victorine, I love you and I must have you! I will have you!"

"But, St. Clare . . ."

"No, you cannot deny me, my love. It would be too cruel. Tell me that you love me, child."

"I love you, St. Clare!"

"Lie back, then, dearest, and let me demonstrate the depths of my affection!"

Her blue eyes opened of a sudden.

"But—wait! Is it quite proper that I stay here with you? Should we not wait till we are wed?"

"Most certainly not—the thing is as good as done already! You have heard me declare my offer for your hand just now. Must we wait to ask permission to enjoy and disport ourselves? No, indeed, we need not," said Lord St. Clare, laughing at his little love's ingenuousness. "Hush, and now let me teach you all that a man can ever teach the woman he loves so well. Know that I love you to utter, sheer distraction. You need never worry about anything, Victorine, my only love: you can always put your trust in me, my dearest. I'll take the very greatest care of you, child, indeed I will. Never forget that."

"Will you?" she asked, all innocence and amazement.

"Why, of course I will, my dear. I always do," said the Viscount, with that purring-soft, brandy-smooth, insistent voice that had, for so many years, and with such sublime success, led his Lordship's chits inexorably down the primrose path of total acquiescence: complete and unrestrained.

In a vestibule near the Red Room, through a spy-hole concealed within a pattern on the wall, Darcher and his wife were watching the scene with admiration and interest.

"His young lordship surely does have a way with the ladies, does he not?"

"*Bien sur*—that he does," said his wife. "Now that the Earl himself has become too old to indulge himself thus, it's good to see the Red Room getting brought back into use once more."

"It reminds me of the old days. His lordship's father—as his father's father before him—were all notorious in the petticoat line. It runs in the Cleremont blood."

"It doesn't run in Master John's blood."

"To be sure it does not—and why ever should it? That young Puritan, that man-milliner, Master John, doesn't have a single drop of Lord Cleremont's blood running in his veins! He's a bastard. Did his lordship Cleremont never tell you?"

"No," replied his wife, astonished. "I never knew that."

"I thought everyone knew. Willby knows. Of course, there's not so many of the old staff still left here. It all comes down to blood. Blood will tell. St. Clare's mother was a de Noialles—a bit like Lady St. Clare in beauty, character, and tastes, while Master John's mother, Cleremont's second wife, was a Pembroke.

"Very high in the instep, the Pembrokes. Very well-to-do, very old family. That's why his lordship got married to her—got her on some havey-cavey deal with the father. Might have been he won her at faro—I'm almost sure of it. Her father was playing deep one night at Watier's, I think it was, and he lost a bundle. The end of it was that either he had to kill himself, or sign over his estates and face a dreadful family scandal, or lose the girl. As the lesser evil of the three, Pembroke consented to the marriage of his only daughter Julia to his lordship Cleremont in order honorably to settle his immense gaming debt. Think of it—to have wagered his daughter away. He died of guilt soon after it happened, and the mother followed suit. Broke their hearts to lose her."

"I never knew!"

"That's not the half of it. As I said, Master John ain't his lordship's son."

"That seems impossible, knowing his lordship. Whose son is he, then?"

"I don't know, but I do know that that's why the Earl dislikes him so much. Never liked the wife he won at cards, either, not by half. His lordship would never touch Julia Pembroke for some reason, though she was a great beauty. That's how he knew she'd given him a bastard, since he'd never deign to bed her down himself.

"He wanted his hands on her Pembroke money, but he kept her as far away from himself as possible—put her in apartments in the old East wing."

"That's like having her live in China!"

"Oh, he'd bring her out for show every once in awhile, but he seemed always to have a disgust of her. I can't imagine why—must have offended him, or perhaps he just wanted to punish her. But that is how it was."

"Scandalous!"

The Viscount draped a silk and Alençon lace dressing gown over Victorine's naked shoulders. He lifted her hair and ran his tongue over the nape of her neck. She shuddered slightly, staring witlessly at the painting of the satyr on the ceiling.

"There, my dear. It wasn't so bad, now, was it?"

Victorine's eyes filled with tears in answer.

"I'll take care of you, my dear," said his lordship reassuringly. "I promised that I would. Remember that I love you."

"Do you really love me, St. Clare?"

"Of course I do. How can you doubt it now?"

"Won't everybody know?" Victorine asked, looked up at St. Clare's face with timid anguish.

"Not a soul, I vow. Your maid has been sent away to London—so there will be no one to have noticed your absence. Your lady mother has been long asleep, as is your cousin. From tomorrow on, Madame Darcher, my valet's wife, will be serving as your lady's-maid—and she is exquisitely discreet, I can assure you. You must doff these antiquated notions of propriety. This sort of thing is done all the time, I assure you. House parties are notorious in that respect."

"I did not know."

"You know now. You have become a woman, and a woman of the world."

He wrapped her in his arms, and allowed the little fool to cry upon his shoulder, till he got bored of it and made her stop. He smiled, showing his brilliant white teeth. He was a devastatingly handsome man. He yawned, and made a gesture toward her, saying, "Now, my child, come to me."

She stared at him, uncomprehending.

"Again?" she said, astonished.

St. Clare sighed with irritation and snapped at her, "Really, you have quite an extraordinary amount of difficulty following the most simple directions, Victorine. Do as I bid you. Now."

And again she did just as his lordship said.

Twenty

A dazed Victorine was returned to her room by Madame Darcher just before dawn, having proceeded step by step, slowly through the long corridors like a somnambulist. Her new servant—if servant she could be called—was under strict orders to give Miss Wells another calming sedative as soon as she was returned to her bedchamber, and to keep her quiet and isolated throughout the day.

Victorine, shaken after her long ordeal, accepted what she was given to drink without any question, and even asked Madame Darcher to give her a bit more of the sleeping-draught. The Frenchwoman was happy to comply. Victorine drifted off into a deep sleep, most thankfully losing consciousness of all that had recently happened to her, thus being saved from more torment from secret, shameful thoughts that kept arising within her mind, like the bleak winter storms on a cold, blue sea.

The day after the Haverford ball dawned bright and clear. Helen Fraley came to Pamela's room to serve her mistress her morning chocolate, and to help to choose her gown and dress her hair. Helen wondered whether, after a good night's sleep, her mistress's mood had improved.

"Morning, Miss Pamela."

"Good morning, Helen."

"Are you feeling a bit more the thing this morning?"

"Yes, thank you. I will wear the new sprig muslin today, I think."

"That will suit you very nicely, particularly if Mr. Whyte will be calling today, which I hear he will do."

"If that is so, he is likely to be coming to see Victorine rather than me," replied Pamela bitterly. "At least as far as Lord Cleremont is concerned."

Helen Fraley clicked her tongue in disapproval, but said nothing. Nevertheless, she wondered why Miss Pamela had mentioned the Earl. What had riven the understanding between her mistress and Peter's master? Why should Mr. Whyte be lavishing his attentions on Miss Victorine, when he so obviously was enamored of Miss Pamela? Could they have quarreled again? It would be a shame—for herself and her Peter as well—if they failed to make a match of it.

"Mr. Whyte coming to see Miss Victorine? That would be odd, wouldn't it? You know, Miss Pamela, there's more odd bits going on that I know about that I'd like to tell you. I tried to say last night, but you were too blue-devilled. I'll wager you don't know yet that Miss Victorine's abigail, poor young Maud Green, has been dismissed. Sent right away back to London. Happened late last night, it did."

"Dismissed? But how terrible! Whatever has she done?"

"Nothing, Miss. She did nothing at all, that's the horror

of it. There's more to it, too. Miss Victorine ain't even been the one who turned Maud off. Mr. Willby done it."

"But Willby had no right to—"

"My Peter says Mr. Willby don't need no right. He just done it."

"When did you say it happened?"

"Last night, during the ball. I'll wager Miss Victorine didn't even know about it until she came to bed, and found Maud not waiting up for her like she always did. Wonder who they got to wait upon her in Maud's stead— probably that old cat, Darcher's wife. She's a weasely one, she is."

"But what could have been the reason for doing such a thing?"

"That's the most fearful part. They said Maud wasn't behavin' proper, and was bringin' down the morals of the whole household; you know what the reason for that was? Maud was caught by Mr. Willby in a closet kissing with St. Clare's man, Darcher. What a lie!"

"But that's impossible; she's much too shy. I could have vouched for her character. Maud would never do such a thing!"

"Course not. That's what I told my Peter. But Peter tells me Darcher pulls his tricks on the housemaids all the time, he's just that kind of scandalous person. Peter says he thinks they all was just looking to get rid of her, had to think up some reason, and got Darcher to do it to her, and get them caught on purpose."

"I can't think why they would."

"No more can I. But there she was the poor girl—you should have seen her, tears streaming down her face as they was—poor Maud was caught up, scolded in front of all the staff, and packed off on a night coach before the blink of an eye."

"Was Darcher not dismissed as well?"

"No, Miss. He's a man, and Maud's a girl. If a man does it, no one cares a fig—they expect that sort of behavior from men, don't they? If Maud gets herself kissed, they say it's her doing, and it's her that's the flighty one. Not true of course, not a word of it—I know Maud, same as you do. Besides, Peter says there have always been strange doings by the staff and the masters of this house."

"Indeed? But poor Maud! I hope she reached London safely. Has she family there?"

"She does," replied Helen grimly. "If she makes it there without being, well, set upon, she'll be right enough. I can't think but that Miss Victorine will take her back. But—I can't imagine how bad it would be for a young girl travelling all that way in a common stage, getting on in the middle of the night. Anything could happen—easy. She could get robbed, she could get kidnapped or killed. It was a terrible thing they done to her last night."

"Yes, it was," Pamela replied. "I think I shall find Victorine, and see that she understands about it. I'm sure she will be most upset. Perhaps we can send someone after the girl."

Pamela walked some minutes away down a side gallery to the wing where Victorine's rooms were situated. She knocked on the door, which was opened by a strange, dark older woman, who failed to step away from the door and give passage to Pamela to come inside.

"You are Darcher, are you?" said Pamela in what she hoped was a quelling tone.

Madame Darcher raised her eyebrows briefly and, seeing no alternative, dropped Pamela a reluctant curtsey.

"Miss?"

"I am come to see my cousin."

Darcher's wife did not move away from the door.

"You will kindly allow me to enter," said Pamela crossly.

The woman again did not move aside, but said, "I am most terribly sorry, I'm sure, but Miss Victorine is not feeling at all well, and she begs to be excused from seeing anyone this morning, Miss Stone. Perhaps you might return in the morning. That would be much more convenient."

Pamela was amazed at the maid's insolence and brushed past her in a moment, saying over her shoulder, "If my cousin is unwell, then I must of course see her. You will be kind enough to take your leave, Darcher."

Madame Darcher hesitated, clearly perturbed.

"Move aside, Darcher, and go away! Now!" said Pamela. "Are you quite deaf, woman?"

Unable to avoid acceding to Pamela's will, Madame Darcher made no further objection, but stood aside, then bowed out of the room to go report the incident to his lordship St. Clare. If Miss Stone was difficult to control now, she might prove difficult later on as well. His lordship must be apprised of the situation.

When Pamela entered Victorine's bedchamber, she was surprised to see her cousin still abed, curled in a crumpled heap amidst a tousled pile of sheets and bedcovers. Pamela called her name several times, and got no response. After the third try, her young cousin finally raised her head and darted a frightened look at Pamela, keeping the covers clutched close beneath her chin.

Poor Victorine did indeed look unwell. She looked, for one thing, as if she might have been crying, and for another, as if she had not slept all night. There were dark circles under her eyes, marring her beauty, and the deep cornflower-blue eyes themselves looked somehow odd.

"What's wrong, my love?" asked Pamela. "I am so sorry to hear you are unwell."

"Nothing's wrong," Victorine replied, her timidity turned suddenly sullen. "Why should you think anything is wrong, may I ask? There's nothing wrong, at all. Nothing at all. And, please, don't call me 'my love.' It's an odious term; it irritates me; I can't bear it—is that quite clear? I have the headache terribly, and I just can't see anyone today, and I don't want to see anyone. Not even you. Darcher said I ought not to."

"Did she, indeed?" inquired Pamela, surprised at her cousin's odd conduct. "And did the ever-faithful Darcher reveal what she thought was wrong with you?"

"Yes. She said I'm . . . out of sorts."

"Oh! How extremely illuminating, I'm sure! *That,* I must own, does seem a perfectly cogent explanation," remarked Pamela wryly. "As explanations go."

As she began to wonder if her cousin might not be even more shatterbrained than she had heretofore believed, she saw Victorine reach over to the bedside table, and help herself to some of the tonic Darcher had provided for her.

"What's that, coz?"

Victorine snatched the blue-glass bottle back from Pamela's hands, and hid it behind the draperies near her bed.

"Medicine for the migraine headache," she replied, defensively. "Darcher gave it to me. It's very important for my recovery. Darcher says I must stay in bed and take my medicine on a regular basis, or my poor head will hurt this way forever."

Pamela reached for the bottle, took it away from her cousin's unwilling hands, and sniffed it.

"It's laudanum, and very potently mixed, I should say. You must be careful of not taking too much, Victorine."

"I'll do just as I wish, Pamela! You're not my mother! You can't dictate to me! I'm not a child anymore!" she cried out, in the rudest possible manner.

"Victorine! What can you be thinking of, to behave to me, or to anyone, in this manner! You should be ashamed of yourself. What would your mother say if she knew?"

At this, Victorine shrieked and burst openly into tears. She sobbed and sobbed, and her small body shook as waves of weeping swept over her. Pamela Stone could only try to wait patiently for her cousin to recover, so she could get a reasonable answer to some questions.

"There, there. Whatever can be the matter with you? Don't cry, you'll make yourself ill. I know you didn't mean to speak to me so unkindly. You say there's nothing the matter, Victorine, but of course there is—it's very obvious. Are you so very unhappy that Maud's gone? Is that it?"

"Maud? Maud's gone?" she cried, weeping even harder. "She is truly gone away? Oh, no! Then I am all alone, truly all alone!"

"You're not alone, you have me. You have your mother, you silly goose"

"But I can't say—oh, how terrible, I had quite forgotten she had gone. I know that someone must have told me. I miss her, Pamela. I miss her so. I can't bear it. Why did they send Maud away?"

"I think that there was some problem among the household staff."

"Darcher said that she did something very bad, but she wouldn't tell me what. But Maud is never like that—and I need her. No, now I remember, they said that she had to go or else everyone would know—"

"Know what?"

"Know nothing," she replied quickly. "I was confused, I didn't mean it. You see, Darcher says that I can confide in her instead of in Maud, but she's so cold, I don't at all like her. Not in my heart."

"You can confide in me, Victorine. You must know that."

Victorine began to weep and weep once more, throwing herself down on her pillow, barely managing to get a few words out.

"But Pamela, that's just the problem, I cannot talk to you. Not to anyone. Oh, God help me."

Victorine turned over in bed, looking around, found the medicine bottle, took a few more drops. Pamela watched her, astonished. Then finally her cousin's eyes started to close, and the tonic put her into a merciful sleep. Pamela tucked the bedclothes up around Victorine, and stroked her brow for a moment, wondering what was the matter.

Whatever could have happened to upset her so? Victorine had always been high-strung and prone to fits of weeping, but this problem seemed somehow different. It was not the reaction of a more than mildly spoiled young girl; it seemed that something had happened to her cousin that was really wrong.

Could some man have tried to steal a kiss from Victorine last night at the ball? Something of that sort might certainly be upsetting to a young girl, but who would have done so? The only men who had paid her any particular attentions at the ball were the Hon. John Whyte and Charles Bellfort.

Charles Bellfort the girl had as good as snubbed, and John certainly would not have pressed any unwanted attentions on Victorine. He was not that sort of person. Could the redoubtable Viscount Campden have cornered Victorine, as he had cornered herself, one drunken evening?

It was not at all clear what had actually occurred—but there was certainly something quite the matter with her cousin.

Twenty-one

Victorine, naturally enough, did not appear at breakfast. The breakfast room was, in fact, unusually thin of company. No gentlemen were present, and only a few of the chaperones, who had left the party early, had come down. The Marchioness of Plimpton was busily inspecting, poking, and criticizing the breakfast offerings, as her granddaughter cringed in embarrassment. She loudly announced that brown bread and tea without milk was the only salutary choice available, and tried to force poor Miss Falk-Duffield to partake of it.

Pamela went down to breakfast not long after having spoken with Victorine; she greeted her aunt, who announced that she herself was feeling not quite the thing.

"Pamela, my dear! I am happy to see you!" Lady Charlton said. "I have been feeling unwell all night and crave company to take my mind off my miseries. I haven't heard a word from Balmore, and I am entirely disconsolate. Where is Victorine?"

"She is also feeling unwell, Aunt."

"Poor darling, she must be quite fatigued, I expect. When did she retire? I don't precisely recall—in fact, I don't recall very much of last night at all, I'm afraid. Very wicked of me, I think, but that's the way it is with life in the *bon ton!* Parties, routs, and balls—a little too much champagne, and too much dancing, and we're all drained of strength. This is why, in town, it is the custom to rise so late in the morning. I should myself have remained in bed, like Victorine. I can't understand why I did not do so. Foolish of me."

Lady Charlton went on to pick at her breakfast, as Lady St. Clare swept into the room with a great flourish and a dangerous look in her eyes. She chose the barest minimum of food, and settled herself next to Lady Charlton and Pamela Stone, favoring them with a particularly brilliant smile.

"Good morning, Lady Charlton. Good morning, Miss Stone. There are quite a few people down early—I confess, I am surprised by it. But where is Miss Wells?"

"Why, she is still resting after the ball, Lady St. Clare," replied Pamela evenly, somehow feeling sure that Madame Darcher had informed her ladyship in great detail as to the nature and depth of Victorine's indisposition.

"Resting, is she? I am surprised by it. In fact, I thought I had noticed Victorine leave the ball last night rather early."

"I'm afraid I did not notice when she left, your ladyship."

"I noticed very precisely. She went out on the verandah just before she disappeared entirely. I believe my husband's brother, John Whyte, left the ballroom at approximately the same time. An interesting coincidence, or so it struck me. My father-in-law told me last night that those two were smelling of April and May. They did seem to be getting along famously last night, wouldn't you say? Or did you not notice?"

"I'm sure Mr. Whyte's amiable nature is appreciated

by everyone, including my cousin," replied Pamela carefully.

"Yes, I'm sure it is. I know that he danced two dances with her last night. Most particular in his attentions toward her. Did Mr. Whyte dance with you? I thought he did not, and I thought it very unusual, for the two of you used to be famous friends, were you not?"

"We are still friends, Lady St. Clare."

"Call me Marguerite. You can't be great friends, however, if he does not dance with you, can you? But perhaps I am bringing up a sensitive subject, and I am so sorry if I have mentioned something that might cause you any pain."

Pamela Stone ground her teeth in stony silence as the Frenchwoman babbled on.

"Still, one must be happy for Victorine's sake, mustn't one?" her ladyship continued, leaning over confidentially toward the two women. "You will not, I think, take it amiss if I offer you a bit of advice. I think that perhaps Victorine may need to be more closely chaperoned, Lady Charlton. Even so amiable a man as Mr. Whyte—a man possessing a sensitive, passionate nature—might be tempted into indiscretion by such rare beauty as Miss Wells possesses. And it cannot be good for her reputation to be thought, well—fast."

Her ladyship's eyes glinted wickedly as she assessed the effect of her inventions on Lady Charlton and her niece.

"I'm sure Victorine would never behave with anything but the strictest propriety," replied Lady Charlton stiffly. With unaccustomed severity, she went on, "I am, however, very much shocked at your having the temerity to criticize my daughter's conduct. To my face."

"Oh, do excuse me then. I am French, you must recall, and we French do not have the least scruples about discussing family matters among family members. However, I meant what I said only in the very best sense. You cannot have failed to see that Mr. Whyte has been paying the most marked attentions to your daughter of late."

There was a rustle of doors and silence as Lady St. Clare waited for Lady Grafton to pass through, and for a footman to leave the room. She lowered her voice to a fine whisper.

"And I must tell you, Lady Charlton, that I heard talk of there having been an—an incident of an embrace— which apparently occurred just outside the ballroom last night. Perhaps it's just talk, of course. In any case, it is of no consequence so long as the two of them actually make a match of it. However, as Victorine's chaperone, I thought you should be informed."

Pamela realized that she and her aunt were being deliberately baited, but wondered what the reason could be. She wondered what to make of this so-called "incident," but was of no mind to inquire of Lady St. Clare.

"Thank you for providing us with such rare gossip for breakfast, Lady St. Clare," said Lady Charlton, acidly. "You must excuse us for not wishing to endure more of your imaginative tales. It is too early for bed-time stories."

"Well! You need not use such tone to me, Madam! I only had your daughter's best interests in mind, I assure you."

"I will look after my daughter's best interests by myself, thank you," said Lady Charlton, rising, and signalling her niece to leave with her, furious with the woman for encouraging the spread of rumors about Victorine. Her ladyship knew full well how much damage the wag-

ging tongue of one spiteful termagant could do to a debutante's reputation.

Pamela as well was furious. Having parted from her
aunt in order to change her clothing, she was beside herself by the time she reached her own apartments, and
flung herself on the bed inside, burying her face in the
bedclothes. She felt humiliated and confused about the
story concerning John Whyte that his sister-in-law had
told at breakfast.

She rang for Helen, questioned her about the story,
and, to her dismay, she found out that the servants' hall
was abuzz with gossip about Mr. Whyte's conduct at last
night's ball.

Two footman had reported seeing the Hon. John Whyte
locked in a torrid embrace with a woman late in the evening. The couple obviously had been trying to hide from
view, for they had been standing talking in a dark corner
of the verandah. The identity of the lady remained unknown, as she had been in shadow at first, and then had
run off into the garden afterward. Mr. John Whyte, however, was so tall that he could be mistaken for no other
person. It certainly had been Mr. Whyte embracing the
woman, and Mr. Whyte's conduct was being soundly criticized below-stairs.

"I can't see why they should make such a fuss about
it, myself," commented Helen, as she placed Miss
Pamela's silver-backed brushes and combs into a nice,
straight line on the dressing table. "When that ferret
Darcher pushed himself onto Maud and kissed her, no
one criticized Darcher, not a word. But as to last night,
I suppose everyone was more surprised that it was Mr.
Whyte behaving in such a fashion, since they don't con-

sider Mr. John as ever having been much in the petticoat line."

"Yes," replied Pamela, stiffly. "I should think that would be it. They must have been very much surprised at such conduct. From the fine, upstanding Mr. Whyte."

Helen realized she had said more than she ought, and excused herself from the room, cursing herself for a fool. She hoped to meet Peter later in the day, and thought that, perhaps from him she could find out Mr. John Whyte's explanation. It would be helpful for Miss Pamela to learn the other side of that story—if there was one.

Helen Fraley had to own herself concerned. Such a thing might mean that Mr. Whyte had given up on Miss Pamela, and that he had taken it truly in mind to take a rich wife. Had the man her mistress was deep in love with really been making love to Miss Victorine last night? Everyone in the servant's hall knew about the Earl's threats to take Melfield away from Mr. John—but had Mr. Whyte buckled under to his father's threats? A strange family, that was for certain, just as Peter had said.

Thinking the tale over to herself once Helen had left her, Pamela knew herself to be shocked. To put the truth to it, she was appalled. Whether or not the woman involved turned out to be Victorine, Lady St. Clare's mean-spirited account of her brother-in-law's behavior did seem to have had a basis in truth.

Certainly the Hon. John Whyte had kissed someone at his father's ball, and he had been indiscreet enough to have been observed by his father's servants. Certainly the woman he had kissed had not been herself, for the place and the time it had occurred were both incorrect. These were facts.

How to explain the facts? The most likely possibility, dreadful though it was, was that the man she wished to marry had been making violent love to her own cousin Victorine, just as Lady St. Clare had suggested. Later in the evening, having spoken again to his father, and not wishing to lose Melfield, which he loved so well and which he had long labored over, what if John Whyte had finally yielded to the pressure of his family to make an advantageous match? This explanation would account for both the incident itself, and for Victorine's odd reaction. A sheltered young girl, having her first kiss stolen from her in public circumstances by an older, more experienced man, might well react as had Victorine.

Of course, to behave toward her cousin in such a way seemed unlike anything she knew of John Whyte's character, and was particularly bizarre after all his declarations of affection toward herself. How could he have betrayed her so easily?

It hardly seemed possible, and yet the facts would not disappear by merely wishing them away. Pamela felt a sense of unease growing within her, along with an urge to leave Haverford at once.

But leaving was, for the moment, quite impossible.

The arrival of two morning visitors, Mr. Bellfort and Mr. John Whyte, was soon announced, denying Pamela any further opportunity for reflection. She tossed on a light shawl, and checked her hair in a pier-glass, before heading for the stairs.

Pamela Stone went down to meet them dressed simply

in her gown of sprig muslin. Her aunt, Lady Charlton, was already in the parlor; she had been asking after Lord Balmore, and had learned to her dismay that he would be delayed in London for at least another day. As Pamela entered, Lady Charlton had begun the daunting task of trying to explain to the two men the nature of Victorine's indisposition in the vaguest possible terms.

Troubled, yet trying to conceal it, Pamela was unable to meet John Whyte's eyes, although she felt his presence acutely. She made a point of seating herself next to Mr. Bellfort rather than Mr. Whyte. Both men noticed her choice with some surprise, but could hardly remark upon it, particularly since the Countess of Grafton chose that moment to join them, bringing along her omnipresent protege, Lord Shelton.

"Good day," chirped the countess. "Shelton came down to particularly to pay his compliments to your daughter, Victorine, who looked so lovely last night at the ball, and of course to your little niece Miss Stone, like these two gentlemen. How do you do, Mr. Whyte? Mr. Bellfort? But where is your daughter, Lady Charlton? Has another gentleman captured her already?"

"The early bird catches the worm, Aunt Grafton," chuckled Lord Shelton, like the flat that he was. "So they say."

"Hold your tongue, Shelton. Where is she?"

"Victorine is feeling a bit unwell today."

"How unfortunate for us! Shelton wanted particularly to escort Miss Wells around the arboretum! Oh, dear, this is a sad shock. For we must, of course, be leaving very soon. As you will, I suppose?"

"Yes," replied Lady Charlton.

"Grafton, Shelton and I will be going on to the Duke

of Portland's place for another house party. I am sure we will see you there—everyone is going, just everyone, it will be just like this last ball! A shocking crush!"

Pamela thought she could hardly imagine a worse fate, but kept an inane smile plastered on her countenance, and allowed her aunt to deal with the marital machinations of her friend, Celia, Countess Grafton.

"Well, my dear. I'm afraid we'll be off very soon, but I wanted you to know how very much dear Shelton has taken to your extremely lovely daughter, Victorine, and that he hopes to spend a deal of time with her in the very near future. Isn't that so, Shelton?"

"Why—yes," replied the young gentleman.

"We must be off and say farewell to our hosts and to our hostess. Don't forget to give Shelton's very best wishes to your delightful daughter!"

After the Countess and her nephew left the room, Mr. Whyte engaged Lady Charlton in general conversation about life in the neighborhood. Pamela found pleasure initiating a discussion with Mr. Bellfort of the temperaments and strengths of various horses in his stables.

Conversation continued on, with the two couples chatting away in a perfectly ordinary fashion, until Willby opened the salon door, and announced the arrival of an unexpected party—Miss Victorine Wells. She had appeared in the doorway dressed in the simplest of morning-dresses, and teetered there unsteadily for just a moment.

"Miss Wells!" exclaimed Mr. Bellfort as he rose to his feet in shock.

For the beautiful Miss Wells had ceased to look at all beautiful; she remained in the doorway appearing wan and haunted. Her blonde hair was most carelessly arranged, and she could manage only the very most sub-dued of smiles. She held out her hand languidly to Mr. Bellfort, who helped her to a seat.

"My dear!" said Lady Charlton. "I can't think what you are about to be coming down to company! You are very obviously unwell, and are not at all in looks. You should return to bed, child."

"Bed?" Victorine replied blankly, her voice whispery and flat, like that of one already gone on to the nether-worlds. "Oh, no, Mama, I do not wish to remain in my bedroom any longer. I have been there quite long enough. Quite long enough in the . . . room."

Everyone was astonished; speaking glances were exchanged on all sides.

She continued on, "And, if you don't mind very much, Mama, I should like to take a walk in the garden at this time. I feel I have a great need for some fresh air. The bedroom air has been . . . so very stifling. Mr. Bellfort, would you be kind enough to offer me your arm? I don't think I am yet well enough to walk alone without aid."

"You're not well enough to walk at all, child! Go to your room, at once," said Lady Charlton, out of temper.

Victorine turned slowly toward her mother, looking her directly in the eyes. Her voice had an odd, new hardness to it.

"Why, no, Mama," said Victorine, with careful deliberation. "I am afraid I cannot accede to your wishes. After all, I am not a child any longer. I wish to go for a walk now with Mr. Bellfort, and I shall do so."

Lady Charlton was taken aback by this unusual show of resolve, but decided not to comment upon it. She herself, when asked, declined to join the walking party, preferring to attend to some letters and direct the rearrangement of her belongings in preparation for their return to London. Pamela indicated her willingness to join her cousin.

"I should like to accompany you, also, if you don't object, Miss Wells?" said Mr. Whyte. "If you would not find my company too fatiguing?"

Pamela held her breath to see how her cousin would react, but she made no special reaction to his words whatsoever.

"Yes, of course," replied Victorine, with a shadow of a smile and an inclination of her head. "You shall come. Charles, Pamela, please do join us. I would like that very well."

So, thought Pamela, *Victorine makes no objection to having Mr. Whyte around.* Whatever the source of her cousin's strange mood might be, she did not seem to hold Mr. Whyte to blame for it. In fact, it was Mr. Whyte's arm that Victorine chose to lean upon when she left the house, Pamela following behind and exchanging pleasantries with Charles Bellfort.

It was most certainly a puzzle, but she soon found herself pleasantly distracted as the two pairs went out into the gardens, and set out choosing a path to walk upon through Haverford Park.

The morning was such a fine one, and the view so exquisitely green, that it had the effect of raising the spirits of all the party. As they strolled along, admiring the landscape, they were each lifted out of their own thoughts, and brought into a state of natural tranquility.

From a distance, they could see the carriages of the various houseguests being loaded with trunks and maids and dressers and sent off to their next destinations. Ladies and gentlemen of the ton as well were being seen off in their shiny, well-sprung travelling carriages, as they, too, returned to London, went off to spend time in Bath or Brighton, or travelled onward to yet another house party and another grand ball.

Pamela's thoughts, as she walked silently with Mr. Bellfort, were many. It occurred to Pamela that they had overstayed their welcome, and that Aunt Charlton should request a carriage to carry them back to London tomorrow morning. Since Lord Balmore was still in town, their swift remove from Haverford would no doubt please her aunt particularly. It was surprising how low her Aunt Charlton's spirits had been in Balmore's absence.

There was merely the matter of transportation to be settled, and all the puzzles of Haverford could be forgotten and put behind them. Once beyond the reach of the Earl of Cleremont, she and Mr. Whyte could probably visit one another once again without putting his livelihood in jeopardy. The first business, however, was to leave the demesne of Lord Cleremont: Lord St. Clare had promised them that he would have them conveyed back to London, and, if that were to prove inconvenient, they could always return by post.

Once they were well out of sight of the house, and the intrusive eyes of Lord Cleremont's servants, the couples switched partners. Mr. Whyte had pulled Pamela's arm through his, and, in a very short time, Pamela was deep in enjoyment of his conversation and his company. It was as if nothing amiss had ever happened between them; he treated her with as much apparent deference and affection as he ever had.

Her pulse raced; her breath quickened merely being so close to him. Nothing at all seemed to have changed since the time that the woman John had been kissing in the shadows of the lilac tree had been Pamela herself.

It seemed impossible not to trust John and yet Pamela was as afraid to do so as she had been at the very first. If he had kissed another woman, as the rumors said, she would be making a fool of herself if she believed him, and Pamela did not wish to be a fool.

"It has been very awkward for us, Pamela, these past few days. I had no idea my father would react as he did."

"How should you, indeed?" she asked.

"I must tell you that, though our problem has been uppermost in my mind, I have still not come close to a solution."

"It would be hard to do so, in such a short time. You have, however, been noticed making quite a show of dangling after Victorine. Your sister-in-law delights in bringing this to my attention."

"What? Can you be jealous? You mustn't give in to such an impulse. I assure you that is only for show—a strategy for buying time."

Pamela knew she should not give way to an unladylike impulse of spite, but a bitter inquiry was out of her mouth before she could bite it back.

"And your encounter with a lady at the ball?" she asked acidly. "Was that a strategy for show as well?"

"What encounter?" asked John Whyte, sharply.

"The one they are discussing with great interest in the servant's hall. The one that took place not in the garden with me, but on the verandah, the very same night. Last night."

"They are discussing it in the servant's hall, did you say?"

"Indeed they are. You were seen."

He reddened visibly.

"I see."

"Do you deny it? Or am I indulging in a flight of fancy myself, now?"

"Please, Pamela. Don't be like that. It's not what you think."

"I'm sure I don't know what to think."

"It's true enough. But it meant nothing."

"Oh, really?" she asked. "Would it seem vulgarly intrusive of me to inquire just who *was* the fortunate recipient of your favors?"

"Not at all," he replied frigidly. "It was Lady St. Clare."

It was Pamela's turn to flood red with embarrassment and outrage.

"How could you do such a thing?"

"She goaded me into it."

"What a shocking fairy tale, John! You must take me for an idiot. Tell me, did I as well goad you into kissing me earlier in the evening? Was it very much the same thing?"

"I was angry with her."

"And that is how you conduct yourself when you're angry? How very singular."

"Stop being such a cat. Can't you trust me, if I tell you it signified nothing but my contempt for her?"

Pamela found tears running down her face, and she hastily brushed them away.

"If that is how you express your contempt, pray, how do you express your affection? Or is it far too indelicate a subject upon which to speculate? No, I'm afraid that the whole story is a little difficult to digest. It is just too fanciful, that, not an hour after professing your desire to marry me, you should embrace another lady, a married lady, in fact your brother's own wife, in full view of the servants, and try to pass it off as the result of a fit of the sullens."

Mr. John Whyte grew cold.

"Once again, you are unable to bring yourself to believe what I am telling you. I should like to remind you of what happened the last time this occurred, but I am tired of these games. There is nothing more to be said. Good day, Miss Stone. God knows I wish you well."

He bowed, and walked back to the great house in company with Charles Bellfort and Victorine, leaving Pamela Stone to follow wretchedly behind.

The two couples returned to Haverford before nuncheon. The gentlemen, although requested to remain, declined, and rode back to Melfield. They were not long astride before Mr. Bellfort spoke to his friend about his concern for Miss Wells.

"From all the time I have just spent in her company, John, I can offer no explanation of the change in her. I am very worried. I should like to take her away from here, if I were only in a position to do so."

"She is with her cousin and her mother," replied John, still angry from his encounter with Pamela. "I feel sure they will look after her. She is temporarily overset, that is all."

"I wish I could believe that."

"There is certainly some obvious explanation. Perhaps at the ball—I don't know, perhaps someone gave her champagne, not realizing the effect it would have on a girl just out of the schoolroom. She may simply have drunk too much champagne for the first time, or perhaps some gentleman was a bit too forward with her. It seems as if she'd had some kind of frightening experience, I would say."

"Who would do such a thing? Anyone but a flat can see what a simple child she is."

"That is so. But, it can hardly be serious. As she is with her family, in a house filled with company, she can't come to real harm. I feel that this illness of hers can only be a temporary indisposition. Don't make too much of it."

"It won't do, believe me," he added bitterly, "to indulge in flights of overactive imagination."

"Very well, John."

They said nothing for some time.

"All right, John, do you intend to bring up your own situation, or do you suppose I am such a flat that I cannot feel your pain?"

"Oh, Charles," said Mr. Whyte almost with relief, "I am not a happy man. As you see. I long for the solitary life I lived before at Melfield. It was simple and uncomplicated. Since I have had the ill luck to tumble into love, my life has been pure hell, and I don't scruple to admit it."

"It has been hell for me as well, John."

"The only one of us with cause for happiness is Balmore. Did you know that, in addition to his own business, the more pressing reason that he set off tonight in such haste for London was to procure a special license?"

"Then he has offered for Lady Charlton?"

"He means to do so once he has secured the license, and I understand he has reason to hope she will accept him."

"At least for one of us," sighed Charles Bellfort, "Perseverance will bring about a happy ending."

Victorine seemed to have been revivified by her walk with Mr. Bellfort; after the gentleman had left, walking back toward one wing of the house, Victorine mentioned to Pamela the particular pleasure she was finding in Charles Bellfort's company. However, strangely, Victorine's indisposition seemed to return and even increase just as soon as she had re-entered the main hall of Haverford. She swiftly retired to her bedroom, and remained there all through the rest of the day.

Talking it over, her mother and her cousin decided that rest was perhaps the best thing for Victorine, and hoped that, by the evening, she might have recovered her spirits.

The two ladies, Pamela and her aunt, spent a quiet afternoon doing needlework, and supervising the packing of their dresses and trunks and bandboxes. They decided not to deal with Darcher at all for the moment; Victorine's things could be packed up swiftly enough if everyone else was ready to go. Pamela was happy to have something to occupy herself, and to keep her mind from dwelling on the bitter scene with Mr. John Whyte.

The St. Clares were nowhere to be found, having gone riding with Lord and Lady Braithwaite to see some hunters a neighbor was offering to sell. His lordship the Earl of Cleremont spent the day, as usual in his book room.

Such was life at Haverford.

Twenty-two

The Earl of Cleremont and Lady St. Clare both graced the dinner table with their presence that evening, although Lord St. Clare had joined his hunting friend for dinner with Lord and Lady Braithwaite. Miss Wells chose to dine alone in her bedchamber, pleading ill-health, and neither of her relatives thought it wise to press her to make an appearance.

Her ladyship St. Clare was ever more gay than usual, and spent dinner time entertaining her odd father-in-law with risque stories he seemed to find most amusing. *They're two of a kind, aren't they?* thought Pamela.

Lady Charlton exchanged a speaking glance with her niece at one particularly shocking story told by the young Viscountess, and was evidently beginning to wonder if Haverford were really a proper place to have brought her daughter and her niece. If this was how the higher nobility behaved, her family members were better off spending time with persons rather less august and rather more genteel.

Over dessert, the more Lady Charlton thought about it, the more she thought that enough was enough. Whatever social benefits the connection could confer upon her daughter they had, no doubt, already conferred them. Any further stay at Haverford could do no good for Victorine and Pamela, and it was beginning to look as if it might do them some harm. Clearly, it was time to go back to London—and then later moving for a stay at Brighton or Bath. Lady Charlton decided to take this opportunity to provoke an exit.

"Your lordship has been very kind in allowing us to stay with you so long. We have enjoyed ourselves immensely, and thank you very much for having invited us. I think the time has come for us to return to London," Lady Charlton ventured to suggest.

"Just as you wish, of course," replied the Earl.

A flood of relief came over Pamela at the thought of leaving Haverford, and the many unhappy memories that had it as their source.

Lady St. Clare's eyes flickered with surprise and displeasure at Lady Charlton's announcement, thinking, *I have not done with these girls just yet. They may not leave this house until Miles has done with both of them.*

"Yes, we shall be sad to leave you," continued Lady Charlton. "However, we have imposed on your hospitality long enough, and the country air does not seem to be agreeing with Victorine."

"Oh, does it not?" said Lady St. Clare innocently. "How uncommon. I always thought the country offered a very healthy atmosphere."

"In general, I think it does. But Victorine, if you had seen her, does not seem to be doing well at all, although I cannot imagine why. I think we shall repair to London as soon as we may, and there consult the famous Dr. Knighton. In fact, come to think of it, it might be a very good thing if Pamela's father were to meet us there, and to consult the good doctor himself, on his own behalf. Perhaps I should send him a note."

"That seems a good thought," replied Lady St. Clare,

her brain working at top speed to turn all information gathered from this conversation to her own advantage.

"My brother, Thomas Stone, has been an invalid for many years now; no doubt it has been many years as well since he has been seen by a first-rate surgeon. There may be new medicines now and new techniques that would be of help to him."

"Of course," said Lady St. Clare. "Of course there may. You are quite right."

"He was used to be a bruising rider, but took a terrible fall, and never really recovered from it, I'm afraid."

"He fell, did he? Why, that's like Miss Stone! Do such accidents then run in the family?"

Pamela's cheeks flushed with indignation, but she pretended not to have heard her ladyship's barb. Instead, she added, "Oh, I don't know about him going to London, Aunt. Papa is so fragile—I don't think I'd dare let him travel so far."

"Nonsense, Pamela. He is my only surviving brother—the one I am most close to. You cannot think I would suggest he do anything that would injure his health, my dear. I feel he is well enough to travel some distance. And I would do anything to make him regain his strength. Lord Balmore swears by this Dr. Knighton, and if seeing a doctor in London would help your father, I think we should encourage him to meet us there."

"Yes, of course, Aunt. You're quite right."

It was an interesting event when, once the ladies had withdrawn after dinner, a message reached Lady Charlton concerning her brother Thomas Stone, so recently the subject of discussion. It informed her of her brother's sudden serious illness, and begged her ladyship's attendance on Mr. Stone at the earliest possible moment. The messenger—for the news was brought by messenger rather than by letter—had apparently left Lincolnshire several days ago, just prior to the ball.

Both Pamela and her aunt were profoundly upset at this news, delivered to them while they were with Lady St. Clare in the withdrawing room.

"We must leave for Easton at once, Pamela."

"Yes, Aunt, I'll get ready."

"I'm sure Lord Cleremont will lend us a carriage under the circumstances."

Lady St. Clare, having overheard their conversation, assured them that either Cleremont or her own husband would of course offer them the comfort of a travelling carriage. She extended her sympathies to the women, and wished them a very safe trip to Lincolnshire.

"However," she added, "I wonder that you consider Miss Wells healthy enough to survive such a long, fast journey when she is in such an unwell condition."

Lady Charlton snapped to attention. "You believe she cannot survive it?"

"Well, it is quite a long way. And I am sure you will be wanting to travel just as fast as you may. You can see how merely the effort of having taken a walk this morning has overset poor Victorine this whole afternoon and evening. Most injudicious of her to have attempted it, I think. Were I her mother, I should never take the chance of letting her undertake such a long, uncomfortable journey." Her ladyship affected to walk away, but kept an ear on the subsequent interchange.

"Pamela, my heavens, I never thought of that! Whatever shall we do?"

"Well, then—one of us must remain here with Victorine, till she is well enough to come. I shall go to Papa by myself then, tomorrow."

"No, dearest, it is out of the question. I cannot allow you to travel alone."

"I won't be alone; I can bring Helen."

"No, I—no, it will not do; you are simply too young. It's out of the question—such a journey at seventeen! Think what would happen if anything untoward—no, I have quite made up my mind."

"Aunt!"

"You will remain here, until I can send some of your father's people after to fetch you back. By that time, Victorine should be much better and well enough to come along as well."

"No, I can't—"

"We will take the greatest care of your daughter and niece, of course, Lady Charlton," interjected the Viscountess St. Clare. "And I think it quite right that you not let Miss Stone travel alone all that way. Who knows what could happen? With the roads being the way they are these days, better not to take the chance. The condition of the roads is so shocking!"

"But, Aunt . . ."

"No. It is settled," said Lady Charlton. "I will be off and gone to nurse your poor, dear father even before you have retired to your bed tonight. In the morning, please explain to Victorine what has happened, why I have had to leave—I do not want to disturb her night of rest. Please ask Mr. Bellfort to inform Lord Balmore of our change in plans. He will have been expecting to get in touch with me."

The rest of the evening was spent in a bustle trying to

get her aunt away, and leaving Pamela little time to think about what lay ahead of her in the days to come. Caught between dislike for her present situation, the quarrel with John Whyte, her intense worry over the health of her father, and frustration over her inability to go to be with him in his illness, she bade her aunt a safe journey, retired to her rooms, and fell into a deep, if troubled, sleep.

Twenty-three

Madame Darcher sidled into Victorine's bedroom a little after eleven o'clock in the evening, shook her awake, and bade her drink a glass of milk well-spiced with laudanum. Victorine huddled in her satin dressing gown, and did as she was bid, saying nothing. She had come to like the soothing drinks that her new abigail gave to her; it was the only way she had survived the day. And the long night before.

As the drug began to have its relaxing effect upon her, Victorine began to wonder what would happen next. Confused, frightened, all day long she had felt so different from her former self; much more mature, but also infinitely more alone, because now she had so many secrets, so many frightening things she was able to reveal to no one.

Her maid began putting out an evening dress for her to wear, made of pale blue silk with deep decolletage in the French manner, and decorated with silver ribands. It was not the sort of dress for a debutante. It was very beautiful and very sophisticated and very fashionable—but very daring. In fact, its cut was far beyond daring: it was just the kind of dress that a well-kept Cyprian might wear.

Victorine stared at the gorgeous creation without comprehension.

"Madame Darcher, it is very late. Why do you bring this dress to me? Am I going out?"

Madame Darcher returned her glance with an astonished one, then smiled condescendingly and ran her fingers along Victorine's long, golden hair.

"But of course you are going out, my dear; you have your appointment with Lord St. Clare. Surely you did not think that his lordship would forget you!"

"I have not seen his lordship all day."

"He is a busy man. But of course, for you, who are so dear to his heart, he will make time. It is certain, child; it is more than certain."

Victorine smiled just a little bit, her blue eyes looking trustingly into Madame Darcher's small, birdlike ones.

"All right, then. Let's get ready. It must be time. I would like to see his lordship, for I have many things to say to him," said Victorine. "But, Madame Darcher, I cannot wear this dress. It is entirely unsuitable. Besides, it does not belong to me."

She ran her fingers enviously over the delicate, gossamer-sheer bodice. Her mother would never allow her to wear such a gown; in fact, Lady Charlton would have forbidden her daughter to associate with anyone who even was familiar with the direction of shop where such immodest garments were made. Some freedoms were simply disallowed to the daughters of gentlemen.

Madame Darcher scowled, and gave Victorine a thunderous look which made her quail, and grumbled sharply, without the least attempt at civility or servility, "Yes, of course you must wear it, Miss! And finish your milk!"

Victorine was taken aback at such treatment at the

hands of a servant. "Very well. I think I shall drink the milk, in any case. I like it very much."

"Of course you do, *ma petite,*" said Madame Darcher, mollified by obedience. "It always helps you. You have been so unwell, you must be careful."

"But I won't wear that horrid dress!"

Madame Darcher smiled an awful smile, and said, as she left the room for a moment, "Won't you wear it? I think you will have changed your mind after a few minutes. After all, you do want to please Lord St. Clare, don't you?"

Victorine made no reply. Madame went on, inexorably.

"You must realize, Miss, that that gentleman went to a deal of trouble to select this style for you himself, and to have your measurements taken off your old gowns, and a special French dressmaker brought all the way out here in the country, working overtime to finish that dress.

"I am sure that, not only do you not wish to cast aspersions on his lordship's taste—which is impeccable— but you do not wish to seem ungrateful for his lordship's condescension.

"Also, of course, that gown is fabulously expensive. If I were you, I would want to show his lordship gratitude, not provincial missishness."

She left. Her words accomplished what she wanted them to accomplish. By the time Madame Darcher returned, Victorine had already begun to change.

Seeing that the time was right, Madame Darcher worked feverishly to prepare her charge properly. Her golden hair was upswept into a Grecian knot at the top of her head, ornamented with a silver fillet that wound its way amongst her curls. Her complexion was so fine that it needed no paint.

The gown that had been selected for Victorine was of the finest, most delicate gauze imaginable, and Madame Darcher took great pains to dampen it so that the skirt-folds would cling revealingly to Victorine's figure, and so that its low-slung bodice revealed nearly as much of Victorine's beauty as might Nature herself.

It was not above than a half-hour later, just past midnight, that Victorine was brought once again to the Red Room, beautifully coiffed and clothed, perfumed with a light rose and violet scent, ready to meet the Viscount. She was conscious of looking her best, and was surprised that the very effort it took to dress herself was helpful in making her feel a bit more the thing—less ashamed and more sophisticated.

Just as she was passing through the door, a memory of the previous evening flashed through her mind, and she became tremblingly afraid—but as it happened, his lordship was waiting right there for her, and when he took her hand, she forgot her fears a little. She was a woman, after all. The guilty thoughts that had plagued her all day were just thoughts, weren't they? The truth was that he loved her. He had said so, had he not? And she loved him. It was far better to keep her mind concentrated on these few facts, the only ones that really mattered.

"My dear girl," he said, leading her to a velvet-covered loveseat, and putting his arms around her waist in an embrace she willingly returned. "How have you been? I have been wretched with worry, for I heard you have not been well all day."

"No. I have been very much indisposed."

"My poor darling child! Indisposed, have you been? How shocking! I do dislike being indisposed, myself! If you have been unwell, I am doubly indebted to you for having come to me tonight. Have some champagne, my darling, won't you? It is an exquisite variety."

And she sipped at her drink, served in a long, delicate fluted glass that had been blessed by the addition of a few drops of the murky liquid from the cut-glass decanter just before the champagne itself was added. It was quite tasteless.

She pulled at her drink as she walked nervously and aimlessly around the room, running her fingers over a piece of mahogany here, a piece of brocade there, tugging at a scarlet damask hanging. The Viscount tapped his foot, consulted his heirloom timepiece, and began to look impatient.

He stepped toward the bed, drawing the hanging draperies back, and motioned to Victorine to join him. Again Victorine felt a thrill of fear pass through her, despite the formidable barrier to negative states of mind the laudanum and champagne together produced. She put her hand to her throat, and felt her own pulse trembling with anxiety. She had been in control of herself until the moment he had pulled back the drapes, and revealed the silken sheets of his lordship's great four-poster mahogany bed.

"Oh, St. Clare—dear St. Clare—I am so sorry."

"Why, should you feel sorry, my heart's love? Is there something wrong?" St. Clare asked disingenuously, while within him, annoyance and irritation fought for dominance.

"Well, St. Clare, I must thank you for this evening's invitation. I wished to come here to meet you tonight to tell you that I must not be your lover any more."

His brow darkened, and his whole face assumed a stony appearance. It was a surprising feature of his countenance that negative emotions passing over his face could so thoroughly disorder his good looks.

"It is not for *you* to tell *me* that our affair is over, little one," he replied in the blackest tones possible, smashing the champagne glass against the granite wall.

"But why ever not?"

"Why not? Observe!"

He went over to her, and took her strongly in his arms. She tried to shrug him off, was unable to do so, and then mutely acceded to his demands for a few moments, letting his hands run over her just he wished. She then tried to escape, but the Viscount prevented her from doing so. Keeping her trapped in his embrace, St. Clare slowly and deliberately removed the lovely, spider-thin blue gauze covering from her body in an urgency born of possessiveness.

Almost more appalled by the outrageous way he had destroyed the expensive gown than by his cavalier treatment of her person, Victorine was brought back to her senses for a moment, and began to fight in earnest to regain her freedom.

"I won't have it! Do you hear, St. Clare?"

"Do shut up, my dear."

"No, don't, St. Clare, don't! Stop! This is quite enough! Do you perfectly comprehend me? It is the outside of enough!"

"It will be enough when I have said it is enough, and not before, child!"

An unusual flash of anger lit Victorine's pretty face.

"You can't do this unless I accede to it! And—and I won't accede to you tonight! I don't want to do these dreadful things anymore! All day I have been shockingly upset about it—I can't eat, I can't think, I can't behave like this one moment longer. Can't you see—I'm not like your other lovers. I'm ashamed of myself, so terribly, terribly ashamed."

"Why should whatever you have on your conscience signify anything to me?"

"You don't seem to understand, St. Clare! I can't do it! I can't be what you want me to be; I wish I could, but I can't. I do love you, I love you most desperately, but I haven't been raised to be able to think as you do about—about such things.

"I'm not a trollop! And the things you make me do—I cannot do them—not ever again!"

"You will do just exactly what I desire you to do, chit," replied the Viscount's frigid voice.

"I won't! In fact, I'll tell everyone in town and country just what kind of man you are! I'll tell everyone what you've done to me! I'll ruin you!"

St. Clare let her go, threw back his head and laughed outrageously for some time, till tears came to him, as Victorine could only stare at him in incomprehension. His black locks shone brilliantly in the light of the branch of candles near them, and, even though they were filled with the tears of laughter, his sapphire eyes shone with a cold blue fire.

"My dear, you possess such a delightful sense of humor, it quite astounds me!" said he, dabbing at his eyes with a lace handkerchief. "Do you mean to say that you actually intend to expose in public all the very interesting things we two have done together? Are you utterly mad? Have you quite lost your senses?"

His eyes narrowed, and they tried to lock her gaze to his own.

"You cannot threaten me, my child—but know this: I

can threaten you. If you don't obey me now, you will spend the rest of your life wishing that you had only had the sense to make yourself pleasant to me in every way."

"You can't make me! I won't be with you like this anymore! It's sneaking and hateful and I hate it! It's not at all the way love is supposed to be!"

His beautiful mouth twisted into an ugly snarl, as he pulled her closely to him, saying, "Mark my words, child, you will do as you are told. You think your ruination is complete already, but that is because you are inexperienced. I assure you that you still have a long way to go; if you are disobedient, you shall be well taught what are the extremes to which a female can sink. It would be an easy enough affair to arrange for you to disappear entirely off the face of this earth. In fact, it happens all the time. More often than anyone knows. How should you like that? How should your honored mother like that, to lose her daughter without a trace?"

Victorine was shocked beyond belief.

"Without a trace? Oh, coming it a bit too strong, St. Clare, are you not? These are surely idle threats. You are a horrid, hardened rake, and a libertine, but for all that, you are a gentleman."

He brought his face close enough to hers that she could smell the brandy on his breath, and close enough that he could not help but feel her terrible, uncontrollable trembling. He broke out into harsh laughter and he laughed at her, loud and long, until tears came to his eyes.

"You really are impossibly naive, Victorine. One wonders how you have managed all these years. You have been living in such profound obliviousness to the real world, and to the real way things are done in it. Are you merely stupid, or is it your upbringing that was to blame?"

"Demon! How dare you insult my family! I was perfectly well-brought up!"

"That is of course, the crux of the problem to some extent. Yes, I suppose your dangerous ignorance is due to having led what is called a 'sheltered life.' A nasty business that is, ignorance, if you ask my opinion on it. Look just where all that sheltering has gotten you, my dear. Saved since childhood from knowledge of the ultimate consequences of your actions, you became a flower just ripe for the plucking, with no more idea of the horrid fates that might befall you than a rosebud."

"It is your lies that are to blame, not my upbringing! You are the one who told me you would divorce your wife!"

"And you are the one who believed what I said! Your cousin Pamela would not give credence to such an utter hum, I can tell you. I adore my wife and always have. Pamela has seen that, because she has a head on her shoulders and a brain in her head, rather than having, like you, a pate stuffed full of novels. Quite different. Pamela will require entirely different circumstances than the ones that succeeded in making you available for seduction."

"You are the one who seduced me!"

"You are the one who allowed yourself to be seduced."

"You said that you loved me!"

"Saying it don't make it so, my dear. Your failure to inspect my motives carefully was a function of your ignorance, as I said, and your own innate, carnal desires. Love, after all, is merely a notion of poets."

"It is not!"

"How would you know?"

"You promised to marry me!"

"Did I?" he said languidly. "How very naughty of me! All in pursuit of the hunt, however, and thus allowable. But I weary of this talk. You are in my power, my dear, fully and completely, and I can do whatever I wish with you. Know it well: I can do whatever I wish.

"Your every breath depends upon my good-will and my good humor, so keep that in mind. You are fully dependent on me, and on no other. Your esteemed mother has been sent away, by my agency, and you are best advised to submit to your circumstances with whatever grace remains to you to muster.

"Is that all quite clear, Victorine?"

She sat down on the side of the bed, and buried her head in her hands, quaking with fear and weeping inconsolably. This display of waterworks seemed to irritate the Viscount, who cast a contemptuous glance at the girl, and poured himself a brandy. He threw it back, and took one other.

Victorine dried her eyes, then turned toward her oppressor, hanging her head, unwilling to meet his eyes directly lest his gaze drain her of what little strength remained to her. She sat there, looking like a broken china doll.

"Well, then, little one, I suppose that you've seen reason now, haven't you?"

"Yes."

"Don't make such a drama of it. It will all be over soon."

"Will it?" she asked in a dead voice.

"Yes, it will. We'll put aside all this unpleasantness now, shall we? The night is young, summer is in the air, and I am in a great mood to enjoy myself, I assure you."

He paused, loosened his shirt, and removed his cravat, then tapped his foot impatiently.

"Well? What are you waiting for? Let's get on with it."

Several hours later, when the Viscount's myriad amusements had finally come to an end, Victorine was returned in a stupor to her room, to enjoy the special ministrations of Darcher's wife, while Lord St. Clare returned to his own apartments.

St. Clare was thinking hard about the near future and making detailed plans. He settled himself into a seat, threw back his head and yawned, while Darcher scurried here and there about the room, picking up his master's clothes, brushing them, folding them, and putting them lovingly away.

Seemingly lost in thought, the Viscount lifted a half-emptied glass of cognac to his lips, with one hand, while with his other hand, he insistently tapped his beautifully manicured fingertips against the brocade covering of his favorite chair.

"By the way, I shan't be needing Miss Wells again, Darcher."

"Over so soon?"

"Darcher, surely you jest. You know very well that I prefer untouched chits. I am surprised at you. Two nights with any one woman is more than enough." St. Clare looked thoughtful and almost petulant, as he yawned again, and pointed out, "It's really only the very first night with a girl that's any fun at all."

"So she will be leaving Haverford soon. Are we leaving as well? Back to the continent?"

"Don't jump the gun quite yet! There is another young woman in this house, Darcher, or had you forgotten? I can hardly consider leaving Haverford until I have made the complete acquaintance of little Miss Stone."

"Miss Stone? The one your brother John wished to marry? That your lordship's father does not like?"

"Yes, indeed. That will make it more amusing, do you not think?"

"Quite so, your lordship."

"I think so. I think I'll inform John about my experiences in detail, afterwards—don't you think? He can hardly call me out—I'm a better shot than he is. It will also provide some small amusement just arranging the most suitable and efficient methods necessary to procure the personal attention of Miss Pamela Stone."

"Indeed. If I may be so bold as to comment, it was devilishly clever of her ladyship to rid us of Miss Stone's chaperone, Lady Charlton, with such dispatch. Long before the time her ladyship Charlton finds out that message was just a hum, your lordship will have already finished making Miss Stone's acquaintance. As it were."

"She's a good woman, my Marguerite. Always eager to promote my interests."

"An excellent wife, sir."

"Indeed. One could not wish for better."

Dawn found Lord St. Clare and his wife in his lordship's spacious bedchamber talking with great animation about the plans necessary to the acquisition of Miss Pamela Stone. Her ladyship was entwined around his lordship; she was stroking his raven hair, and he was stroking her full, accommodating body, both husband and wife lounging in bed while tangled in a cascading mixture of immaculate cotton bedclothes and silken duvets.

As always, at this point, the two were gleefully involved in plotting the next chapter of their hunting game; they did so while pouring the dregs of last night's cognac into steaming cups of West Indian coffee topped with fresh dairy cream, and consuming the delicious contents. From time to time, one of them popped a fresh strawberry dipped in brandy and sugar into the other's mouth.

"It will be naturally more exciting dealing with Miss Stone than it was with Miss Wells, Marguerite. It must be."

"Why, *mon cher?*" asked his wife, who was raptly drawing a long line down her husband's chest with her fingernails.

"Different kind of girl; different kind of strategy. Miss Wells was a target almost too easily accomplished to be really interesting, to really give one that gratifying jolt that betokens success."

"Oh?"

"Quite. It is like the second stage in the siege of a city: it can't proceed in precisely the same manner. One can't get rid of Pamela Stone's maid in just the same way that Miss Wells's maid was got rid of, using the same old tired tactics. And this one is an inherently more complex situation: one had to rid oneself of the watchful eyes of Lady Charlton. Then there's the girl's maid and my brother to remove from contention. Oh, it's a much more interesting proposition, I assure you. Therefore, more satisfying, upon the enterprise's successful completion."

"*Tiens,* the girl's maid doesn't signify. Lady Charlton is already gone. You need only be rid of John—if only for a few hours. You are sending him off tomorrow, as I understand, are you not?"

"Yes, I believe that tomorrow dear John will ride happily out over the fields pursuing what he believes to be a mission useful to his future contentment with his Pamela Stone!" The Viscount laughed wickedly. "No need to worry on his account. By the time he returns, it will all be over. And I will have secured his future unhappiness. I can't wait to tell him. It would be great fun if he were to call me out. I haven't dueled since Venice— have I?"

The Viscountess purred, and ran her hand down the well-muscled thigh of his lordship. He continued speaking, adjusting his body just a bit in response to her touch.

"Stroke of genius with regard to Lady Charlton, my dear. Darcher was complimenting you only this evening. Very well done. Subtle. Elegant."

"Yes, it did go wonderfully well. Myself, I would not have so easily believed an oral message brought by an unknown messenger, but her love for her brother, thankfully enough, blinded her judgment. It's like that, *l'amour, n'est-ce pas?*"

"I'm afraid I wouldn't know," replied his lordship, stiffly.

For just a moment, it seemed as if the Viscountess might take offense at this remark, and the cold, distanced manner in which it was made, but in the end, she decided it was better merely to ignore her husband's heedless statement.

"I think," said her ladyship carefully, "we had better give orders that Miss Stone's food is to be drugged as well. Starting tomorrow noon—*demain*. At about the time that John goes off. Don't you suppose? Or would tomorrow morning be better?"

"Perhaps a touch with her bed tea in the morning, and then a bit more and a bit more, so that by the early afternoon she reaches a state in which she is completely open and tractable."

"Very good. You prefer afternoon to evening, my love?"

"I harbor no prejudices in this regard. I merely enjoy having the opportunity to—er, indulge my predilection for entering that tender place where none has gone before. In the case of Miss Stone, I believe, that chances for success are better if I act with dispatch. My window of opportunity is but a narrow one."

"Indeed."

"How shall she come to my room, darling? Ought I to have her escorted there?" he yawned.

"Nothing so ungenteel. I'm sure we can find some reason for her to arrive of her own accord, in the course of her daily business. I particularly like the idea of finding a way for her to go voluntarily to her own ruination. *Ce serait bien bon*—it has a thrilling feel to it. And then, once she arrives at the Red Room—there will be nothing but a vast evening of diversion."

"Yes, indeed," replied his lordship huskily. "You're a precious woman to understand my needs so very well, Marguerite."

"Oui, mais pour quoi pas, mon cher? Just as long as you have a *leetle* something left over afterward for me, your fond wife."

She ran her hands through her husband's hair and kissed him until he responded to her. They made violent love and then lay together in his lordship's bed, deeply content.

It was raining steadily when Pamela awakened, and the grey weather reflected her own mood extremely well. In the humid air, her wrist ached terribly from the time she had fallen off the grey mare, and she was worried about her family—her father and her cousin. She was also a bit concerned about herself. Once again she was ashamed for the way in which she had rung a peal over Mr. John Whyte. This time he would be unlikely to forgive her.

Pamela felt herself becoming infected by a depression that seemed to spring from the very walls of Haverford itself. She had to get away, and soon she would. But she also had to be patient until her aunt returned, or until Victorine's health improved, and Lady Charlton sent for them.

Pamela rubbed her wrist for a few minutes without much good coming of it, then rang for, received, and drank a hot cup of Darjeeling tea with cream and sugar. She got dressed almost carelessly, hardly talking to Helen Fraley more than to bid her good day, and then dismissing her. Dressed in a simple morning dress, not having taken as much care with her toilette as she normally did, she went in search of Victorine.

She found her cousin in her room, still abed, a mass of yellow curls almost lost in the enormous feather pillows; her cousin looked for all the world like a girl who had been invalided all her life. To judge merely by Victorine's pallor and lack of energy, she was apparently feeling even more poorly than she had the day before.

Pamela simply could not account for her cousin's sudden ill-health; she dreaded having to break the news to Victorine that Lady Charlton had gone away. It seemed that there was no way to tell her the truth without risking her falling into another one of her distempered freaks.

To be sure, learning of the absence of her mother in such a weakened, vulnerable state could only hurt the girl.

As spoiled a child as she was, Victorine was honestly attached to her mother; she was not merely dependent on her. Would her mother's absence lead her further on in this decline? Pamela feared that further decline was very likely, and she could not think what the source of Victorine's distress might be, or how the situation could be ameliorated.

Pamela put a hand on her cousin's forehead to feel for fever, and her cousin's sky-blue eyes sprang open; as if lost in a dream, she thrashed around in the bedclothes wildly, then looked straight at her cousin without recognizing her. She pushed Pamela's hand away roughly, and cried, "No, don't! Don't touch me!"

"Victorine, it's me. It's Pamela!" said her cousin, trying to bring Victorine back to reason.

Victorine seemed to recognize Pamela's voice, and she quietened down immediately; she settled herself back on the pillows again and breathed easier, though her small hands were clutching the cotton sheets with a desperate strength, as if a good grip could keep her from being swept away into oblivion.

"Just you, is it? Pamela? Well, that's all right then," said Victorine, with just the ghost of a smile passing across her face.

Pamela pulled the bell rope to desire two cups of hot chocolate to be brought up to the room; these arrived in very good time. Setting the lovely patterned cups down next to the bed, Pamela began to coax her cousin to drink up the dark, hot, soothing liquid contained therein. Oddly, Victorine refused to drink a drop she was offered until her cousin did so—but once Pamela had shown her, by example, that one could take a sip and come to no harm, the chocolate was gratefully accepted. The dreadful thought crossed Pamela's mind that her cousin's mind had become seriously deranged.

As if she read what Pamela had been thinking, Victorine announced, "I'm afraid, you see," as if this explanation of her odd behavior would suffice.

"Afraid of what?"

"I'm afraid of what they give me."

Pamela was nonplussed. Directly, Pamela decided that the no-nonsense tone her own governess had been used to employ when Pamela was a child would be just the thing to shock her young cousin out of her distempered state.

"Victorine, don't be silly! Afraid? Now that, my dear, is being foolish beyond permission. What is there to be afraid of? You're letting your imagination carry you away. You must stop reading those novels of Mrs. Radcliffe's. Life is not like that."

Tears welled up in the once-lovely eyes.

"But you don't understand, Pamela. You don't understand what has been occurring here . . . at Haverford."

"You're quite right. I don't understand. Please tell me what is the matter with you."

"I will, but promise not to tell Mother. You must promise you won't tell Mother," she said in a piteous wail of a voice.

"All right, dear, I won't. Oh, and by the way, your mother—" and here Pamela had to pause while she suppressed the tears that had risen in her own throat, thinking of her only remaining parent, and fears for his health and safety. "Your mother had suddenly to go away last night, so she won't be joining us again for a few days."

"Go away?" said Victorine, wildly. "Mother has gone away? Why?"'

"There was a message arrived about my father saying that he was dreadfully ill, suddenly ill, and that he needed his sister to come to him immediately. I wanted to go to him, but Aunt Charlton refused to let me, and insisted on going herself. I could not stop her. In any case, it is temporary. She will be back soon, so you must try to get better."

"Oh, no, no. Oh, God, I am done for!" Victorine shrieked. "I am abandoned; I am all alone here!"

"You're not alone!" replied Pamela with a hint of irritation in her voice. "I'm here."

"You don't understand—it is terrible beyond all things! Oh, Pamela, why did we all not go away with Mother? Why did we stay?"

"It was thought you were too unwell to endure the long journey."

"Then it is my fault we have stayed on in this terrible house! Oh, God, again it is my fault!"

"Victorine, you are making no sense!" interjected Pamela, with growing exasperation, suppressing a strong desire to administer a strong, salutary slap to bring her cousin back to reason.

"You don't know, you don't know, you don't know," were the only words interspersed between Victorine's sobs. Pamela, seeing her cousin lost in such strong hysterics, realized that she could do nothing with her or for her, threw her hands up and left the room.

In the corridor she ran into Madame Darcher, who curtseyed to Pamela with apparent deference and inquired if the young Miss Wells was feeling more the thing today.

"Not at all, I'm sorry to say," Pamela answered curtly,

not wishing to cause any more talk than there had been already.

"How shocking! Have you any orders to give regarding her care?"

"Why, yes. Have you any laudanum?"

Madame Darcher barely repressed a smile. *Yes, Miss, I do have some laudanum. And both you and your cousin have just consumed quite a bit of it.*

"Well—yes, Miss Stone. I believe I can procure some."

"Then please give Miss Victorine a few drops just as a sedative. She's very upset."

"Certainly, Miss."

Madame Darcher bobbed another curtsey, and watched with some satisfaction as Miss Stone walked rather unsteadily down the long hallway.

Later on in the morning, after the rains had cleared, Mr. Bellfort and Mr. Whyte rode over once again from Melfield to Haverford. They rode side by side, saying very little, each man lost in his own thoughts, their horses walking through the damp fields at a stately pace suitable to reflection.

Mr. Whyte was still smarting from his encounter with Pamela Stone, though, in all fairness, it would be hard for any woman to countenance her avowed lover's embrace of another woman—much less such a woman of fast reputation such as Lady St. Clare. He could hardly blame Pamela for holding the incident against him, and yet, it pained him that she felt she could not trust his innate honesty and his respect for her.

The two gentlemen had received a hasty note from

Pamela in the this morning relating the tale of Victorine's continuing illness, and the unexpected departure of Lady Charlton to go to the aid of the ailing Mr. Thomas Stone. Although the letter cost the author something in terms of loss of face, Miss Pamela Stone requested that they call, and lend her their advice on how she should proceed.

Mr. Willby greeted the visitors with his customary perfect correctness, and showed them up to the parlor, where they were announced to Miss Pamela Stone. Miss Stone had been sitting in the parlor for some time, attempting unsuccessfully to embroider a fire-screen. She seemed today, quite unaccountably, to have entirely lost her former capacity to match silks or thread a needle with dispatch.

Her state of mild disorientation, however, was such as to make transparent her true feelings. Immediately she saw the Hon. John Whyte, an unmistakable look of relief and happiness flooded her visage, and she approached him without reserve, extending to him her two hands.

In an undertone meant for her alone, he whispered, "Please believe that, whatever has passed between us, at the very least I remain your friend, ready to help you in any way I may."

She blushed with mortification and embarrassment as he took her hands in his and pressed them, meaningfully. Whatever doubts and fears she might have entertained about him dissolved fully in the warm light of his presence and, oppressed by events as she had been of late, she could not help but feel deeply comforted by his gesture of support.

"Thank you so much for coming. You are both very kind, very kind indeed. I'm afraid my cousin has grown much worse. As I wrote you, my Aunt Charlton has had to leave—because my father has taken ill—and I am afraid I am somewhat at a loss as to what to do. Do sit down. I wish you would advise me; I am somewhat overset by this unfortunate concatenation of events."

"Pamela," said Mr. Whyte, "I think it is time you should leave here. You look unwell."

"I should like to more than anything, but how can I? As my aunt pointed out, Victorine cannot travel in such a state."

"I believe Victorine should be seen by a doctor, Miss Stone, and the truth of whether she can or cannot travel should be determined by him, not by us," interjected Mr. Bellfort. "If your mother were here, I would strongly advise her to send for one at once. I must advise the same to you. I am extremely worried about Victorine's health, I do not scruple to tell you. If she is worse today, as you suggest, there is not a moment to lose."

"I think you are right, Mr. Bellfort. I will request Lord St. Clare to send for a doctor right away. I had thought yesterday that Victorine looked unwell merely because her nerves were overset. But today, she seems so much worse that I fear for her. I know how dangerous the influenza can be."

A footman appeared, bringing them some tea and cakes, and all conversation had to be interrupted until the servant had left and had closed the salon doors behind him.

"Are you quite sure your cousin cannot travel?" asked Mr. John Whyte with a grim set to his mouth. "Unless the doctor were to forbid it absolutely, surely you would both be better off at your father's home, remaining under the aegis of Mr. Stone and under the care of Lady Charlton."

As Mr. Whyte was saying this, and before Pamela could answer, Lady St. Clare came into the room, immediately preceded by her characteristic cloud of musk-rose perfume. She sat down next to Mr. Whyte and favored him with her most scintillating smile.

The Hon. John Whyte, inwardly revolted, maintained perfect composure and treated her ladyship with utter civility. No one, seeing his extremely correct conduct, could tell how deeply he disliked this woman.

Pamela maintained her composure only with the greatest of effort; she noticed both how possessive and coming her ladyship was toward her brother-in-law, and how formal, cold, and correct he was toward her. She kept strongly in mind his expressed desire that she trust him, trust his conduct, and trust his respect for her.

The Viscountess, having greeted the visitors and inquired after their health, lost no time inserting herself into their conversation.

"I could not help overhearing what you said about our guests. But of course poor Victorine cannot travel, John! What can you be thinking? It is quite out of the question! I have just seen her myself, and she is delirious," opined Lady St. Clare, turning toward Pamela in order to better ring a peal over her head.

"Of course, Pamela, I attribute the shocking fact that you did not ask for a doctor to be sent to Victorine *at once* to your deep dismay at learning of your poor father's illness and to your shock at Lady Charlton's departure. And of course, you are perhaps still too young to be capable of acting with proper dispatch and maturity—as one must in such a difficult family situation as this. You will be pleased to know that I, in contrast, have already sent for Dr. Talborne to come to us as soon as possible."

"Thank you so much," replied Pamela, not bothering to hide the coldness in her tone. "I think Victorine's condition very poor indeed, and was just this minute discussing the measures that should be taken to help her with these gentlemen. Her condition is sufficiently frightening that I should not be surprised at all if she begins running a high fever very soon. That would, you see, explain her delirium."

Lady St. Clare raised her eyebrows in a gesture of innocent surprise. "You think she may conveniently develop a fever to explain two days of delirium? Well, I hope it may be so!"

The Viscountess cast down her eyes in a helpless gesture, shook her head, and went on, "Otherwise, lacking the presence of any physical malady, it would seem that it is the poor girl's mind which . . . well, perhaps it is best not to mention more at this time."

But the fear that Victorine might have suffered a blow to her sanity had already been planted firmly in the minds of her listeners.

"Thank you once again, Lady St. Clare," said Pamela primly. "Your continual attentiveness to our needs must form an occasion for gratitude, and I must express my sense of obligation."

"Very wise of you, child. Now, I wonder if such fits as Victorine's have ever happened to others in your family? Sometimes these things do run in the blood—but of course, it would be Lady Charlton who could tell us about your family history. Always skeletons in the best of closets. So sad that she had to leave us or she could have told us all about your family! So intriguing!

"But it is settled, so let us now talk of other things! Best not to dwell on unhappy events beyond our control.

Now, I have some interesting news for our Mr. John Whyte. John, my dear, had you heard that an old retainer of your mother's seems to have come visiting in the neighborhood? Old Derwent, Edgar Derwent, I think your father said to me, who used to be in charge of Julia Pembroke's fortune. Has he told you?"

"I have not met my father today, Ma'am, no."

"Are you not intrigued by this news?"

"Why should I be so?"

"Well! I am sorry if I intrude. It is merely that I understood you had been making inquiries here and in London, about what was the disposition of the Pembroke inheritance that was to come to you through your mother. And I believe this Derwent knew details about that which even his lordship Cleremont did not know, something about funds separate from those that were lost by that bank's collapse. Or so the Earl believes. I had thought you would be in alt hearing of such information."

"I have an interest there, yes."

The Viscountess leaned closer to Mr. John Whyte, lowered her voice, and held him rapt in private conversation for some time. Seeing them in this intimate proximity, Pamela Stone began to wonder just when his sister-in-law had begun trying to relate to Mr. John Whyte in such an ingratiating, cloying, forward manner. She realized that she was feeling very jealous and possessive of John, and she also realized that she was, herself, feeling increasingly more dizzy and unwell. It must be an infectious influenza, just as she had thought.

She struggled to maintain her composure, but she wanted to sleep, or at the very least to lie back in her seat; that, however, would be unladylike. Seeing Mr. Whyte and Lady St. Clare increasingly lost in conversation, she tried to focus her attention on what they were saying. She could hardly make it out.

Unable properly to follow their dialogue, jealousy of Lady St. Clare arose once again in her wandering mind. Surely John could feel no attraction to that creature, the Viscountess! Surely if he kissed that creature at the ball she must have ensnared him, somehow. Surely he had not lied to cover his feelings—had he? There was so very much she did not understand! And she wanted so very much just to retire to her bedchamber and rest.

John Whyte was still gravely questioning Lady St. Clare. "This Derwent had details about the disposition of my mother's portion? How do you know this?"

"Cleremont told me, and St. Clare said so as well. You know how clever Miles is with figures. He always knows where his every penny is coming from. Always."

The door opened, and the exquisite figure of the Viscount St. Clare entered the salon. His bearing was regal, the cut of his coat superb, his intricate tie a muslin masterpiece of expertise. His tasselled Hessians were champagne-buffed to diamond brilliance; a quizzing-glass dangled at his waist. With a flick of his left wrist he opened his snuff box, took a bit, and dusted off his long, delicate fingers. He was a magnificent beast fully cognizant of his own magnificence.

"Yes, I *am* clever with funds, aren't I, dear?" he smiled, showing his teeth.

"St. Clare! How delightful! Do join us! I was just telling John about Edgar Derwent!"

"Ah, forget about him, John! It's just useless rumors. Can't imagine why Marguerite pays them any attention. I assure you that I do not."

"Rumors?" asked John Whyte. "Which ones?"

"Well, they *say* that Derwent knows what became of all your mother's money—that which was lost on 'Change when you were so young. Or was it in a bank? I can't recall," said the Viscountess. "Derwent kept the records of the rest."

"I'm sure there's nothing to it," St. Clare said with evident boredom. "I wouldn't give it a second thought, John. Just a hum. Probably the wrong Derwent, anyway. You know how dotty Father can be."

"Where is this man staying?" asked Mr. Whyte.

"I think I heard he was at the Boar's Head in Wilverton. Or was it Tiverton? Hardly signifies, does it? My dear boy, you're *not* thinking of going off on a wild goose chase looking for Derwent, are you? That's all water under the dam. Whatever there was of Julia Pembroke's money, it's all gone for nothing now. So many fortunes have been lost in just that way, it is hardly to be thought an unusual occurrence. Best not to get your hopes up, man, but deal with reality as it is. Speaking of which, how is the divine Miss Wells? I understand she is indisposed once again today. Dashed sorry to hear it, as you may imagine. Worst of bad luck."

"It is true that she is still unwell, your lordship," interjected Pamela.

"Sorry to hear it; indeed I am. Has a physician been sent for?" asked the Viscount, opening his box again deftly and taking another pinch of snuff.

"Yes, thank you. Your wife has kindly sent a man to bring a local physician, I believe."

"I expect Miss Wells will be better soon. I certainly hope that may be so."

Mr. John Whyte, fading out of the conversation, was thinking about what his brother had said. Should he pursue it? There was little to be lost and much to be gained. All he had thus far uncovered, in his inquiries as to the disposition of his mother's London monies, was that it was quite likely that she had had several sources of funds. That being the case, it was more than reasonable to follow up any lead that presented itself, no matter how slim. If the Derwent possibility turned out to be just a paper chase, how could it signify? Taking out a few hours this afternoon to track the fellow down and ask a few questions could hardly make matters any worse than they already were, could it?

Twenty-four

Lord and Lady St. Clare bid their guests a smiling fare-well, but did not remain to see them to the door, leaving that office to Pamela and the butler. The two gentlemen made a point of having a private conversation with Pamela Stone just as Willby withdrew.

"Miss Stone," Mr. Bellfort whispered so the footman could not hear him. "Please, try to get yourself and Victorine away from this place as soon as ever you may. You may count on me for any assistance."

"Thank you so much. I will do so. Once the doctor arrives, I will ask his permission to take Victorine away. If he thinks she is well enough to travel, I shall send word to Melfield and to Fairmont." They shook hands warmly, and the Hon. John Whyte approached to take his leave.

"Pamela," John Whyte whispered, "Do take care of yourself."

He pressed her small hand meaningfully, and looked deep into her honest green eyes. "Trust me. I don't want to lose you, Pamela. It has taken me all of my life to find you."

"I am sorry to have been such a hornet, John."

"I never wanted a bread-and-butter miss in any case."

"Well, you have not got one, it appears. You have won the heart of a gently bred termagant in her first season."

Mr. John Whyte had to laugh.

"You're delicious, my dear. Believe me, the next time that woman tries to enveigle me, I shall find other ways to punish her."

"I hope so. If you must punish anyone in that extremely fast manner, I do hope that, considering all my dreadful follies and my unhappy tendency to jump the gun, as it were, you will be kind enough to do so to me. Some evening. In the moonlight. Soon."

"You, my pet," he replied, "Are becoming much too forward. Punish you I shall, and in just that sweet manner."

He swept her hand to his lips, and as he bade her farewell, she lost her balance, and swayed against him. He caught her in his arms, and looked at her with concern.

"Are you quite all right, Pamela?"

"Yes, of course, just a bit light-headed. It's the strain of Victorine's and my father's illness. I haven't slept well these past nights."

"Of course not. My dear, please, take care of yourself, do you hear me?"

"Yes, John."

"Trust me to find a way that we can be together."

"I will, John."

"I think you should leave here just as soon as possible. Charles quite agrees; we have discussed it at length. The atmosphere is quite unsuitable, and now that your aunt has been called away, I cannot feel comfortable with the two of you living here with Lady St. Clare to look after you. I find her—not of a character suitable to a chaperone, quite frankly."

"Do you not?" Pamela asked, with a wry gleam in her eyes.

"No, and this is not the time to discuss it further. Should this local doctor feel that Victorine's health would be seriously impaired by travelling long distances, we have begun looking for an alternative place for you to stay, somewhere not more than a half hour or hour's drive distant.

"In fact, there is a sister of Charles's living not far from here, Lady Flood, whom we are trying to contact. I will try to arrange that you leave to stay with her this afternoon or this evening at the very latest. Don't worry; do not be concerned. You are not alone. Charles and I will look after both of you."

He took her hands in his and clasped them tightly for a few moments. Her heart fluttered in her chest and she smiled for what seemed the first time in many days.

"Thank you, John. I am so very uncomfortable here now. Particularly without Aunt Charlton."

Just then Lady St. Clare came out into the front hall.

"Why, I thought you'd gone long ago, gentlemen! I should have seen you to the door myself, I know. Do forgive me," she said with barely disguised belligerence, eyeing the now-intertwined hands of Mr. Whyte and Miss Stone with a frigid and envious glance.

Pamela blushed, removed her hands from John Whyte's, and turned away; she realized their imprudence, and feared that the Viscountess would go and tell John's father what she had seen, thus setting off a chain of events whose end would be uncertain.

Noticing the fear on Pamela's face, her ladyship's scarlet lips turned up in a sneer that dissolved into a small, cold smile. She put her own bejeweled hands possessively upon Mr. Whyte's sleeve, and had the satisfaction of seeing Pamela stiffen, clench her jaw with determination, and turn away.

"John, my dear—I am happy to have caught you. I think your father wants to have a word with you. It seems that he is concerned about Miss Wells," she said with a searing look at Pamela.

"I shall go to him, then," replied John Whyte, "And then be off about my business. Good day, ladies. I shall see you later at home, then, Charles, shall I?"

He bowed and left.

Every time I am parted from him, thought Pamela to herself, *it seems as if part of myself is gone, too. And this time, inexplicably, I feel more lonely at parting from him than I ever have before.*

Lady St. Clare must have noticed the look of sadness on Pamela's face, for she lost no opportunity to throw a barb her way, as the doors closed behind the gentlemen. "Such an attractive man, John Whyte, isn't he? Isn't Victorine lucky to have caught him?"

"Has she caught him?" Pamela inquired evenly.

"Well, according to the Earl, and assuming that she recovers, which is, I suppose, by no means sure, it should be quite a settled thing."

"And according to Mr. John Whyte?"

"Well, but my dear, if he doesn't do as the Earl of Cleremont wishes, he will be forced to go into," and here she shuddered slightly, "into business! How shocking that would be! And of course, if he has no money at all, he cannot even really succeed in business, can he? So what will become of him? Shall he be a highwayman, then, to earn his bread? No, surely anyone can see that it would be far better if he married Miss Wells. Everyone thinks so; it is perfectly plain.

"If I were a friend of his, as you so obviously seem to be, Miss Stone, I would certainly advise him to take the prudent course. Any other action would be, I think, disastrous."

Torn with guilt and apprehensiveness about what would come of all this, Pamela made no reply.

"And, if you do not mind accepting the advice of your hostess, it is rather unseemly to be holding hands in public with a man who is all but betrothed to your cousin. Particularly when your cousin is so ill. It is really not the thing, Pamela. Is it?"

At this outrageous comment, Pamela turned on her heel, and strode away from the scheming little Frenchwoman. She was thus quite unable to perceive the small and horrid grin of triumph that defaced the Viscountess's otherwise lovely visage.

John Whyte entered his father's book-room, and waited some time for the Earl of Cleremont to look up from his reading. He then cleared his throat and began, "Excuse me, Father, but I am given to understand you wish to have speech with me before I leave?"

"Dear little Marguerite told you, did she? Yes, I do wish to have speech with you, John. Just wanted to tell you once again, with utmost clarity, that I haven't changed my mind about my plans for your marriage. And I shall not do so in the future."

"I had not expected that you would, sir. I am well acquainted with your resolute character and implacable disposition."

"Then we understand each other, do we, boy?"

"Perfectly, sir."

"An heiress, or nothing."

John inclined his head slightly, seething inwardly.

"There is a third alternative. You may remain at Melfield, unmarried, as you are, living on the Melfield income. I just don't want you breeding behind my back, as it were. If you want to give this Stone chit—or another one—carte blanche, we can discuss that. I'm not an ogre, you see. I understand the needs of young men."

His son suppressed a strong desire to rip his forebear into small shreds, and inclined his head once again to indicate that his father's words had been heard.

"Very well, then. You may go."

The Honorable John Whyte left his father's presence, furious once again. The situation became clearer every day, every moment: he *must* track down this person Derwent; no matter how, he *must* find an income of his own. To continue to remain at his father's whim and mercy was completely insupportable.

Pamela went into her chambers, drew the drapes, and lay down on the bed, her arm crossing over her forehead. She dozed for some time, then woke to find her eyes had become quite sensitive to the light. It hurt her so: she felt she longed for dark places, secret places where she could freely dream the dreams that were beginning to infiltrate her mind, like ocean waves whipped up into spindrift by a strong wind.

Helen Fraley tiptoed into the room, and peered down onto her mistress's prostrate form, surprised to see her laid abed. Pamela blinked herself awake.

"Oh, Helen—is that you?"

"Yes, miss. What is the matter with you?"

"I'm quite tired, rather knocked-up, I'm afraid. It's just the strain; the strain of all of this."

"I'm sorry to hear about your poor dear pa. You must be terribly worried."

"I am that."

"Well, rest then. Your aunt will take good care of him, and send for you just as soon as she may."

"Perhaps I shall rest, then."

Helen Fraley watched as her young mistress's eyes began to flutter closed. *I'm afeared for her, and that's the truth,* she thought to herself. *Don't know what's been going on here, but I just don't like the look of it. Don't like how it all smells.*

Helen walked out of the room, and decided she must contact Peter Welish. It was time, she realized, to bring in outside help to assist Miss Pamela and Miss Victorine. She couldn't like them being here without any more protection than came from that Lady St. Clare. Helen could not approve of the way that lady dressed or the way she conducted herself. There was something very vulgar about her indeed.

Thus, acting upon the very the best of intentions, the faithful abigail Helen Fraley, in order to arrange to bring assistance to her two young ladies, left her mistress behind at Haverford, asleep in her room, and quite alone.

Pamela slipped into an odd sleep, full of many broken, unquiet dreams, and was awakened well after nuncheon by a servant, unknown to her, who brought her a pot of freshly made tea. She was grateful for the beverage—it was just what she desired.

"Where is Helen?"

"She's gone off on an errand, Miss."

"What sort of errand?"

"Why, I'm sure I wouldn't know, Miss."

"Did she ask for the tea to be brought?"

"I can't say, Miss. Quite prob'ly, though 'twas Cook what told me to bring it, 's all I know. Ye missed nuncheon, after all, and everybody noticed."

"Thank you."

Drinking the tea made her feel a bit refreshed, if still languid. Pamela decided she had contracted the influenza, very surely. What a thing—first Victorine, then Papa, and now her own health uncertain! Bad things coming in threes.

Still, she knew she must check on Victorine, and so managed to right herself, make herself tidy, and make her way to her cousin's rooms. She felt rather guilty at having left Victorine in such hysterics earlier in the day, but thought that the laudanum drops must have allowed her cousin to have some sort of a rest. When would the doctor arrive? she wondered impatiently. When could they leave this place?

Victorine, to her surprise, was awake and alone, sitting in an armchair with a shawl wrapped tight around her, staring out of the window. She didn't notice Pamela enter her room, but looked at her in an almost uncaring way when she came nearer.

"Victorine?"

No answer.

"Victorine, can you please tell me what's the matter?"

No answer. The blue eyes staring out into space.

"Victorine, I don't know what has happened to you, but I know it is a very serious matter indeed, or you would never behave in this way, would you?"

Victorine nodded agreement.

"Now, we two have known each other all our lives, haven't we? And you know you can trust me, don't you?"

Two large tears like pearls slipped down the poor girl's cheek. A horrifying thought entered into Pamela Stone's head for the first time.

"Has someone—has someone taken . . . I don't know how to put it more delicately . . . has anyone taken advantage of you, Victorine?"

No answer. More silent tears. Many more silent tears, one after another, running in a slow cascade down Victorine's face.

"My God. Can you tell me who it is?"

A shake of the head. Tears again. Many more tears, but not a sound.

"Victorine, listen to me. You are safe now. I don't know what has happened to you, but the details don't matter at all. I will see to it that you are safe, and see to it that we leave this house by this very evening. I promise you that. Are you well enough to travel a little distance, just to get away?"

A nod of the head in agreement.

"Don't be frightened. Whatever may have happened, we will get you away from here, do you hear me? And then you will be well again, do you hear me? You will be fine, I promise. No matter what has happened, I will see to it that it is all made right."

Victorine turned her beautiful face, now deathly pale and stained with a thousand tears, toward her cousin, and asked in a shaken, childlike voice, "How shall it ever be all right again, cousin?"

Pamela threw her arms around Victorine and hugged her until at last her cousin hugged her back and buried her face in her shoulder, sobbing hopelessly, uncontrollably, inconsolably.

"Oh, God—do you fail to comprehend my meaning, cousin? I am a ruined woman! How can you bear to soil your hands with the horrid touch of me?"

"My dear, hush. Oh, my poor, sweet, dear! Who can have done this to you?"

But her cousin had once again beaten retreat into her lost universe, her world of mute numbness, and to that painful question, there was to be no reply.

Twenty-five

Despite an increasing dizziness and general sense of disorientation, Pamela was able to pack Victorine's things into some trunks, and then return to her own rooms to ask Helen Fraley to finish doing the same for herself. Helen, unfortunately, was still nowhere to be found. The person who came in response to a rung bell was the nameless servant who had supplied her earlier with tea, and who could give her no idea what had become of her own maid.

Nevertheless, Pamela sent the girl downstairs with instructions that a carriage was to be placed at their disposal as soon as possible, and orders that Helen Fraley must be located immediately. She set about packing up her belongings all by herself.

The girl returned with the news that Helen was thought to have gone over to Melfield to meet Peter Welish. Pamela cursed her situation in the most genteel manner possible; how could she leave without Helen? What could Helen have been thinking, to go off jauntering like that, without leave? Tracking her down only meant more delay, and Pamela felt instinctively that there was no time to lose, that their exodus had to be accomplished immediately.

Some minutes later, there was further unhappy news. The scrupulously correct Mr. Willby sent, by means of the young serving girl, to Miss Stone his most sincere regrets that he was unable to order a carriage put to for the use of the two young ladies until he received direct instructions to that effect from his lordship the Earl or his lordship Viscount St. Clare.

"Oh, drat the man! But I suppose it is quite proper. Tell Willby, if you please, that I therefore desire to see the Lord Cleremont at his lordship's very earliest convenience, in order to beg this favor of him."

"Yes, mum. I'll tell Mr. Willby, mum."

Not long afterward, Miss Pamela Stone was ushered into the august presence of his lordship, the Earl of Cleremont. He looked his visitor up and down in a weary, bored manner, and waited for her to name her business. She said nothing, but stood patiently until he was forced to address her.

"Do you imagine yourself to be viewing the Elgin Marbles, young lady? If that is the explanation for your having come here to view me in silence, I must inform you that I am sentient and may be spoken to. Just why have you sought this private interview?" his lordship inquired.

Lord Cleremont yawned, and went on, "I do hope you haven't come here to beg me for my permission for you to marry my younger son, for I assure you nothing could persuade me to assent to such a disastrous match for him."

Miss Pamela Stone sank into a scarlet fury, and bit back her words, asking only for what she had come to ask for.

"If you please, your lordship, I should like the favor of borrowing a travelling carriage to take my cousin and myself away from here."

"My dear Miss . . . Stone, is it? I wonder greatly that you and your family should assume that we at Haverford are running a stagecoach service for our guests."

Pamela flushed red with humiliation.

"Do my words embarrass you, child? Just as well. I am glad to see you come to some consciousness of your encroaching behavior."

It took all of Miss Pamela Stone's good breeding to keep her from flinging a most stinging set-down at his lordship, but she kept quiet, though she was appalled at being so mistreated.

"Your travelling plans are naturally no business of mine, although I should like to point out that I have already extended myself so far as to put my own best chaise at the disposal of that aunt of yours so she could see to the sudden illness of your father . . . which I trust is not all just a hum? Most inconvenient for me, as you may imagine. I may be a peer of the realm, but just how many carriages do you suppose I keep at one time, girl? Eh?"

Pamela made no reply and the Earl continued his remonstrance.

"I think you demanding in the extreme after all we have already done to assist you; if you require yet *another* travelling carriage, you had best apply to my son Miles. You are his guest, after all, not mine, and I keep only the two carriages in these increasingly expensive times, you understand, and cannot spare the one that's left. After all, why should I? You and your family are nothing to me. Miles has several carriages, so if you wish to importune anyone, importune him."

Pamela replied, in her most frigidly correct manner, "I thank you so much for your kind condescension, my lord Earl."

"Not at all. I am very happy to help any of these tiresome late-staying ball guests to remove from Haverford and leave me in peace. In particular I am happy to assist you to leave Haverford. The sooner you stop trying to entangle the affections of my dear son John, the better it will be for everyone. Won't it?"

Pamela did not dignify this comment with a reply. She merely curtseyed and left the room. She shivered and pulled her shawl around her as she walked down past the main gallery.

Once in the corridor, perhaps due to the stress of the day and such a disquieting conversation, Pamela found herself having a bit of trouble walking and focusing her eyes. She had to lean against the wall of the corridor for support, and thought it best she should retire to her room for a bit in order to recover herself and wait for Helen's arrival.

The arrogance of Lord Cleremont! The colossal arrogance! Never had she been treated in such a manner! She made her mind up to finish her packing, find the Viscount, and apply to him for the use of his travelling carriage at once. If it were not forthcoming, she would leave her bags, take her cousin, and escape to Melfield on foot.

In nearby Tiverton, Mr. John Whyte was making inquiries at the Boar's Head Inn after a certain person calling himself Edgar Derwent. The white-haired, ruddy-faced innkeeper regarded Mr. Whyte with some suspicion, as he offered him a tankard of ale.

"Derwent? What business be he in?" asked the innkeeper. "And who might you be, sir, if I may be so bold as to ask?"

"I'm John Whyte of Haverford, the Earl of Cleremont's second son. I'm interested in finding out what has become of this Derwent, as I'm told the man was, some years ago, my late mother's man of business. My mother, Julia Pembroke, was Lord Cleremont's second wife; she died when I was still a boy. I heard that there was such an Edgar Derwent lately to be found here. Do you know anything of this fellow? Can you tell me where he might be found? It's most important."

The man fixed John Whyte with a greedy gaze and said nothing, waiting.

John Whyte held out a guinea, and the inn-keeper paused no more than a moment before taking it into his hand.

"Derwent? Julia, Countess of Cleremont's man of business? No, I can't recall him, but I do recall that there was a deal of talk about her fortune just around the time that the poor lady died. I can't put my finger on what it was; it's been a long time, and I'm getting so old, if you catch my meanin'."

Mr. Whyte held out another guinea. The man took it.

"Don't think it was any good kind of story, though, as best I recall. You must keep in mind, sir, that that scandal took place a long time ago; I disremember the details of what happened. Edgar Derwent, did you say?

"No, that ain't right. No, the man's name wasn't Derwent—come to think on it, her ladyship's man of business was a good customer of mine at that time. Knew him a bit, I did. I kin recall his face, but what was his name? Devlin? Darwin?"

A third guinea was put on the counter and duly pocketed.

"Why, sir, that's kind of you, and, Lord bless me, I kin

remember now! His name wasn't Derwent, it was Durward! That's it! Harry Durward! Thick-set fellow, with a
good brain in his head. The soul of honesty, if that's what
you're worrying over. How came you to think his name
Derwent?"

"My source was clearly in error. It has been so many
years, after all. Where is this man Durward, then? I heard
he had come here. Is that, at least, true?"

"Well, no, I don't believe that's true. Harry don't live
in these parts, no more."

"Would you know where he has gone, or is there anyone I might ask?"

More money changed hands.

"Well, now, I seem to think Harry Durward went to
retire up North. Sure, there was a lady here in these parts
he was particular friendly with, by the name of Anna
Halpern. She still lives in Barlowe on a farm called Wall's
End. You might ask after him there, sir."

John Whyte gave the innkeeper a last note for his
trouble, and set off in the direction of Haverford for the
nearby village of Barlowe. He went off so fast, that his
horse was nearly winded by the time they arrived.

Helen Fraley reached the Melfield farm in time to
catch Peter Welish before he had left the farm to do his
normal rounds of errands, deliveries, inspections, and the
like. When Mr. Whyte was in London, Peter's work was
that of a gentleman's gentleman, but once they were back
out in the country, there was too much work to be done
managing the farm for Peter to spend all his time as a
valet. That's why Peter liked working for Mr. John

Whyte—good wages, fair treatment, and a good variety of duties in town and country.

Helen arrived out of breath, rather a bit dishevelled, with her crop of curly red hair whipping around her head; she had run over the fields most of the way from Haverford, needing more than an hour to do so.

"What's this? Helen? What's the matter, luv? You're not telling me you came all this way on foot?" he asked, sweeping her into his arms for a welcoming kiss.

"The carter took pity on me, and gave me a ride. Listen, Peter, we're trying to go away from Haverford, the young misses and I. We have to leave, right away. There's something wrong going on; I can feel it. Can you get a message to your master and to Mr. Bellfort? Perhaps you can arrange for a post-chaise?"

"Yes, I can, but not without Mr. Whyte's permission, and he's not here."

"Where's he gone? You must find him."

"It can wait till the master returns, surely. He said he'd be back in a couple of hours' time."

"It won't wait. Miss Pamela's not been herself: she's sickening or something like. Both the young misses aren't well, and I'm real worried for them. Miss Pamela's been trying to leave on her own, but I don't know if she can. They've no carriage or horses of their own. If Mr. Whyte and Mr. Bellfort would just come and help them to get out of that horrid place, I'm sure that everything would turn out all right."

"Fair enough to get 'em away, then, but why the mortal hurry? It looks queer enough that you ran off to see *me*. If the young ladies were to leave suddenly, in the company of the two gentlemen, it will just make a scandal.

Do you really think they can't wait for Miss Victorine's mother to send for them properly?"

"You haven't seen how they are, Peter. They're not well, I tell you—neither one of them. I'm not pitching you a whisker, I swear it. That house and all those people are just as you said—they're not right, none of them. I took some tea given to Miss Pamela this morning, and it smelled—it smelled odd, like. I think someone in that house means to do them a great mischief, and will do so while her ladyship's not there to look out after them. You can tell Mr. John and Mr. Charles I said so, if you think it will bring 'em to Haverford any quicker."

"Devil take it, lass, you think someone's been drugging them? That's a different tale altogether. That news'll bring the gentlemen riding down straight away, I warrant. Don't go back, lest they do to you what they did to Maud. Stay here, and I'll track down Mr. Whyte and Mr. Bellfort and bring 'em there quick. Don't you worry."

Having given Helen a peck on the cheek and a fond pat on her bottom, Peter Welish set out for Fairmont, Mr. Bellfort's estate, which marched with Melfield; he felt sure Mr. Charles Bellfort would know of Mr. John Whyte's whereabouts, and his exact plans. Peter knew his master said he'd gone to Tiverton. Mr. Bellfort might know the rest of John Whyte's afternoon's engagements. It wouldn't do to go off half-cocked in the wrong direction, and even if he was able only to locate Mr. Charles Bellfort, Mr. Bellfort would be able to give orders on what should be done.

Pamela Stone was sitting in her bedchamber, looking down at her own two hands. They seemed completely unfamiliar to her. Her entire sense of reality was shifting, slowly shifting. It was hard to put together two reasonable thoughts in a row; she could not recall how long she had been sitting in her room. She felt her will dissolving into a soft and sensuous haze in which everything that had seemed so terribly important just a few minutes back had ceased to matter in any way at all.

There was a knock on the door. The door opened. It was that silly maid of Victorine's, Madame Darcher. She was saying that Pamela should follow her to go and meet the Viscount so that the carriage could be ordered to take her and her cousin away to Easton.

A great vagueness had descended upon Pamela's consciousness, as if she were inspecting the succession of her thoughts from a great distance.

Carriage? Why did we need a carriage? Ah, yes, of course, we are going to leave Haverford. I must needs ask St. Clare's permission to use it. Now I recall.

Very well, thought Pamela to herself, as she walked unsteadily after Madame Darcher through the halls and the galleries, up a long stone staircase, walking for a considerable distance. I will follow this woman, and I will ask for the carriage, and then I will lie down to take a nice, long nap. I need a nice, long nap. It's been such a difficult day.

When she reached the door that Darcher indicated, having walked for what seemed like a very long time, she was completely exhausted, and longed to curl up on a settle and have a rest.

Madame Darcher opened the great door for her, and inside she could see a beautiful room decorated in scarlet velvet, with the Viscount St. Clare within, looking very handsome, smiling at her and extending his hand to her.

She held out hers, he took it, and pressed it to his lips.

"Father sent word that you wanted to see me. How can I be of service to you, Miss Stone? I am so glad you were finally able to find time to come to me, my dear," said the Viscount, indicating a velvet-covered carved mahogany chair to her left.

"You are glad I came?" said Pamela in a far-off, disoriented manner, as his lordship escorted her into the room. "What a pretty room you have up here! So many paintings! And so many mirrors!"

"All the better to see your lovely face in, my child."

Pamela found herself giggling inancly. "Why, your lordship, you sound like a character in a fairy tale!"

"Do I, my dear? Here, have a glass of this tonic. It will do you good; you seem a bit weary."

"Yes, I am that, Lord St. Clare."

"I can see on your pretty face that you've had a trying day. What a horrid shame! Of course, it's been difficult for you, poor dear. Everything has been going wrong of late for you, hasn't it? My father was too harsh with you today—I could tell; he's old, and he gets easily out of temper. I do apologize. Believe me, you have my full sympathy."

"Lord Cleremont didn't give us use of his carriage. May we please have the use of yours?"

"The carriage? But of course you may! There could be no question of it! You may use it with all my compliments!"

"Then Victorine and I shall be taking our leave now. Thank you for your gracious hospitality."

"I'm so sorry that you must go, but, of course, your family responsibilities are paramount. However, I couldn't think of letting you go until you have had some refreshment. Here," said he, pouring out a glass of amber-colored liquid.

"Oh! Thank you so much for your kindness, this is exactly what I needed! Mmm—it tastes a little like one of those French liqueurs, the ones those monks make, chartreuse, I think they call it."

"It is a tonic much like that, but with additional restorative ingredients. I know you now are burdened by many cares, many cares. My condolences on your father's illness."

"Poor father! How horrid of me—I had almost forgotten—my mind keeps wandering, terribly. Why do you suppose that is? I don't feel at all myself. Of course, if I'm not myself, who am I feeling like, that's the question. Isn't it?"

She giggled another inappropriate giggle, then caught herself.

"Oh, do forgive me, your lordship. I'm knocked-up and rather giddy."

"Don't give it a thought. You must be very tired. I'm sure you must be very weary indeed, Miss Stone. Why don't you have a seat here, my dear?"

He patted a sofa, and she came to him. His ravenous eyes caught hers, and held them in a mesmerizing grip. She began to breathe faster.

He caught her hand, and helped her to the sofa. She was so near to him, he could smell the sweet perfume of her breath.

What a virile man the Viscount is, Pamela was thinking to herself, as thoughts of every hue danced about within her befuddled mind. *What a very handsome and magnetic man.*

How attentively he is looking after me. I do love the

taste of this punch. Or is it tonic? What did he call it?
Ah, yes, a restorative tonic. It makes me feel deliciously
languid and warm.

"You must be entirely overset, my child. Let me help
you off with that shawl. It is quite warm in here, I find."

And as his lordship slipped the shawl off Pamela's
shoulders, his lips found the nape of her neck, which his
lordship began to shower with a long series of tender
kisses.

The Hon. John Whyte was coming back to Melfield
from Barlowe when he saw Peter Welish riding like the
wind in the general direction of Fairmont; when Peter
saw his master, he hailed him, and they both pulled their
horses up short.

"Oh, sir, I've been lookin' for ye!" he said, breathless.

"Yes, Peter?"

"I'm afraid there's some trouble, sir. My Helen came
to me from Haverford. It's the young ladies, sir, Helen
says they need to get out of there right now, sir, she thinks
something no good's been going on there. Can you come
now, sir?"

"A moment. What things have been going on?"

"She thinks the servants have been lacing the young
ladies' drinks with—something, I don't know what, medicines, or such-like. She's real worried, and wants that you
and Mr. Bellfort come by and take the misses somewhere
safe right away."

"The devil you say! Peter, you ride to Bellfort's."

"I was just on my way there."

"Get him, and have him meet us at the great elm in
front of Haverford Park. Have him bring a weapon—

sword or pistol, doesn't signify. He should bring his man, too—we may need him. I'll wait at the elm tree directly after I get my pistol. We'll get Miss Wells and Miss Stone out of that damned place if we have to take our leave riding two on a horse. Drugs, by God! Someone's going to pay a dear price for this mischief."

They wheeled their horses and rode off.

"Oh, sir, Whatever can you be doing?" cried Pamela.

"I am kissing the nape of your neck, Miss Stone. Isn't it obvious?"

"But you mustn't *do* such a thing!"

"I just did, my dear. Was it terribly unpleasant? I shouldn't think so."

"Not precisely, but—my God, what have you done to me? What am I saying?"

"I have no idea, really. And furthermore, whatever you have to say about it doesn't signify at all. It is time to further our acquaintance, Miss Stone," said his lordship, holding her tight within a powerful embrace.

Lady St. Clare had not been content to watch the long-awaited seduction of Miss Pamela Stone from the spyhole, so had secreted herself in an arras well-concealed by thick velvet hangings. She thus had an excellent view of the ongoing proceedings and was enjoying herself immensely. It was far more engaging than any Drury Lane melodrama, and her husband far more charismatic to watch even than an actor like Kean.

When her husband had first begun touching Miss Stone, the drowsy young girl had tried to push St. Clare away, but he merely caught her two hands easily in one of his, and proceeded to implant his kisses all over her soft, white bosom while she cried for assistance that, naturally enough, did not appear.

He then let her go, walked casually over to the champagne, poured himself a glass, and drained it. He carefully poured another glass of champagne for Pamela, offered it to her, and in return, received its contents full in the face. He wiped his countenance with a handkerchief, but did not seem fazed in the least. He even smiled a little, apparently amused by her attempts at resistance.

"Oh, dear God! Let me out of here!" she cried, and ran for the door, struggling with the handle and beating on it with her fist.

"It's locked from the outside, my dearest. You may try it once again, if you wish."

"You monster! You are the one who turned my dear sweet cousin into—into a damaged person, into a ghost of the beautiful girl she was before!"

"Yes, I am the one. And you are right—along with losing her maidenhead, poor Victorine *has* quite lost her looks. What a pity! Had she remained more attractive, I might not have gotten around to knowing you so soon, Miss Stone. But she had begun to bore me. A pretty enough child—and then, tragically, but two nights afterward, she became—not so pretty. And never very bright."

"How can you speak of her that way! I demand that you release me at once! You are a devil! A libertine!"

The Viscount St. Clare laughed and laughed, shook his head in apparent wonder, and tossed another soothing glass of champagne down his throat.

"Good God, girl—of course I'm a libertine! Do you expect a libertine to release you? You must have taken leave of your senses. You've arrived at last in this special chamber, and I welcome you, with all my heart. Once I have taken from you just what it is that I desire of you—your maidenhead—I shall let you go. But not before."

"I'll scream so the whole household will waken!"

"Now you sound like your silly cousin Victorine. She screamed too, and what did it avail her? Nothing. A great deal of planning, I should point out, has gone into this room; it is very well designed, and it was designed with the purpose in mind of achieving a sanctuary of utter privacy. And it has always worked well, I assure you.

"I do hate to repeat myself, but I will tell you just what I told your darling little feather-headed cousin: you are very far away from the rest of the household, and this room is entirely built of thick stone. No one is going to hear your screams; no one is going to come and rescue you."

Pamela could not speak, and Lord St. Clare continued on in his bored, faintly amused fashion.

"It is a very classical situation. You are a well-educated young lady; I'm sure you can appreciate that. You are entirely in my power. Entirely. I have left nothing to chance: I want you to understand that very well."

Pamela almost wanted to laugh when she heard this; the last time anyone had said such a thing to her had been in fun, and by someone who valued her, even loved her; now it was said to her in deadly earnest by a man who had no morals at all.

"Now, Pamela, take a few moments to consider your position in a rational manner. You shall give me what I want of your own free will—more or less—or I will ravish you and take from you what I want in any case. Is that perfectly clear?

"You may take some time to think about whether you wish me to act with, or without, your consent. It is completely up to you, my child. Completely.

"Willing or unwilling, Miss Stone—it's all the same to me. I'm afraid there's no time to contemplate deliverance, or even to pray for it. Your fate, my dear girl, was sealed the very moment you were unwise enough to enter into this room."

Twenty-six

The Hon. John Whyte and Mr. Charles Bellfort, Peter Welish, and Bellfort's man Adam Hackney rode full out up to the Haverford stables, pulled up their horses in a fever, and jumped down, not bothering to wait for anyone to see to their horses.

The four entered the house from a door at the rear, while footmen stepped back to let them pass, intimidated by their air of sheer determination. Following John Whyte's lead, they ran up the back stairs to the chamber where Helen had said Victorine was staying. Miss Wells was still resting abed, her blond hair scattered like a halo over her pillow. She was unattended.

"Miss Wells!" cried Mr. Bellfort. "Please—we have come to take you away. Will you come with me?"

Victorine tipped her sweet face up at him, and looked at him as if he were her savior, saying, "Oh, please, Charles, if you only *would* take me away! Now, please, Charles; take me away, now!"

"Take her now, man. Get her to your house at once. Miss Wells, how long will it take us to reach Miss Stone's room?"

Victorine thought for a long moment.

"Pamela's room is perhaps ten minutes away, it's in the Old West wing, but I don't believe she's in there."

"Where might she be?"

"I think that they've brought her to—the room. The other room."

"The room? What room?"

Victorine's most far away and childlike voice replied, "The one that's very, very far away, and made of stone, and if you scream there, they tell you no one will hear your screams. And they can't hear you, I can tell you, because I screamed and screamed and screamed, but nobody ever heard me."

"What are you talking about?" said Charles Bellfort, aghast. "Victorine, what has been done to you?"

"Oh, Mr. Bellfort, please, don't ask me! I'm lost! Sunk beneath reproach! How can you bear to touch me—I'm so ashamed!" and she threw her arms around him, weeping onto his broad shoulders.

"My dearest girl, you need feel no shame in front of me, I assure you. I have always had the very greatest regard for you, and will continue to have that regard, no matter what difficulties may have befallen you. Please understand that I mean just what I say. I am not a small-minded person. Listen to me—I love you, Victorine."

He took her hand in his; trust and tenderness shone out from his eyes. She managed to give him a small, quivering smile.

"Tell me what has happened," he said softly, with neither curiosity nor rancor. Victorine looked at the ground, and a tear slipped down her cheek.

"Is it that you been mistreated?" Mr. Bellfort asked, tenderly brushing a few dishevelled wisps of golden hair away from her brow.

Victorine nodded slowly in reply.

"Who did it? Was it St. Clare?" demanded John Whyte.

Victorine hesitated, at first frightened a little by Mr. Whyte's display of anger, and then she nodded her assent. Both men paled visibly, then their pallor swiftly transformed into a livid anger.

"By God, there's viciousness rampant in this damned house! Take her back to Fairmont, Charles; you may need Adam as well to get her out, so take him. Peter and I will search for Pamela."

"It will be my honor to take her into my care. Come, my dear. You will need a cloak." Mr. Bellfort took her arm and led her away to safety; she clung to him gratefully, trustingly.

And Victorine, leaning on the strong arm of Charles Bellfort, was freed.

Moments later, the Hon. John Whyte burst into the leathered silence of his father's study, and demanded to know what had become of Miss Stone. His father, enraged at this heedless violation of his sanctuary, glared at John, saying, "I don't know what's become of her, and furthermore, I don't care. Now, get out of here! And get out of Melfield! Do you hear? I've had enough of your stupidity!"

"I don't give a damn about Melfield, Father! And I don't give a damn about you and your libertine heir! Can it be that you don't know what is going on under your very own roof? I doubt it very much. Are you that blind and deaf as well?"

"Damn you, puppy! Get out of here! Forever!" roared

the Earl, throwing another glass of sherry down his thin, withered throat.

The Hon. John Whyte's voice dropped to a low, un-yielding note.

"Tell me where Miles has taken Pamela. Miss Wells says she's been taken somewhere deep within the house— you must know where she is. Where, Father? Where within this dreadful travesty of a castle could Miles take her if he didn't wish to be found?"

"Father? Hah! I'm not your father, you stupid young bastard! Your mother was nothing but a whore! A rich whore, but a whore nonetheless! You're Webster's brat, much good may that do you!"

"Don't you dare to speak of my mother in that way!"

"Why should I not? Her stupid father got foxed, and lost his daughter in a game of faro! What a joke! I won her for her money, and she never bedded me, I'll tell you, because I never bedded her! You hear me? Never once touched a hair of her vile, pious body! Never once! Never wished to!"

It took all of John Whyte's great strength to refrain from relieving this vile old man of his ability to speak or act ever again, but, once again, he remain in utter control of his emotions.

"Tell me where Miles is."

"I don't have to! I'm not going to! I'm telling you about your mother—how much it pained old Pembroke to have to give her up to me: he knew what I was, only too well. I only took her, 'cause I knew it pained him. His daughter was good for absolutely nothing—except for payin' the bills. That's where Julia shone!"

The Hon. John Whyte took the Earl of Cleremont by

his thin, frail shoulders, as Cleremont began to cough and to wheeze, struggling for breath.

"Ring that bell, puppy. I need my medicine," growled his lordship.

"I'll ring it when you've told me where he's taken Pamela."

"How the devil should I know? I'm too old for that sort of thing, don't you know that? Pull that bell rope, bastard."

"Tell me where she is," said John Whyte in a hard, uncompromising voice, starting to shake sense into the old man.

His father's face grew red with rage. "She's up in the tower! No, in the dungeon! How the blazes should I know? You ring that bell, do you hear me?"

"No."

"It's none of your business what Miles does!" cried Cleremont, wheezing, and gasping for breath again.

"As you wish, Cleremont."

John Whyte backed to the door and added, "I am happy to learn that you and Miles and I don't share even one single drop of the same blood. If you were any kind of man at all, you would be ashamed of your son. Be sure that I'll find Miles, and that I'll see him hang for this work he's done!"

The Earl began screaming and screaming with rage, "Ring the bell for my man, damn you to hell! Miles'll be up in the tower, I warrant! Much good it will do you. Remember, Miles is a peer of the realm—you'll never see him hang, no matter what he's done! I did the same myself when I was his age! He's just a man, with a real man's desires, not some weak, pious man-milliner like yourself! Pull the bell rope! Pull it, bastard! Or do you want to kill me? It'll be your neck on the gibbet, then, I promise you!"

"Which tower?"

"The South Tower, stupid fool; that's where our family's always takcn our tarts!"

John Whyte firmly rejected the thought of striking down the man he had for so many years regarded as his closest kin, a man whom he had always tried to treat with filial respect; he pulled the bell rope. He looked at the earl's thin and wrinkled face with undisguised contempt.

"Stay here with him, Peter, till his own man comes, then come after me. But make sure he comes to no harm."

As Lord Cleremont's furious ravings continued behind him, he shut the door and ran toward the passageway leading to the South Tower, Charles Bellfort's pistol ready in his hand.

His Lordship, the Right Honorable Miles Whyte, Third Viscount St. Clare, had been forced to employ conduct unbecoming a gentleman in order to deal with the intransigent Miss Pamela Stone. His lordship had accomplished this feat with nothing to show for the struggle but a blue bruise near his left eye, and a long bloody scratch where his unwilling companion had had the unmitigated audacity to rake her nails across his cheek.

St. Clare, no longer fully dressed, was still trying to convince Miss Stone of the necessity of swift compliance with his carnal ambitions when the sound of a struggle outside the oaken door reached his ears, but he paid no heed, intent on first winning the battle closest to him. Pamela, on her part, was intent upon rising above her drugged state in order to wield her best weapon against him—her wit.

"Pamela, my dear," Lord Cleremont was saying ingratiatingly to that glaring girl, "you must know that your vast beauty is merely enhanced by your fury."

"Oh, spare me! God, St. Clare, not *that* old chestnut!" cried Pamela, her voice filled with contempt. "I know of nothing more ludicrous than a hardened rake who resorts to banalities to have his own way with a wench."

Tears, pleadings beyond count he was immune to, but it was this vicious home thrust that proved the last straw for Lord St. Clare. His patience fully exhausted, he had decided on taking the insolent chit by force when he heard a soft cry of surprise escape from Darcher's lips. He heard the sound of a mill and then a sick, thudding noise.

The key in the iron lock rattled loudly; the door was thrown back, and John Whyte strode into the room.

"John! Thank God!" cried Pamela, trying to cover herself, tears welling up in her eyes as she tried to pull up her ruined gown.

"I'll kill you for this, Miles," John Whyte said, with great civility to the Viscount. His pistol was pointed and cocked. "I shall kill you."

Before his lordship could offer the favor of a reply, Lady St. Clare stepped out from behind the hangings, walked to the bed, and pointed a long-nosed, well-polished brass pistol at Miss Stone's head. The first, disorienting thought that passed through Pamela's astonished mind was that her ladyship seemed oddly overdressed for an armed woman.

Marguerite Perigord de la Tour, the Viscountess St. Clare, was dressed as if for some grand ball, in a gown of blue gauze over a silk underskirt; her thick black locks were piled high upon her head, with one diamond-and-pearl crescent winking through her curls. Her ladyship's delicate neck, wrists, and earlobes were ornamented with a set of dazzling diamonds. She shot an almost flirtatious glance at the Hon. John Whyte.

"Why, John! *Mon Dieu!* What a very nice surprise! How very nice to see you, as ever! What brings you here? Do you as well care to enter into a spot of fun?"

"Get away from Pamela, you shameless jade."

"But I don't *want* to get away from her, my dear boy. I want to kill her. Didn't you know that? I tried to do so once before, when she was on horseback in the Park. Don't you recall?"

Pamela stared in bare astonishment at the lovely, vicious Viscountess, asking, "Why ever should you wish to kill me? What ever have I done?"

"I suppose, my dear, that you have done nothing at all, boring little chit that you are. However, *Monsieur* Whyte likes you very much, and that, for me, is reason enough.

"That was why I wanted to kill you then, and why I wish to kill you now. Throw your gun down now, John Whyte, throw your gun down at my little feet—and, see? My ankles are charmingly turned, do you not agree? But I digress. Throw your gun down now, John, or I shall be forced to—to—how do you say *een Eenglish?*—I shall be forced to blow her head off."

John Whyte glowered, but did not immediately surrender his weapon.

He asked, "What assurance have I, ma'am, that you will keep your word?"

Lady St. Clare laughed her small, attractive, bell-like laugh.

"No assurance at all, *mon cher.* Keep your gun if you wish. I really can't be bothered, in any case, either way. I prefer to take her life right here in front of you so you realize completely well that you are to be parted from this silly girl for all time."

Pamela asked again in a small voice, her eyes unable to leave off looking at the gun that was still pointing toward her left temple, "Please, your ladyship. One moment more of your time. I did not understand: once again, could you please explain why should you want to do this to me?"

"I just told you, you silly fool. Are you quite deaf? You are a threat to me. You always have been, and as long as you exist, I will be unable to do as I wish with him. With Mr. John Whyte. You see, *I* like him. And I want him. And I will have him, whatever the cost."

"You will?" interrupted his lordship St. Clare, suddenly turning toward his wife.

"Why yes, dear. Surely you do not object!"

"I do object!"

"But Miles, I have kissed him, that night at the Haverford ball, and he is utterly delectable. I want him for myself alone, and I am going to have him. I am going to keep John here, in this room, for myself. Forever. *Toujours!*"

"You are not! I do not permit it!"

"How can you talk such nonsense to me, Miles? How many little girls have you brought up into this room, with my full help and cooperation, for you to deny me anything of a similar nature? Tell me that!"

"You can have any man you want—except him!" shouted the Viscount, banging his fist on the mahogany center table, till the cut-glass decanter crashed and broke on the Aubusson-carpeted floor, spilling its contents, and creating a deep, dark-maroon stain.

"I told you, I don't want any man *but* him! I love him!"

"Love him? Love him, do you?" shouted Viscount St. Clare, his face livid. "Damn you, woman, I don't care if you bed him, but love him you shall not! You're my wife! Does that mean nothing at all to you? I'll kill you, you doxy, do you hear me?" and he sprang at Lady St. Clare, grabbing for her gun, wrenching her wrist savagely.

As soon as the angle of the muzzle shifted, Pamela ducked down, and then she bolted, running as fast as she was able into the Hon. John Whyte's arms, the ultimate sanctuary. John quickly turned over the center table, unbound Pamela's wrists, covered her in her shawl, and enfolded her in his strong embrace, rocking her back and forth as if she were a frightened child whose nightmare could be taken away merely by the security of loving contact.

"Don't be alarmed," he whispered to her. "Peter Welish will be bringing help soon. You are quite safe here with me now."

The two of them stayed behind the overturned table, watching with incredulity at the scene that continued to unfold in front of their horrified eyes. The Hon. John Whyte kept a pistol pointed at Lord St. Clare and his wife, but no shot could he fire; direct intervention in their deadly marital quarrel was not to be considered.

The Viscount struck the Viscountess full in the face; she returned his blow with a stinging slap. They struggled on fiercely, each one an even match for the other; they tumbled from one side of the room to another, overturning furniture and breaking glassware in a flurry of fury, until, of a sudden, the gun exploded with a deafening report, and Lord St. Clare doubled over and slipped to the ground.

Dark red blood began to issue forth from a wound near his stomach, and Lady St. Clare, her hands flying to her cheeks, a look of deadly horror on her visage, began howling in unmitigated anguish, like a dying beast.

"Miles! Oh, *Dieu! Merde!* I didn't mean it, Miles!" she cried, cradling her husband in her arms, and kissing his forehead, his cheeks, his white aristocratic hands.

"Know you didn't, dearest. Silly mistake," whispered his lordship to his wife, clutching her hands in his and kissing them.

"Oh, Miles, don't die! Don't die! You know how much I love you, don't you? Don't you?"

"Yes, love."

"That other—was just a momentary passion. I don't care for your brother a bit. It doesn't matter what I said— it wasn't true! I don't love him! I never did! I don't give a damn about him, not really, not deeply—I swear it!"

"Know you don't. Know you loved me, wench," gasped the Viscount, struggling to maintain consciousness with decreasing success.

"I can't live without you, Miles, *mon cher, mon cher.* I'll get a doctor, now. Just you wait, all right? Promise me you will wait a while," she said in a voice of utter desperation. *"Un moment!"*

"Don't go away to get him, Marguerite. Don't leave me, dearest. I'm all done, I fear. I don't blame you, dear girl, you must realize that. You've been a good wife to me, and a good, true, unselfish friend and lover. Always helped me with whatever I wanted to accomplish. Thank you, darling. For everything."

"Miles!"

"I'm sorry. This is the end, love. I cannot wait. *Adieu, ma chere.*"

"Miles!" she shrieked in terrifying tones, as his lordship's head, which she had been cradling so tenderly in her lap, fell slack and silent. For a few moments she let her fingertips idly trace the features of her husband's face, then stroked his cheek once or twice with a trembling hand, and gently let his body down on to the carpet. She came over to the bed, removed a silken pillow from it, and brought it back to set softly beneath the Viscount's now still head.

Then, sitting next to his body, she rocked back and forth on her heels, keening.

"Il est mort! Je suis morte! Morte!"

The Viscountess St. Clare looked up at the ceiling, with a helpless, disbelieving expression—as if seeking to inquire of her Maker how this dreadful event could possibly have come about, and then her ladyship howled most pitifully once again. As a cascade of tears poured down her face, she flew into hysterics, tearing at her own clothes, tearing at furniture, throwing across the room anything her hands could take hold of, destroying in her fury of anguish whatever she could reach.

Suddenly she turned on the Hon. John Whyte and Pamela Stone.

"You! It's you who are responsible for all this!"

Putting Miss Stone safely behind him, John rose to his feet. Taking no chances, coming slowly forward toward her while keeping his pistol pointed directly at her, in a slow and even voice, he tried to a reason with Lady St. Clare.

"Marguerite, there's nothing more you can do for him

here. Come downstairs with me. We must fetch a doctor for Miles right away."

"*C'est imposible! Pourquois?* A doctor for Miles? *Imbecile!* It is too late for doctors—my Miles is dead! He is dead!*"

"Marguerite, you should sit down now; you're beside yourself with grief. Listen to me: let him go, and sit down now."

"It's all that wicked girl's fault. Nothing would have happened if she had not come between you and Miles! She's the one! It's her fault! Her life is forfeit—I'll kill her!" she shrieked, suddenly pulling a razor-sharp stiletto knife out from a sheath hidden in her garter; its blade glinted in the light.

"No! Let go of the knife, Marguerite!"

Lady St. Clare rushed at Pamela, but John Whyte was blocking her the way. Not wanting to kill his sister-in-law, and realizing she was no match for him, being so small, he turned over his pistol to Pamela, and grabbed at the stiletto in her ladyship's hand. She hacked viciously at him with the knife, but to no avail.

In an instant, he had wrapped his hands around her wrist and twisted the small but deadly knife out of it; it clattered to the bare floor near the edge of the rug. John let go of the disarmed woman. The Viscountess dropped to her knees and began sobbing once more, her head in her hands.

After a moment, she looked up at them again, and screamed at them in contempt, "You don't understand, either one of you! You're both too stupid, and far too bourgeois to understand the meaning of true love! I spit on your delicate, spineless love! Do you understand? I loved that man; I loved my husband Miles, and I did for him what made him happy, regardless of what it cost me! *That* is unselfish love!"

She walked over to a hanging, and pulled the thick velvet curtains apart, revealing a tall, mullioned window. She unlocked it and opened it, leaning out as if to savor a breath of fresh air after having been trapped in an airless room. Then, light as a deer, she jumped to the window-sash and balanced there precariously for a moment. Her beautiful face was stained with the trails of endless tears, maddened by grief and passion.

"You don't know what love is, either one of you! I wish you well of your vile, puny, pious love! I'll show you what love is like! Love is when you cannot live without the one you love! As I cannot! *Je ne veux vivre sans mon mari!*"

And, as John Whyte tried desperately to reach the sill in time, her ladyship threw herself out of the window, hurtling down and down and down to the slate flagstone courtyard.

Pamela shuddered and turned away, to bury her face in John Whyte's broad shoulders. They held each other close for several moments, silent in the face of death.

"How horrible," said Pamela Stone, unable to cope with the evidence of her senses. "Quite horrible."

She averted her eyes from St. Clare's body as a feeling of sickness and dread began to overwhelm her. She shook her head, and trembled in disbelief and disgust.

"They were both . . . entirely insane," said the Honorable John Whyte.

"A perfect match," noted Pamela dryly.

Twenty-seven

It was late spring of 1817, and the Right Honorable John Julian Whyte, Fourth Viscount St. Clare, and his wife, Pamela, Lady St. Clare, were entertaining Mr. and Mrs. Charles Bellfort at their small but picturesque farming estate, Melfield, when news reached them of the death of the Viscount's sire-by-law, Bertram Francis Whyte, Seventh Earl of Cleremont.

By that time the fruit tree blossoms that had been blooming in the Melfield orchards had already begun to fall, scattering the ground with a white and rose-pink petal-blanket.

Mr. and Mrs. Bellfort, a particularly devoted couple whose union had recently been blessed with the advent of a beautiful baby girl, were quick to express their condolences. This was purely a matter of form, since they, like everyone else in polite society, were well aware that the old Earl Cleremont and his heir, John Whyte, Viscount St. Clare, had been utterly estranged for nearly a year, since the scandalous demise of Miles Whyte, the Third Viscount, and his wife, the former Marguerite Perigord de la Tour.

His lordship refolded the thick sheet of hand-pressed paper and laid it on a table.

"So, Father is gone. I wish I could grieve for him."

"Just as well Lord Cleremont's out of his pain, John," said Charles Bellfort. "However little you liked him—and he you—he is better off out of his suffering. That last attack he endured was already near to overwhelming."

"Quite true. I do not like to think of him, or anyone, suffering such pain. However, I cannot be expected to overlook all of his excesses, or ever to forget what he did to my mother."

"No, one cannot be expected to forget such things," said her ladyship.

"It would be un-Christian not to forgive, and yet, speaking frankly, there is a hardness in my heart toward that man that will never leave me. The selfishness of him! An irresponsibility almost beyond comprehension, that he squandered on his stable of expensive incognitas and on faro my mother's vast fortune, which comprised the best part of the entire Pembroke estate. Compared to his waste, the part of Mother's fortune lost in the bank on Berners Street was a mere pittance."

"That was, I own, a particularly timely conjunction of events," said Mr. Bellfort. "Only by means of the Berners Street embezzlement was the Earl's shocking misappropriation of the rest of the Pembroke money so successfully concealed."

" 'Misappropriation'? A feeble noun, Charles, and quite unsuited to its ponderous duty," said her ladyship. "Recall that, according to Harry Durward, old Lord Cleremont was one of London's most enthusiastic buyers of precious love trinkets. Considering which, one expects to see a hatchment put up over the door at Rundell and Bridge's immediately when they hear the sad news."

This dry remark provoked a peal of wry laughter from her husband, and smiles all around the company.

Victorine Bellfort added, "It is an odd thing, but one would think that even Cleremont with his odiously expensive tastes would have found it difficult to dissipate such a vast fortune as your mother's so quickly, and so entirely"

"True, and one cannot but despise him for such profligacy," said his lordship with a shake of his head. "Better to have spent the money on the tenants, and on improving the properties. So selfish. Such a waste."

"Well, it is fortunate that he was not your father after all, is it not?" commented his wife.

John laughed.

"Why, my dear? Did you fear that I, sooner or later, would learn profligacy? That I should turn to gaming and light-skirts? Squander a fortune buying priceless ruby necklaces to distribute generously among my barques of frailty?"

"Priceless ruby necklaces? What an interesting thought. Were you aware, my dear, that I myself am prodigiously fond of red?"

"John, be careful—this is Pamela's way of angling you for jewels," said Victorine, with a smile. "Now that you have succeeded your father, I am afraid there will be no way of satisfying her mercenary nature."

"Yes, my father warned me about her, time and again. Dash it all! Why do I keep calling him my father? An old habit, and hard to break, though I was most relieved to learn I was not a blood relation. However, at my age, to discover that my natural sire was the old Duke of Webster—what an extraordinary thing! I remember well that, during Cleremont's absences, which were very frequent, Webster was used to spend a great deal of time at our house, during the months before his death. I did not wonder at his presence at the time, for I liked him very well. He was a good, kind man, the old Duke. I certainly remember his many kindnesses to my mother. I think they must have loved each other very much."

"That being the case, and both of them knowing perfectly well your parentage, it was rather surprising—was it not?—that your name did not appear as one of the beneficiaries's in the old Duke's will," remarked her ladyship, as she shifted the Fifth Viscount St. Clare, Thomas Stone Whyte, from a soft cloth on the carpeted floor back onto her lap, and there dandled his young lordship.

"Perhaps not," replied Victorine Bellfort. "His grace the Duke would naturally have preferred John to be acknowledged and accepted by the Earl of Cleremont as his legitimate second son, and thus occupy a much more respectable position in society than would a mere by-blow—even a Duke's by-blow."

"Victorine! Such language! I am very much surprised at your frankness, my dear!" said her husband, with amusement. "However, I admit I think your reasoning very sound. To have mentioned John's existence in his grace's will would be to tell the world what no one wanted to have bruited about."

"I should think that would account for the Duke's omission. It is understandable, though it would have meant a lot to me at one time to have had a proper personal fortune," said his lordship, exchanging a speaking glance with his wife.

"Perhaps Lord Cleremont had, in fact, promised Webster he would acknowledge you as his own son and look after you. It was to his advantage; however little Cleremont liked your unfortunate mother, he would have disliked earning the public reputation of a cuckold even more."

"Just as his own son Miles disliked the thought," added her ladyship, acidly.

"Now, now—that episode is long gone, and best forgotten, Pamela," chastised Charles Bellfort, in his soft-spoken, naturally mediating manner. "Remember that we have all of us been lucky enough to fulfill our most heart-felt desires," and here he threw a loving glance at his own beautiful wife, "and should rest gratefully within our happiness, not dwelling on the errors of the past."

"You're right, Charles, as usual," added his lordship. "At any rate, however ironic it is, as a result of his death, from today, Pamela and I must go into mourning."

Lord and Lady Balmore interrupted the conversation at this moment, entering into the salon, looking well-rested and content.

"Mourning?" said Lord Balmore, striding to take a seat. "You are really going into mourning for that old goat?"

"I suppose they must, dear," said Lady Balmore, choosing a seat next to her husband. "May we sit with you a while?"

"How are you today, Balmore? I trust your ladyship is well? Have you seen Thomas Stone?"

"We are both well, and your father-in-law is doing very well, also, though he is presently sleeping."

"Balmore completely wore poor Thomas out with a devastating game of chess that lasted all this morning. Balmore can be terribly ruthless, you must know."

"I am only ruthless when it comes to getting what I want," he said to his wife, who blushed prettily in return, looking nearly as young and fresh as her daughter, Victorine Bellfort.

"So, my esteemed Countess," said John, turning to his own lady. "What orders shall I send to Haverford?"

"I should like to have Haverford cleared of every stick of furniture belonging to that horrid man, and have it swept clean, and aired, for perhaps a week. Then, we must start all over again, and make the place the gracious manor it always should have been."

"On my own part," added Lord Cleremont, "I intend, over the next few years, to make Haverford an estate one can only admire, from the great house right down to the humblest cottage."

Pamela looked thoughtful. "I will send directly for a needlewoman to make up my blacks, though it is naught but hypocrisy to feign a display of grief over a man who did us such wrong."

"It is the way of the world, Pamela, nothing more. It is a matter of fitting in with the fabric of society. For myself, I privately shall consider this year of mourning as a year of mourning for my beloved mother, and one of mourning for my true father.

"So, friends. On this day, for us another chapter of life opens. What shall we do with ourselves? Since Mr. Thomas Stone is resting, and thus can spare his dear sister and his brother-in-law's company for an hour or so, shall we all go out and take the air together?"

"Pamela? Victorine? Lady Balmore? It's a very fine day, and good walking weather. Shall we all go out together and enjoy the spring?" asked Charles Bellfort.

This plan was quickly agreed to. Nurses were summoned, and infants kissed and consigned into their care. Light shawls and straw bonnets were duly donned, parasols opened, and the three handsome couples strolled out into the freshness of the country air.

The new Earl and Countess of Cleremont walked together arm-in-arm, admiring a bank of multicolored wildflowers. Mr. and Mrs. Charles Bellfort followed them at a short distance, with Lord and Lady Balmore trailing behind. They talked with one another upon various light topics, and then lapsed into a silence born of contentment.

The couples disappeared into a copse of rhododendrons, which drew from all of them remarks of delight and admiration. It was like a fairy-land, averred Victorine Bellfort, with so many spring-scarlet clusters of blossoms, and pink blossom-clusters, and lavender ones, tucked in amongst glossy, forest-green leaves.

Suddenly, as they entered into a shadowy part of the wood, following a path lined with delicate white lilies-of-the-valley, they all fell into another, deeper silence.

As they continued to admire the gentle beauty which the ending of spring had brought, each individual was moved by recognition of the worldly happiness that finally had been bestowed upon them—a happiness profound and unalloyed.

ZEBRA REGENCIES
ARE
THE TALK OF THE TON!

A REFORMED RAKE (4499, $3.99)
by Jeanne Savery

After governess Harriet Cole helped her young charge flee to France — and the designs of a despicable suitor, more trouble soon arrived in the person of a London rake. Sir Frederick Carrington insisted on providing safe escort back to England. Harriet deemed Carrington more dangerous than any band of brigands, but secretly relished matching wits with him. But after being taken in his arms for a tender kiss, she found herself wondering — *could* a lady find love with an irresistible rogue?

A SCANDALOUS PROPOSAL (4504, $4.99)
by Teresa DesJardien

After only two weeks into the London season, Lady Pamela Premington has already received her first offer of marriage. If only it hadn't come from the *ton's* most notorious rake, Lord Marchmont. Pamela had already set her sights on the distinguished Lieutenant Penford, who had the heroism and honor that made him the ideal match. Now she had to keep from falling under the spell of the seductive Lord so she could pursue the man more worthy of her love. Or was he?

A LADY'S CHAMPION (4535, $3.99)
by Janice Bennett

Miss Daphne, art mistress of the Selwood Academy for Young Ladies, greeted the notion of ghosts haunting the academy with skepticism. However, to avoid rumors frightening off students, she found herself turning to Mr. Adrian Carstairs, sent by her uncle to be her "protector" against the "ghosts." Although, Daphne would accept no interference in her life, she *would* accept aid in exposing her spectral spirits. What she never expected was for Adrian to expose the secret wishes of her hidden heart . . .

CHARITY'S GAMBIT (4537, $3.99)
by Marcy Stewart

Charity Abercrombie reluctantly embarks on a London season in hopes of making a suitable match. However she cannot forget the mysterious Dominic Castille — and the kiss they shared — when he fell from a tree as she strolled through the woods. Charity does not know that the dark and dashing captain harbors a dangerous secret that will ensnare them both in its web — leaving Charity to risk certain ruin and losing the man she so passionately loves . . .

Available wherever paperbacks are sold, or order direct from the Publisher. Send cover price plus 50¢ per copy for mailing and handling to Penguin USA, P.O. Box 999, c/o Dept. 17109, Bergenfield, NJ 07621. Residents of New York and Tennessee must include sales tax. DO NOT SEND CASH.

ELEGANT LOVE STILL FLOURISHES –
Wrap yourself in a Zebra Regency Romance.

A MATCHMAKER'S MATCH (3783, $3.50/$4.50)
by Nina Porter

To save herself from a loveless marriage, Lady Psyche Veringham pretends to be a bluestocking. Resigned to spinsterhood at twenty-three, Psyche sets her keen mind to snaring a husband for her young charge, Amanda. She sets her cap for long-time bachelor, Justin St. James. This man of the world has had his fill of frothy-headed debutantes and turns the tables on Psyche. Can a bluestocking and a man about town find true love?

FIRES IN THE SNOW (3809, $3.99/$4.99)
by Janis Laden

Because of an unhappy occurrence, Diana Ruskin knew that a secure marriage was not in her future. She was content to assist her physician father and follow in his footsteps . . . until now. After meeting Adam, Duke of Marchmaine, Diana's precise world is shattered. She would simply have to avoid the temptation of his gentle touch and stunning physique – and by doing so break her own heart!

FIRST SEASON (3810, $3.50/$4.50)
by Anne Baldwin

When country heiress Laetitia Biddle arrives in London for the Season, she harbors dreams of triumph and applause. Instead, she becomes the laughingstock of drawing rooms and ballrooms, alike. This headstrong miss blames the rakish Lord Wakeford for her miserable debut, and she vows to rise above her many faux pas. Vowing to become an Original, Letty proves that she's more than a match for this eligible, seasoned Lord.

AN UNCOMMON INTRIGUE (3701, $3.99/$4.99)
by Georgina Devon

Miss Mary Elizabeth Sinclair was rather startled when the British Home Office employed her as a spy. Posing as "Tasha," an exotic fortune-teller, she expected to encounter unforeseen dangers. However, nothing could have prepared her for Lord Eric Stewart, her dashing and infuriating partner. Giving her heart to this haughty rogue would be the most reckless hazard of all.

A MADDENING MINX (3702, $3.50/$4.50)
by Mary Kingsley

After a curricle accident, Miss Sarah Chadwick is literally thrust into the arms of Philip Thornton. While other women shy away from Thornton's eyepatch and aloof exterior, Sarah finds herself drawn to discover why this man is physically and emotionally scarred.